THE INCUBUS'S ASSISTANT

CHARMED AWAY TEMP AGENCY
BOOK 1

AMY PADILLA

ISBN: 9798325154942

ISBN: 9798999351999

Imprint: Independently published

Social Media Manager: Aspen Tree E.A.S.

TRIGGER WARNING

This book contains one scene of dubious consent. The characters are not hurt or troubled over the event, but if this type of scene bothers you, consider skipping the spicy scene in chapter 2.

Your mental health is very important! If these themes are at all triggering to you, please consider another book.

Love you!

Rule # 1: Never fall in love with your incubus.

CHAPTER ONE

Rule Number 2 of being a feeder: honesty is key.

Okay, so technically, Avery didn't sign up for the job. There was nothing wrong with it. Being a feeder was like any other job. Waiter, mailman, feeder. You apply online, go in for an interview, and do a drug test to see if you're clear headed when signing the paperwork. Lots of Supes needed sustenance and, if you were willing to feed them, they generally paid pretty well.

It's not what Avery signed up for, though.

He'd been working for a temp agency for the past two years. The pay wasn't great, and the jobs were sometimes horrendous, but he liked the variety and the flexible schedule. It gave him time to work on his novel. He knew the likelihood of a human getting published was slim, but it was a lifelong dream and he wanted to see it through, even if it took years to do it.

He had just finished a job at a shipping plant, filling in for a chimera secretary who apparently was also the company therapist. No one seemed to care that he wasn't the normal secretary, and they showed up in droves to complain to him about their lives and ask for advice. It was actually really interesting, and he'd been sad when the real secretary came back from her vacation and he had to move on to a new job.

Avery was rarely in the temp agency proper. He job hopped so often, he usually only showed up if he needed to fill out paperwork or if there was a staff meeting they weren't allowed to skip. But at the end of every job, he had to come back to write up a report of the job and the experience and receive his newest assignment. He waved to Doreen, the only other human in the office and the friendliest receptionist he knew, and dropped into a chair in front of an empty desk. None of the temps had an assigned desk, since they weren't around much, but this one was his favorite because it was right next to the window overlooking the city. He logged into the company computer and pulled up the documents he needed, filling them out carefully so maybe in the future he could be sent back. He wanted to hear more about the love triangle between the vampire, the werewolf, and the demon.

He was just finishing when his boss came rushing out of her office, the snakes that made up her hair all in a tizzy. Medusas weren't as dangerous as other humans liked to pretend they were. Morana was trained as a child to control her ability to turn people into stone. Avery could look her in the eye without issue, and he did so now as she hurried to his desk.

"Avery! Good, you're here. You just finished your last job, right?"

"Uh, yeah. I'm just finishing up the paperwork now. Are you okay?" Avery asked, concerned. His boss was normally the picture of calm. Nothing could shake her patient exterior. Except now, she looked almost panicked.

"No. I mean yes, I'm fine. I need you on a job. Mariella was supposed to take it, but she called in sick *again*. This client is very high profile, and if things go poorly, we could lose a huge account. I know you're supposed to have a few days off, but this is an emergency. I'll put in a word for you to get a bonus if you take it."

Blinking rapidly, Avery tried to catch up with her chaotic rant. Everyone normally got two days off between jobs, and he'd been planning to work on his novel, but he could see the desperation in Morana's bright red eyes.

"Okay, sure."

Her shoulders sagged with relief, and the snakes on her head all seemed to collectively sigh. Avery had to purse his lips to fight off a laugh. It wasn't polite to comment on a medusa's snakes, but Avery had always loved how animated and emotional they were.

"When did you need me to go?"

He was hoping to at least have time today to get a few pages out, but Morana dashed those hopes before he could even get the thought fully formed.

"Now. I need you to go now. If you hurry, you won't be late."

She grabbed Avery's arm, pulling him out of his chair and nudging him towards the exit. He barely had time to grab his messenger bag before she was forcing him out the door, snatching his phone to plug the address into his GPS app.

"I'll fill out all the paperwork for you and finish what you were doing before. Go straight to the top floor, CEO's office. You'll be working for Mr. Hawksley. Now hurry!"

She shoved his phone back into his hand and physically pushed him down the street toward the station. Avery stumbled over his feet, shooting her a stunned look over his shoulder as he hurried toward the subway. If he didn't know his boss any better, he'd be upset about the way she treated him. But Morana wasn't an unkind boss. She was actually very fair and understanding if things didn't work out and a company sent him home before he even started because he was human. Not all Supes liked working with humans. Whatever job this was, it was important enough to Morana that she skipped all protocol to get him there. He didn't even know what job he'd be doing.

Since he knew she wouldn't be rushing him if it wasn't important, he sprinted to the subway. He dodged around the droves of Supes in the station, shoving his way into the subway car just as the doors closed. He had just enough time to yank his bag out of the way before it got caught in the doors. While he waited for his stop, he looked up where exactly he was headed. When he realized, his jaw almost hit the ground.

Spellbound Corps was the leading supernatural company in the country. Probably in the world. Avery read in a magazine once that it started off as a small business in someone's garage. The founders created spells and gadgets to make life easier for Supes who didn't have the capacity, or the opposable thumbs, to work ordinary jobs. They were now the leaders in magical innovation and had the most diverse personnel in the city.

It made more sense now why Morana was so panicked. The temp agency worked closely with Spellbound Corps, and losing that contract would be catastrophic for the agency. It did make Avery a little nervous about whether or not they'd accept his presence. The company was literally created for Supes, and they might not like it if a human showed up to work for them.

Well, there was nothing he could do about that. At least if he showed up, they'd be more likely to accept a little lateness so he could find a replacement. He hoped he wouldn't need a replacement, though. He was good at his job, adaptable to most situations, and a quick study. If they gave him a chance, he knew he could pull off whatever they put in front of him.

His punctuality was even more important now, so the second the doors opened at his stop, Avery dodged through them and tore out of the station. Spellbound Corps was easy to find, given that it was the tallest building in the city. A lot of little buildings of different sizes combined to form a massive skyscraper, with green spaces dotted on most of the roofs. Avery had to crane his neck to take in all of it, and he was pretty sure the top was in the clouds. Lucky for him, he wasn't afraid of heights.

Pushing through the rotating glass door, he tried not to gape at the company entryway. The marble floors actually sparkled and the floor to ceiling windows let in tons of natural light. It was also stuffed to the brim with Supes of every different race and color. And size, apparently. Avery had to dodge out of the way when a pair of golem guards stomped past him. They could squash him in one step if they weren't careful.

Slipping through the crowds, Avery stopped at the front desk, sucking in a deep breath to calm his frantic panting from running all the way here.

"Can I help you?" The hydra behind the desk stared at him with no less than three of its dozen heads. Avery never knew where to look in situations like this, so he focused on the one in the middle as he answered.

"I'm Avery Whitman. I'm from Charmed Away Temp Agency. I'm supposed to be meeting a Mr. Hawksley?"

She blinked a few times, the ridge of her brow wrinkling as she studied him. Avery held his breath, waiting for the inevitable dismissal. But the hydra only pressed her lips together, her tail snagging a temporary badge from her desk and handing it to him.

"Top floor. Use the gold elevator; it will bring you straight there." She paused, her eyes narrowing slightly. "You don't have a sensitive stomach, do you?"

"Uh... No?"

She huffed, clearly not convinced but unwilling to argue with him about it. She jerked several chins toward the turnstiles behind her desk.

"You'd better hurry. Mr. Hawksley doesn't appreciate tardiness."

"Right. Thanks. I'll just—"

She had already moved on to helping someone else, so Avery shut his mouth and headed for the turnstiles. He had to press the badge to the screen on top before it turned green and allowed him to pass. He edged his way around the lines of people waiting for the elevators, stopping in front of the last one on the right, the only gold elevator in the bunch.

There was no one else waiting in front of this one, and he got a few funny looks when he pressed the button to call for it. He ignored the stares, shuffling into the elevator after the doors opened and a few people offloaded. Right before the doors slipped closed, a little green goblin darted inside, giving him a once over before ignoring him completely.

The hydra's question about sensitive stomachs made more sense when the elevator shot towards the top floor at dizzying speeds. Avery clutched the handrail on the wall in a death grip, praying his stomach didn't stage a revolt. When it slowed to a stop at the top floor, he felt almost as green as the goblin, and his hands were clammy as he stepped off the elevator.

"You get used to it," the goblin commented, finally looking at him.

"You promise?" Avery croaked, taking a second to breathe through the nausea.

The goblin chuckled, bobbing his head. "Yes. I felt the same way you did for at least a week when I started here. Are you a new recruit?"

"I'm a temp. I'm supposed to be reporting to Mr. Hawksley."

The goblin's forehead wrinkled in surprise. If he had eyebrows, they'd be in his hairline. But he had neither eyebrows nor hair, so it was irrelevant.

"I see. Well, his office is on the left. You can't miss it. And... good luck."

Well, that wasn't ominous at all.

CHAPTER TWO

Ozen was starving.

His stomach tightened uncomfortably like it was trying to eat itself. If he didn't find a feeder soon, he'd perish, and he couldn't allow that. He had a company to run. He glanced at his clock, his frustration rising with every passing minute. His secretary, Collette, was supposed to be here already with another feeder who better suited him. Usually he personally went through an agency for such things, but the last feeder they sent him had been a disaster. The man was obstinate and demanding, and he continually interrupted Ozen's work to ask for attention. He seemed to be under the impression that signing on as Ozen's feeder meant they were in some kind of romantic relationship. Which was ridiculous. Ozen didn't date. He had far too much work to do.

After firing the last feeder, Ozen was ready to admit defeat. He couldn't keep a feeder for longer than a few weeks at this point. Collette promised she'd vette the next one herself and bring them here before his morning meeting. He didn't want to face the board while distracted by his stomach.

A knock on his office door caught his attention and he barked out a quick, "Enter," his attention still on the paperwork in front of him. He swore he'd read the same paragraph three times and it still wasn't filtering through his starved brain.

"Mr. Hawklsey?"

The voice was unfamiliar, and when Ozen looked up, he didn't recognize the man standing just inside his office. He assumed it was the feeder, since he had no other scheduled visits that morning. The feeder was petite, probably no taller than 5'7", with a slim build and a cherub face. Golden curls topped his head, and bright blue eyes stared back at him. A deep inhale told Ozen the man was human, twenty-seven years of age, and—

A virgin?

What in the great goddess's name was Collette thinking? There was no way a virgin could tend to his needs.

"My name is Avery Whitman—" he began, but Ozen cut him off.

"You can't be serious. Does she really think someone with zero experience can do what is required?" he snapped. He'd mostly said it to himself, but the young man overheard him and took another step forward, his hands clutching the strap to his messenger bag.

"I can assure you, I can do the job. I'm a quick study and I've got a knack for adapting to new environments. There isn't any challenge I haven't met so far."

Maybe in his professional life, but there were obviously things he'd forgone in his private life. Who in this day and age was still a virgin at twenty-seven?

Still, the man was pleasing to look at and Ozen liked his determination. If he signed with the feeder agency, he obviously knew what he was getting into. It wouldn't hurt to test their compatibility. Collette wouldn't send him here without reason.

"Fine. Close the door and come here."

Avery hurried to do as he asked, which was a point in his favor. Ozen liked a certain level of obedience. It made the process easier. When Avery stopped just on the other side of his desk, though, Ozen resisted the urge to roll his eyes. He pointed directly next to him, pressing his lips together to hide his scowl.

"I said come here."

With only a moment of hesitation, Avery rounded the desk and stood in front of him, his plump bottom lip caught between his teeth as he bounced on his toes. Standing this close, Ozen could taste Avery's nerves in the air. That wasn't surprising, given his virgin status. Hopefully it wouldn't be an issue, because he was so hungry, he was beginning to feel delirious.

"Bag down. Take off your pants and bend over the desk."

Avery's eyes went as wide as saucers and he didn't move to follow Ozen's orders. Ozen's eyes narrowed.

"Well?"

"I, uh— What—"

Another pang of hunger stabbed through his gut and Ozen's patience wore out. He didn't like using his abilities to move things along; it defeated the purpose of feeding if he was using his magic to do it. But with Avery's nerves, they'd still be standing here three days from now. Drawing just enough of his magic to lower inhibitions, he let it sweep through the room, focusing on the young man in front of him.

"Do you want me?"

"Y-Yes."

"Do you want me to make you feel good?"

"Yes." His reply was more breathy, and he swayed toward Ozen slightly. He drew back on his powers just a little. He wanted Avery relaxed, not drugged. That wasn't consent. He tried again when the fog lifted from Avery's gaze.

"I need to feed, little one. Will you allow me to feed from you?"

Avery blinked a few times and Ozen worried he'd deny him. He had to admit he too preferred when he and his partner had time to talk first, but the pain in his gut was making him dizzy and he had a meeting to get to. Thankfully, Avery dipped his chin in agreement. Cupping it, Ozen lifted Avery's face to force him to look at Ozen properly.

"I need your words, little one. Yes or no?"

"Yes. I just— I've never—"

"I'll be gentle," Ozen assured him, though he worried that was a promise he wouldn't be able to keep. It would take all of Ozen's facilities to keep from attacking the smaller man. He never went this long between feeds before. He hoped Avery would be a better fit than his previous attempts at finding a feeder, because he wasn't sure if he could continue like this.

"Take off your pants, little one, and let me see you."

Avery reached for his belt with shaking hands, and Ozen felt as his incisors lengthened in anticipation. The smell of Avery's arousal was tinged with anxiety, so Ozen pushed out a little more of his magic, soaking Avery's senses and drowning out his anxieties. A small moan escaped Avery's lips and his erection tented his briefs as his slacks dropped to his ankles. His hands still trembled at his sides, but he came willingly when Ozen guided him closer by his hips.

Leaning forward, Ozen ran his nose along Avery's length, breathing in the scent of him. Citrus and musk, with a hint of sex from the wet spot blooming around the head of his cock. Ozen flicked his tongue out for a taste, biting back a groan as the salty sweetness teased his senses. His hunger compounded and urgency filled his veins. He promised Avery he would be gentle, but that choice would be taken from him if he didn't speed this up. Dragging Avery's briefs down his legs, Ozen let them pool at his ankles, darting his tongue out for one quick lick before turning Avery to face his desk.

"Bend over. All the way. That's a good lad."

Avery's breath quickened, anticipation bleeding into the lust coming off him. It didn't take away from it, though, and it was enough that Ozen was responding already. The tethers of his magic wrapped around Avery, siphoning his desire as he squirmed on Ozen's desk. Already, the pain of starvation was subsiding, and he could think clearly enough to be gentle. His magic coated his fingers in slickness and he palmed one creamy cheek of Avery's behind, opening him up for Ozen's gaze. He felt Avery tense, some of the anxiety coming back, but thanks to the desire saturating the air, Ozen kept his patience. He stroked over Avery's puckered entrance until Avery relaxed and his moans drowned out the nervous processes in his mind. He pushed back against Ozen's hand, instinct guiding him to seek more pleasure. He tensed when one finger pushed inside, but a quick pulse of magic relaxed him again, and when Ozen added another, Avery didn't flinch.

Normally, Ozen was focused only on getting inside his feeder, surrounding himself in as much desire as he could. But with Avery's inexperience, now wasn't the best time to force that kind of connection. Besides, he was getting plenty just from Avery's response to his fingers alone. It was a curiosity he'd need to evaluate later, as normally it took a lot more to satiate him. Avery squirmed and moaned, pushing back to meet

Ozen's hand. When Ozen crooked his fingers, pressing against Avery's prostate, Avery cried out, and a tidal wave of lust and desire hit Ozen square in the chest, lighting him up inside. He pushed in another finger, attacking that little gland until Avery's sobbing, pleasure soaked cries filled the room.

Avery's thighs trembled, his body tensed, and Ozen could feel in the air that Avery was close to his release. To avoid a mess, Ozen withdrew his fingers and spun Avery around, ignoring his cry of protest. He swallowed Avery's cock in one swift movement, and Avery's head flew back, his release exploding onto Ozen's waiting tongue.

Ozen let the desire and pleasure fill him to bursting, and his eyes slipped closed from the relief, his own pleasure dancing across his skin. It had been a while since he was able to share pleasure with his partner. He had been coupling only to feed, and the quick trysts rarely ended in his pleasure. But Ozen felt his cock throb in his slacks, need replacing hunger in his gut. He almost contemplated taking Avery to his bedroom to continue exploring with him, but the look on Avery's face made him pause. There were tears on his flushed cheeks, and he looked overwhelmed. Ozen felt his chest tighten, and for the first time in years, he felt the urge to provide aftercare. He carefully redressed Avery, avoiding touching his sensitive cock. Once he was dressed again, Ozen scooped him into his arms, carrying him to the leather couch Ozen kept against one wall. Once Avery was settled, he stepped back, intending to head to the ante office where he knew Collette kept a mini fridge with water and juice for him and visitors.

Before he could reach the door, it burst open, an apologetic Collette rushing into the room.

"I do apologize, sir. I know I'm late. The feeder got lost and—" She came to an abrupt halt when her eyes settled on Avery. Her brows drew together tightly and her frown pulled at her lips. "Who's this?"

"What do you mean? He's the feeder," Ozen said, but when Collette's eyes widened, he started to doubt that statement. He looked back at Avery, who still had a dazed look on his face. Avery never specifically said he was a feeder. But if he wasn't the feeder, then who was he?

"Mr. Hawksley, the feeder I vetted is waiting by my desk. Did... Did the young man say his name?"

He could hear it, the accusation in her tone. She was worried he forced the issue on some random stranger due to his hunger. Which, as much as it bothered him to admit, had some truth to it. He'd assumed Avery was from the feeder agency and had acted accordingly, and while he was almost certain he hadn't used enough magic to coerce Avery, he still felt guilty.

"He said his name is Avery Whitman."

"Avery Whit—" She blanched, her head whipping to look at Avery again. "You— He— What did you do?"

"Collette. If you'd let me explain—"

Her eyes were so wide, Ozen could see the whites all around the irises, and the more upset she got, the more her voice rose. If he wasn't careful, his secretary would lose control and unleash a banshee scream on the office, and then they'd all be in trouble.

CHAPTER THREE

Rule Number 6 of being a feeder: trust is earned, not given. Don't give your incubus any reason not to trust you, or the contract could be terminated.

Avery felt warm and fuzzy, his limbs made of jello and his brain full of cotton. He'd never experienced that kind of pleasure in his life. Sure, he participated in some hasty solo sessions when he needed to clear his head, but he wasn't obsessed with the idea of sex like his friends from high school were. In college, he'd been too busy studying to keep his scholarship. And then his mother got sick and he had to drop out to help her and life got in the way. And then suddenly he was twenty-seven, still a virgin, and too embarrassed to do anything about it. A virgin in college was easy to explain. An almost thirty-year-old virgin was a secret he'd been determined to take to his grave. He figured he'd meet the right person, things would happen naturally, and he'd never have to admit that he had no experience.

Granted, up until he stepped inside Ozen Hawksley's office, he'd thought he was straight. Well. Sort of. He'd assumed he was, since he hadn't really given much thought to it. All his friends were straight, so he'd just assumed when he eventually found someone he was interested in, it'd be a woman. Maybe that was one of the reasons he was still a virgin at his age. He hadn't been interested enough to try because he had been looking at the wrong gender.

He didn't spend much time dating, and the few dates he went on every year were awkward and always ended the same way—with him counting down the minutes until it was over and with the woman saying she'd just like to be friends. He was never too disappointed when he went home alone. He was more interested in not coming home to an empty apartment than he was interested in sex.

And then Ozen asked Avery to feed him, and his mindset shifted. He knew part of that was Ozen's magic; it filled the air and made him feel drunk, wiping out the fear and confusion that'd filled his veins. But he'd felt the magic draw back, like cool water running through his system, clearing the fog from his mind. He knew he could say no when Ozen asked him again. He just... didn't want to. He had an opportunity to deal with an issue he'd been embarrassed about for years, and with an incubus, he was almost guaranteed to enjoy it. Sure, he'd never thought about anyone playing with his ass, but Ozen had been gentle. He'd felt nothing but plea- sure until he came so hard, he felt his soul leave his body, and Ozen had to physically carry him to the couch to recover.

Avery let himself drift in those happy feelings for a while. He figured it was fine, since Ozen never said anything to hurry him along. It was only when a shriek that bordered on painful cut through his daze that he blinked back to reality. Ozen was standing a few feet away, his hands up in surrender as a woman with long black hair and a smart skirt suit screamed at him. Avery recognized the pitch black gaze. That, combined with the screaming that was getting more painful by the second, told him what she was. Banshee. If someone didn't stop her, she might accidentally kill him. Humans were especially sensitive to banshee screams.

Covering his ears, he forced himself to his feet, nearly toppling since his knees still felt like jello. He stumbled, which caught the attention of Ozen and the banshee as well. Her tirade stopped, and her fury died off, worry replacing the anger on her face.

"Oh, Mr. Whitman, I'm so sorry. You never should have been put in this position. I hope you didn't think you had to—"

"I didn't. I mean, I asked for it. No, wait, that doesn't sound right. I knew what I was doing?" He was making it worse, and he felt a blush steal up his cheeks. It was one thing to feed an incubus; it was another thing entirely to discuss it with someone else.

The banshee didn't look like she believed him, but he didn't know how to explain himself without admitting he agreed to have sex with a perfect stranger because he was tired of being a virgin. The more he thought about it, the more embarrassed he felt.

"Avery. Did I ever make you feel like you had to feed me?"

Ozen's question made him relax. That was an easy thing to answer.

"No. Never."

"Did my magic make you feel you weren't clear headed enough to consent properly?"

Avery pursed his lips, considering his words carefully. "I mean, at first I felt really drunk. But!" He saw the banshee whip her head toward Ozen, ready to start screaming at him again. Avery hurried before she could start. "But then you pulled it back, and you asked me point blank. At that moment, I was fully aware of myself and my decisions. I promise."

It was still really embarrassing to admit, but Avery kept his chin up. He didn't want Ozen getting into trouble because of Avery's decision. He was hungry, he asked nicely, Avery said yes. End of story.

The banshee didn't agree. "Did you feel like you had to feed Mr. Hawksley as part of your job?"

That made Avery hesitate. So, technically, that had been the first thought that crossed his mind. Since Morana never told him what job he was being sent for, he'd assumed it was something administrative, since that's where he thrived. He saw the empty desk outside Mr. Hawklsey's office and thought that proved him correct. So when Mr. Hawksley asked Avery to feed him, he'd automatically assumed it was part of the job. Mr. Hawklsey had acted like everything was normal, and it wasn't like he forced Avery to do it. He asked permission first.

He hesitated too long, apparently, because the banshee shot a scathing look at Mr. Hawklsey. "I understand you were hungry, but this is unacceptable. I don't know what I'm going to say to his boss when I call her. You—"

Avery blanched. "Uh, we're not really going to tell Morana about this, right? She would fire me if she knew I was having sex on the job."

"You were coerced, dear, none of this was your fault," the banshee said dismissively, her glare still locked on Mr. Hawksley, who looked downright ashamed of himself.

"No, wait! He didn't force me! He asked! I knew I could say no if I wanted. Yes, I figured it was part of the job, but I didn't think that I didn't have a choice in the matter. If I didn't want to do it, I didn't have to accept. It wasn't like he said my job was on the line if I didn't."

Both Mr. Hawksley and the banshee studied him like they were trying to find the lie in his statement. They'd find none. Avery was one hundred percent into what happened between him and Mr. Hawksley. He wanted it to happen. Though he wasn't sure if it counted as him finally having sex. Did fingering count?

"If you're sure..." The banshee still frowned deeply and her gaze was suspicious, like she didn't quite believe him. But she'd have to outright call him a liar if she didn't stop pushing, so she let it go, taking a deep breath and releasing it slowly.

"Now, Mr. Whitman, you were actually hired to take my place as secretary. I understand if that makes you uncomfortable or no longer appeals to you. I'll call your manager and—"

"I'm fine! Totally fine!" Avery assured her, waving his hands a little wildly to ward her off. "I've been in a secretary position plenty of times, and I promise to do the job well."

Her eyes softened a little. "I'm sure you will. Come join me at my desk and I'll give you the rundown of the position. Mr. Hawksley, you have a meeting downstairs. I'll tell the feeder to meet you at lunch."

Something about that bothered him, but he kept his mouth shut, watching as Mr. Hawksley stalked out of the room without another word, his face a stoic mask. The expected feeder was in the ante office, but Mr. Hawksley ignored him, much to the feeder's confusion. He was a pretty man, with long eyelashes framing bright green eyes and a trim figure. He wasn't wearing a suit like the rest of the office; his clothes were more casual and form flattering, showing off his lithe muscles and a strip of skin below his belly button. Compared to Avery, it was easy to tell who was the feeder and who was the awkward temp.

"I apologize, Calvin. Mr. Hawksley has a meeting to get to. You'll speak with him at lunch. Feel free to wait here if you wish, or there is a cafe downstairs. I suggest you don't be late a second time. I won't have another incident thanks to your tardiness."

Her icy tone would've made Avery flinch if he'd been on the receiving end. Calvin only blinked at her, one perfectly plucked eyebrow arching in question. Someone had a superiority complex.

The standoff between the feeder and the banshee was brief, and when Calvin finally left the office and headed toward the elevators, the banshee sighed heavily.

"I thought I vetted him properly, but after that display, I'm beginning to think he was acting to get the job. I hope I'm not wrong... It's been difficult finding a feeder that is compatible with Mr. Hawksley. I'm almost wondering if I should cancel my trip." She muttered that last part to herself, and Avery worried he'd be out of a job before he even started. Because apparently feeding Mr. Hawksley this morning didn't count.

"You don't think he can find a feeder on his own?" Avery queried.

The banshee sighed again, and the tension in her face said she needed the vacation more than she was willing to admit. "He can, and there are agencies that he's used in the past, but there is a common theme amongst feeders these days. They seem to be more and more flippant and cause more trouble than they're worth. I promised him after the last disaster that I'd find one myself that suited him better. I never even considered that they would fake their sincerity during an interview." She stared at the door a while longer before shaking herself like she was clearing her thoughts and returning her attention to Avery. "Well, enough about that. I'm sure Calvin will do his job well enough. I haven't properly introduced myself. My name is Collette Sable, the executive assistant assigned to Mr. Hawksley. He has a whole pool of secretaries, and they'll be around to help you if you need it. You said you've been a secretary before?"

CHAPTER FOUR

Ozen's mind was turbulent the rest of the morning.

He constantly lost focus and his thoughts trailed too often to the blonde-haired cherub who'd wandered into his office and offered himself to a starving incubus. Ozen had never felt so well fed after only one session with a feeder, especially one that didn't go farther than touching. Avery's desire was intoxicating, and he found himself wishing more than once that he really was the feeder.

He banished the thought every time it entered his mind. Avery was there to replace Collette while she was on her reprieve. Every few years, Collette went home for a month to be around her people and recharge her magic. He'd almost forgotten about it entirely until last month when she reminded him of her upcoming absence. Ozen hated when she was gone; she knew him best and wasn't afraid to put people in their place if they disturbed him while he was working. Though if Avery was as efficient in his work as he was at feeding an incubus, perhaps Ozen had nothing to worry about.

When Ozen returned to his office, Avery and Collette were missing. Ozen assumed she was giving Avery a tour of the office and explaining her job, which was what much of her schedule had been blocked off for today.

Ozen couldn't decide if he was thankful or disappointed that Avery wasn't there.

Opening his office door, he was immediately greeted with the smell of sex. Avery's scent permeated the entire room, and Ozen felt himself harden in his slacks. He wasn't still hungry; Avery had more than covered that this morning. But the sounds of Avery's cries, the image of the little human bent over his desk, it all came back to him in a rush.

He lost track of how long he stood there, replaying the memory and breathing in Avery's scent. Long enough for his best friend and business partner to pop up behind him.

"What are we staring at?"

Snapping back to reality, Ozen forced himself forward, dropping into his desk chair and ignoring the spot where Avery had been bent over it that morning. He was an incubus. Sex was a necessity and never a distraction. He needed to focus on his work.

Taron followed him into the room, plopping himself down in one of the chairs on the opposite side of the desk. He was more than used to the smell of sex in Ozen's office. Since the arrangements he made were all business, he refused to invite feeders into his home. His feeds always happened here in his office. It was why the walls were soundproof and he had both a bathroom and a bedroom hidden on the other side of the wall behind his desk.

"Did you need something?"

"Got an idea I need to run past you. I was pretty drunk when I thought it up, so I'm not sure if it makes sense or not."

Sometimes, Taron and Ozen did their best thinking while drunk. It was how they came up with the weight reduction spell so the golems could use the elevators. Granted, it took another year to actually have a working spell, but the initial idea was found at the bottom of a bottle of whiskey.

Ozen put out his hand, taking the notes Taron must have scribbled down during his last drunken revelry, though scribbled might be too kind a word. Ozen couldn't make sense of what he was looking at, no matter which way he turned the paper around.

"What is this?"

"No clue, but it felt important at the time."

Ozen sighed, pressing the button on his desk that connected to

Collette's office. Sometimes she was the only one who could make sense of Taron's scribbles.

Only, it wasn't Collette who answered. When the office door opened, it was Avery who stepped inside, his smile tentative and a little shy.

"Can I help you with something, Mr. Hawksley?"

"Where is Collette?"

"Mrs. Sable went downstairs to look for the feeder you were supposed to meet this morning." A deep flush overtook Avery's face and his gaze dropped to the floor. "Is there something I can help with?"

Taron sat up when Avery came in, curious at the new arrival. His curiosity only grew when he noticed Ozen's tight grip on the papers. It wouldn't surprise him if his pupils were blown. He wanted another taste of the man across the room, and being this close to him wasn't helping. A mischievous grin flashed across Taron's face before he pointed to the papers in Ozen's hand.

"We were hoping she could translate my poor penmanship. I jotted something down and now can't make sense of what I'd written. It felt important when I wrote it."

Avery edged closer, a little unsure of himself. That was Ozen's fault for taking advantage of him this morning. He was still kicking himself for not being more specific in his questioning. He should have been more cautious. He had only himself to blame, though the hunger had a part in his recklessness.

To reassure him, Ozen offered Avery the papers. "Usually Collette can suss out what Taron writes when inebriated. It's fine if you can't."

He had to mask his expression when Avery's fingers brushed against his own when he took the offered papers. One touch and his magic rose to the surface, pushing against his skin to taste the delicious energy of the man in front of him again. He tampered it back down, keeping his face blank. Avery didn't notice Ozen's struggle, but Taron did. His mischievous look only grew the longer Ozen and Avery were in the same room.

"Uh... It looks like it's describing a prototype for an energy converter for thunderbirds. You want to use their power on the electricity grid?"

Taron's eyes lit up, momentarily distracted from Ozen's discomfort. "Oh! Yes, I remember now! And not technically. That would create issues with thunderbird rights. But discharge from a thunderbird causes issues with electricity all the time. Electric companies spend a good deal of money cleaning up after them. If we can convert their discharge into safe electricity that doesn't harm the lines, thunderbirds won't have to avoid the city."

The idea had merit, and if accomplished, could ease the struggles thunderbirds often had with travel. Current laws forbade thunderbirds from entering the city unless in human form due to the damage they caused.

"You should bring this idea to research and development. After Collette rewrites it into something legible."

"I can do that, if you want," Avery offered.

Ozen opened his mouth to refuse, but then he remembered that Collette was leaving and he'd have to rely on Avery to do these things eventually. The task itself wasn't a difficult one, since Avery seemed to be able to understand Taron's handwriting. Ozen's reluctance was personal in nature. He wanted to interact with Avery as little as possible, since he brought out a need Ozen hadn't felt in an age.

"Sure, thanks," Taron said amiably. "Just make sure to write my name on the bottom. Gotta give credit where credit is due, ya know?"

Ozen scowled at Taron's lack of professionalism. That had always been true, though. It was the reason they created this company together. Ozen was better equipped to deal with people in a more professional manner.

Avery didn't seem to mind Taron, and he bobbed his head in agreement, but his gaze flicked to Ozen, like he was waiting for Ozen's permission to do as Taron asked. Ozen's blood heated at the immediate obedience from the temp, and smug pride filled his chest when he dipped his chin. Only with Ozen's permission did Avery hurry off to do what was asked.

"He's cute. New feeder?"

Once again, Ozen was forced back to reality. He ripped his eyes away from the door where Avery had disappeared and grabbed the paperwork he'd been looking at this morning before Avery's arrival.

"No. He's Collette's replacement for her vacation."

"Ah. Forgot about that. But you want him to be your feeder. You wouldn't have been staring at him like that if you didn't. What's the issue?"

Taron knew better than anyone the struggles Ozen faced with finding a decent feeder. He was there when Tristan left, and he knew how many feeders he'd gone through since. His interest in finding Ozen a feeder wasn't intrusive. The leer when Ozen admitted what happened this morning was.

"Wait. You just assumed he was your new feeder and told him to bend over your desk?" he asked with a wide grin.

"I was starving, Taron. I would've asked you to bend over at that point."

"Gross. Don't change the subject. So how was it? Did he at least help before you realized what an idiot you were?"

Ozen scowled at the dig before admitting, "He did more than help. I'd barely touched him before my magic started feeding from him. I doubt I'll need to feed for at least another few days after that experience."

Taron's eyebrows shot skyward. "Woah. So why isn't he your feeder again?"

"Because that's not what he was hired to do," Ozen snapped.

"But he agreed to it, right? Maybe he's interested in the job."

Ozen's mouth watered at the thought of Avery becoming his official feeder. He'd be well fed, that was for certain. And he couldn't forget the need that filled his veins afterward. For the first time in years, he might actually enjoy his feedings. But Avery didn't ask to become a feeder. He had no prior experience with the job. And if he wasn't interested, Ozen would only make things more awkward than they already were.

Taron must've seen the longing in Ozen's face, because he pushed a little. "It couldn't hurt to ask, right?"

"Yes. It could."

CHAPTER FIVE

Rule Number 16 - Jealousy is an unwelcome emotion in a feeder. Refrain from
unwanted outbursts and keep a level head. It's a contract, not a relationship.

Avery was just finishing the write up of the proposal when he realized he
never asked the man his name. He felt like an idiot, but in his defense,
Ozen had been looking at him.

He had never thought of a man as beautiful before, but Ozen fit the
bill. Ozen's features were mostly human. Only his eyes gave away his true
nature. Avery had heard incubi, like many Supes, used glamours to fit more
easily in the world. Avery couldn't tell if magic was being used, he was only
human, so he had to go off of what he saw—flawless honey colored skin,
chiseled jaw without a hint of scruff, straight nose, plush lips. His hair was
platinum, shined like silk, was tied out of his face in a low ponytail, and
made those blood red eyes pop. He was tall with a lithe frame and he wore
a very expensive suit.

He was the stuff of fantasies, and Avery couldn't get him out of his
head. The morning played on a loop in his mind; the pressure of Ozen's
fingers, the cold desk against the warm skin of his cheek, the pleasure that
reached heights he didn't realize existed. He had survived his whole life
with only his right hand for company, and now that the flood gates had

been opened, the need for more swam through his system like syrup, thick and warm, making Avery's movements more sluggish than normal.

"Let's try this again," Mrs. Sable's voice interrupted his thoughts, making him blink rapidly. "Calvin, you sit right there. I'll speak with Mr. Hawksley. Has anything come up while I was gone, Avery?"

"Just this," Avery replied, holding up the piece of paper. "I was asked to rewrite it into something legible for the research team."

She came around the desk, took the paper from Avery's hand, and sighed. "Taron. I swear, that man's handwriting gets worse by the day. And you can understand it?"

"Yes," Avery nodded. "I've been working as a temp for years. I had to learn to read messy handwriting to do well at my job no matter where I was sent. Reading a golem's handwriting was a true challenge."

She huffed out a small laugh, handing Avery back the paper. "Truly. They're much better suited to physical jobs rather than the written word. Alright. I'll be right back. We'll run through the schedule when I return."

She disappeared into the office after a quick knock, closing the door firmly behind her. It was odd; Avery couldn't hear a lick of what was going on inside. In all the jobs he'd worked at, he'd at least hear the murmurs of voices from his desk. Nothing came from Mr. Hawkley's office, despite the knowledge that he wasn't in there alone.

Avery's mind once again drifted back to this morning. He hadn't thought to be quiet, and could barely remember his own name at the time. Was it possible he wasn't overheard? That would be a relief.

A heavy sigh from near the door drew Avery's attention. The feeder, Calvin, looked annoyed, studying his nails like he had somewhere better to be. Avery couldn't imagine where. Feeders' schedules were almost as flexible as temps. Once their charges were fed, they were free to do as they wished. Besides, Avery would jump at the chance to feed Mr. Hawksley again. There wouldn't be another place in the world he'd choose over experiencing that kind of pleasure again.

The office door swung open, and Mrs. Sable came out, the man with the bad handwriting following behind her. He stopped in front of Avery's desk, a smile on his face, but Avery's focus was on the feeder as Mrs. Sable beckoned him. He sauntered into Mr. Hawksley's office like he belonged there, all confidence and sex appeal. Meanwhile, Avery stumbled over his words whenever he was in the presence of the beautiful incubus. A healthy amount of jealousy filled Avery's gut as the door swung shut behind him. That had been him a few hours ago. Now he'd have to be happy sitting outside the office, knowing what was happening inside.

"Did you finish it already?"

Avery's focus snapped back to the man in front of him, who had a grin on his face like he could hear the thoughts swirling through Avery's head. He felt his cheeks burn and he ducked his head to hide his reaction, gesturing to the transcribed page he was almost finished with.

"Almost. I realized I didn't catch your name to sign on the bottom though. I apologize for being so thoughtless."

The man's chuckle was low, drawing Avery's attention back up to his face. He was a good-looking man, with jet black hair and light purple, almost lilac eyes. His skin was like melted chocolate, and his body trim. After experiencing pleasure with Mr. Hawksley, Avery was scrutinizing every man he encountered, searching for a similar reaction. So far, there hadn't been one.

"My name is Taron Cunningham. Ozen is a dear friend of mine."

Avery nearly swallowed his tongue. "You're leaving out the part that you're his business partner and co founder of the company. I'm so sorry I didn't realize sooner."

Taron waved his hand dismissively, like that part didn't matter. "No need to apologize. It's your first day. Though good for you for knowing the names of the leadership already. I'm the one who didn't introduce myself properly."

True, but neither did Avery. He'd been so focused on Ozen that he hardly noticed Taron's presence.

With Taron's name finally added to the bottom of the page, Avery handed him the transcribed document. "I'm Avery. I can bring that downstairs myself if you want, but I'm a little worried I'll get lost without a map. This place is a little intimidating."

"True. We didn't plan it that way. It just works with the large amount of supernaturals in the company. Some don't get along well with others."

That made sense. Some Supes had longstanding animosity with different species, and while working here they might be able to overlook those perceived enemies, it was better not to seat them next to each other.

"Do you like working as a temp?" Taron asked out of nowhere.

Avery frowned at his random question. "Yes?"

"What parts do you like the most?"

While Avery didn't understand the strange shift in conversation, he didn't mind answering questions about himself. It was normal for people to want to get to know him, even if he was only going to be in a position for a short time.

"Well, I like the variety. I like meeting new people. But I think the most valued part for me is the flexible schedule. If a schedule doesn't work for me, I don't have to stick with it for too long. That way I have more free time to work on personal projects." He didn't say anything about his book. That was a secret he shared with absolutely no one.

"Free time," Taron nodded like he agreed with the sentiment. Avery's frown deepened and he was about to ask where all this was coming from, but Mr. Hawksley's office door swung open, and Mrs. Sable came out. The feeder followed behind her, looking just as put together as when he'd gone in. Avery released a breath he didn't realize he'd been holding, glad that at least outwardly, it didn't look like he had fed Mr. Hawksley while he was in there. Mrs. Sable had been with them, but Avery didn't know much about the feeders or their work, so he wasn't sure what limits they had on privacy.

Mr. Hawksley's call button buzzed, and Avery leapt to his feet to answer, earning a smile from Mrs. Sable. He'd always been diligent at his job. No one would need to know it was his eagerness to see Mr. Hawksley that made him so quick to move.

Poking his head into the office, he studied the incubus sitting behind the desk. There was tension around his eyes that hadn't been there before, his lips pressed tightly into a thin line. Something was upsetting him, and Avery felt overwhelmed with the urge to fix it.

"Mr. Hawksley? Is there something I can help you with?"

"I need these taken down to my accountant, Mr. Martell. Twenty second floor. And I'll need a coffee upon your return."

Hurrying across the room, Avery took the file Mr. Hawksley handed to him, disappointment settling in his stomach when his fingers didn't brush against the incubus's like they had earlier.

"Right away, Mr. Hawksley. Is there anything else?"

"That's all for now."

Avery was slower to leave than he was going in, stealing as much time as he could with the incubus before he left the threshold of his office and the door closed quietly behind him. Then it was a race to get Mr. Hawksley's needs met as quickly as possible. If he thought the stairs would've been faster, he would've taken those. Instead, he squeezed himself into the overly full elevator, tucking himself into the corner out of the way of a group of satyrs discussing a new project they were working on. He had to wriggle to get out on the right floor, and he took a moment to fix his hair before heading down the hall to another reception area, this one with a witch manning the phones. He pointed Avery in the direction of Mr. Martell's office, and Avery followed the directions to a T, finding it without issue.

After knocking on the door to no reply, Avery tried the knob and poked his head inside when the door swung open. "Mr. Martell?"

"What?" a craggy old voice snapped from behind the messy desk.

"I have a file from Mr. Hawksley for you. Should I leave it on your desk?"

"If you want me to lose it," he growled. "Gimme a minute."

Avery waited, bouncing on his toes. He needed to get back upstairs to make Mr. Hawksley's coffee. Mrs. Sable walked him through how he preferred it, and he didn't want the incubus to have to wait.

Finally, after a few agonizing minutes, the desk chair moved and a goblin with a long hooked nose and wrinkled skin clambered into the seat. He looked irritated, dropping a few nuts and bolts on top of the nearest pile of papers. "Damn chair keeps sinking on me."

"Oh. Did you want me to ask someone to order you a new one?"

Mr. Martell squinted at him. "You're new, aren't you?"

Avery hadn't realized it'd be that easy to tell. This was a big company, after all. "Uh, I guess you could say that. I'm a temp for Mrs. Sable. I'll be Mr. Hawksley's assistant for the next month."

He snorted but didn't seem to care either way, wiggling his fingers for the file. He flipped it open, grunting as he read over the documents inside.

"Another feeder. Let's hope this one lasts longer than the last one. He almost starved to death before he found a replacement."

CHAPTER SIX

Ozen didn't think it was possible for his new feeder to be worse than the last, but apparently, he was wrong. Calvin hadn't even needed to feed him yet, thanks to Avery's assistance three days ago, but he was already on Ozen's last nerve.

"But why?"

"I told you I'm busy. I'm not here for your entertainment," Ozen snapped. Maybe Ozen should consider going to those incubi clubs to feed. There was no contract involved and a little more risk, but his interactions with feeders would be short and to the point.

"Why are you punishing me? You haven't even touched me yet!" Calvin complained.

Ozen had explained the first day that he'd fed before Calvin's arrival and wouldn't need him for a few days. Granted, he was getting hungry now, but the idea of feeding from Calvin was almost abhorrent. There was only one person he wanted to feed from, and it was the one person he couldn't have.

Like he was summoned from Ozen's wayward thoughts, a gentle knock at Ozen's office door preceded Avery's arrival. He was the picture of professionalism, taking up the reins of Collette's duties with grace and efficiency. He couldn't ask for a better assistant, aside from Collette herself.

There was a strong possibility that the only reason he considered Collette better was because Ozen had zero interest in feeding from her. Meanwhile, Avery was a distraction he didn't want but needed all the same.

"Mr. Hawklsey, the documents you were waiting for have arrived. And I moved your meeting with the Crescent Coven to next week. Apparently, there's a ritual happening this week and they've gotten overwhelmed with preparations."

See? There wasn't a better assistant than Avery. Which made it so much harder when Avery stepped up to his desk to hand him the documents and his scent teased at Ozen's senses. Ozen had no response when Calvin came close, but Avery merely had to look in his direction and he was salivating like an idiot.

Giving himself a firm shake internally, he banished the overwhelming need from his system, gesturing to the inbox on his desk. He got it specifically so he wouldn't accidentally touch Avery. It made everything worse if he did.

"Thank you, Avery. Have you been settling in alright?"

Avery bobbed his head, bouncing on his toes on the other side of Ozen's desk. Ozen noticed early on that Avery almost never stopped moving. If he didn't have a task to do, he'd seek one out. Taron said the secretaries already loved him, despite a few having issues with humans. Apparently, Avery didn't count.

"Yes, sir. I'm doing fine. Can I get you anything else?"

The urge to make up some reason to keep Avery close sat on the edge of Ozen's tongue. He bit down on it to keep himself from saying anything he'd regret, answering Avery with a quick shake of his head.

"Alright. I'll be at my desk if you need me."

After the door shut quietly behind Avery, Calvin's scoff drew Ozen's attention. He was sitting on the sofa, his arms crossed over his chest as he glared in the direction of Avery's desk.

"What now?"

Calvin's scowl grew and Ozen regretted acknowledging him immediately. In his experience, acknowledging a fussy feeder would only bring drama he wasn't interested in dealing with.

"Your assistant is the worst. I'm glad he's only a temp."

That surprised him enough to ask, "Why?" like a complete fool.

Calvin seized the attention he was giving him, spinning around and gesturing with his arms as he ranted. "He's a pretentious asshole! He doesn't even acknowledge my existence! He's always falling over himself to make you happy, but he can't even be bothered to bring me a drink? It's a stupid elevator ride! It's not that far!"

Ozen resisted the urge to roll his eyes, but only just. "Avery is not here for you. His job is to assist me. If he was away from his desk every time you whined for something, he wouldn't be able to do his job effectively. You are perfectly capable of getting your own beverages."

Petulant feeders were worse than needy ones. Ozen knew he'd pay for pointing out the flaws in Calvin's logic, but he wasn't going to listen to the brat disparage Avery. Avery was accommodating, and when he brought in snacks and drinks, there was always a cup for Calvin. But Avery wasn't going to go out of his way to fulfill Calvin's every whim. Calvin wasn't satisfied with the coffee from the break room. He wanted something special from the shop on the first floor and demanded more than once for Avery to bring it to him. That wasn't his job, and Ozen wouldn't allow it even if Avery offered. He was needed here doing his work more than he needed to serve Calvin.

"I'm your feeder," Calvin pointed out with a pout. "Shouldn't I be treated better than a ghost?"

No. Ghosts were quite useful, especially in testing spells. There was no risk of death involved, which helped during some of the more volatile experiments. Ozen knew better than to say that out loud though.

"You are well paid and offered plenty of luxuries to fulfill your role. My assistant isn't one of them. I'm not interested in discussing this further. I have work to do."

With a huff, Calvin launched to his feet and stormed out, slamming Ozen's door so hard, the framed picture next to it crashed to the floor. Ozen sighed heavily, rubbing his fingers against his temples. For a moment, when someone knocked cautiously at his door, he worried it was Calvin coming back to apologize and pout some more. He was grateful when Avery stuck his head in, frowning at the broken frame before turning to face Ozen.

"Is everything alright?"

He closed his eyes, blocking out Avery's hypnotic gaze and the seductive sway of his hips when he came fully into the room. He was sure Avery didn't do the action consciously, which made it that much more difficult to watch. If he thought for a moment that Avery was interested in being his feeder, he'd jump at the chance. But Avery was professional as always and gave him no indication that he wanted a repeat of before. Besides, he'd already signed a contract with Calvin.

Instead of answering the question, Ozen instead asked, "Has Taron chosen the restaurant for our lunch this afternoon?"

"Yes, sir. Yoshida's at noon."

Every time Avery called him sir, a shiver shot up Ozen's spine. He contemplated for the hundredth time asking Avery to stop, but he couldn't deny himself the small thrill of such a simple word. Avery didn't mean it like Ozen wanted, but it didn't hurt anyone to let him pretend.

"Thank you. I'll be joining him directly after my meeting. Feel free to take a long lunch. You've more than earned it."

A bright smile lit up Avery's face, making Ozen's conviction falter for a moment. There was something wrong with him. There had to be. There was no other explanation over why he was so obsessed with this one human. The feeding hadn't even lasted that long, no more than ten minutes. It didn't make any sense.

"I appreciate that, Mr. Hawksley. I brought my lunch today, but I've got some personal things I can get done from my desk."

Always so pragmatic, his new assistant. Ozen was curious about what he had to do, but he pushed the curiosity aside, gathering his phone and wallet before standing to head to his meeting. Avery rushed ahead of him, grabbing his coat from the rack and holding it out for him. The weather had just begun to turn, so he didn't need the layers most days, but today was dreary and he appreciated Avery's thoughtfulness.

"Oh, it started drizzling earlier. Do you need an umbrella?"

Ozen shook his head. "That won't be necessary. My driver will have one. Enjoy your lunch, Avery."

"You too, Mr. Hawksley!" he called after him, a friendly smile on his face.

Only once Ozen arrived at the restaurant did he realize he probably should've fed before he left. Regular food did its job, but the nagging to feed his magic would distract him from his work if he left it too long. He pulled out his phone while following the host to his table, sending a quick text to Calvin to meet him in his office after lunch. He wasn't Avery, but Ozen needed to eat. He couldn't let it go on as long as he had before.

Taron was late but appropriately apologetic, dropping into his seat in a rush. "Sorry, sorry. My meeting with the research team went long. They're trying to avoid bringing a thunderbird in for consultation because of all the regulations with them. I told them that's stupid. We can't help the thunderbirds unless we're working with one to understand their magic better."

"Talk to Maverick. He's not afraid of a little red tape. And I believe he's friends with a thunderbird. He mentioned something at the charity event last month."

After that conversation, they steered away from work. It was important for the both of them to have time where they weren't focused on work or they'd end up workaholics. Ozen was worse than Taron was, because Taron at least took vacations, but these twice weekly lunches were a step in the right direction.

They were just finishing up when Taron asked about Avery again. "Have you talked to your assistant about your obsession with him?"

"I don't have an obsession," Ozen snapped.

"Touchy, touchy," he teased. "Oh, hey, look. Avery chose the same restaurant as us."

Ozen's head whipped around too fast to hide the fact that he might, maybe, have an obsession. He scanned the restaurant hopefully before realizing Taron was screwing with him to prove his point.

"I truly dislike you."

He snorted, his eyes dancing with mischief. "No you don't. You're just grumpy because the object of your obsession isn't here."

"For that trick, you get to pay for lunch," Ozen growled, tossing his napkin onto the table more roughly than he'd intended. It was smart to feed after this. He had the tendency to get grouchy when the nagging hunger got too insistent. And maybe if he fed from Calvin, the obsession with Avery would fade.

"Oh come on, don't be that way," Taron cajoled, handing the waiter his card as he passed. "I'm just trying to help. You haven't even looked at your new feeder, but whenever Avery is in the room, you can't look away. There's nothing saying you can't ask—"

"There is!" Ozen argued. "He's my assistant! I had extremely low expectations on Collette's replacement, but Avery has gone above and beyond to take care of my needs, sometimes before I realize I need something. I can't risk losing him, at least not before Collette returns. Besides, I have a feeder already, so please, drop the subject."

Taron put his hands up in surrender. "Alright, alright. I'll let it go. For now."

Ozen's frustrated groan only made Taron laugh.

CHAPTER SEVEN

Rule Number 5 - A feeder should maintain calm poise in stressful situations.

Something was wrong with Mr. Hawksley. During the first week working with him, he was kind and patient. The second week, he was professional, if a little curt at times. He was never unkind to Avery, just sometimes a little distant. Which, after what happened on his first day, Avery wasn't surprised about. So when he arrived at work the following Monday and Mr. Hawksley was so frustrated that steam was practically coming from his ears, Avery was taken off guard. In all the prepared material Mrs. Sable had left him regarding his job, none of it covered what would put the incubus in such a foul mood.

Everyone on the floor seemed to notice, despite the soundproofing in Mr. Hawksley's office. There was a layer of tension in the office, and through the glass separating his desk from the rest of the floor, Avery noticed dozens of apprehensive glances in the direction of Mr. Hawklsey's office. When one of the secretaries from the pool stopped by to give Avery a report from finance, she practically bolted from the room the second Avery took the file. To Avery's knowledge, arachne didn't spook easily.

By the time lunch rolled around, Avery's concern was too much to bear. He didn't feel like it was a smart idea to ask Mr. Hawksley directly, but after stopping by for a meeting the week prior, Mr. Cunningham told Avery to call if he had any questions. At the moment, he had plenty.

Avery wasn't familiar with every direct line in the building, so instead he called down to the switchboard. Mrs. Sable had introduced Avery to the friendly kraken who worked in the basement (with a company provided salt pool to soak in during work hours) and the kraken said Avery could use his expertise instead of memorizing numbers. He answered on the first ring, his voice chipper and perky.

"Spellbound Corps, how may I direct your call?"

"Hello, Alvin. It's Avery, Mr. Hawksley's assistant." Technically, he could just tell Alvin where he wanted to be transferred, but it felt rude not to acknowledge the kraken.

"Oh! Hello, Avery. How are things going up there? I heard rumors that the boss is in a foul mood."

So the rumors were so wide spread to reach Alvin? That didn't seem good.

"Yes, that's what I'm trying to handle. I don't know him that well, though, so I was hoping you could connect me to Mr. Cunningham's office?"

"Definitely. They've been best friends for years. Taron is the quickest insight into Mr. Hawklsey's moods. Let me transfer you. And be careful, okay? You're only human."

A plastic smile pulled at Avery's lips. "Thanks for worrying about me. I'll be careful. Have a good day, Alvin."

Alvin was only being kind, but the reminder that Avery was only human and seen as weak amongst Supes dug a little. Avery was perfectly capable of handling himself around Mr. Hawksley, thank you very much. He'd survived feeding him, didn't he?

The phone rang twice after Alvin transferred him, and when Mr. Cunningham answered, he sounded harried.

"Cunningham," he answered quickly.

"Hello, Mr. Cunningham. This is Avery, Mr. Hawksley's assistant. I was wondering if I could have a moment of your time to ask a question."

Mr. Cunningham hummed, sounding distracted as he replied, "For a moment, sure. But I've got a meeting in ten."

"That's fine. This shouldn't take long," Avery reassured him, rushing to ask his question and stop bothering the man. "I'm worried about Mr. Hawksley. He's been... difficult this morning, which seems like a complete one-eighty from last week. I was wondering if you had any insight on how I can make his day better?"

"When was the last time he fed?"

Avery blinked. "Oh, um... I'm not sure."

While he wasn't actively avoiding Mr. Hawksley's feeder, he tried his best not to interact with the man. He was worried the feeder would be able to see the jealousy on Avery's face. He had actually been pleased that he hadn't run into him today.

"If he's hungry, he's a real bear. Call his feeder. If that doesn't work, you can call me back after my meeting and I'll come check on him myself."

Well, shoot. So much for not having to interact with the feeder. "Thank you, Mr. Cunningham. I really appreciate your help."

"Please, call me Taron. Only people who want money call me Mr. Cunningham."

Avery bit back a laugh. First world problems. "Taron, then. I can make my own money."

Taron laughed, some of the tension in his voice fading away. "My meeting should be over in an hour. Let me know how it goes."

"I will. Thanks again."

After Taron hung up, Avery summoned the will to call the feeder, but as he picked up the phone on his desk, he realized he didn't have the number. He hadn't thought he'd need it. And he doubted Alvin had it. That meant he'd have to talk to Mr. Hawksley about it. Which kind of defeated the purpose of calling Taron.

He contemplated leaving it be, everyone was allowed to have a bad day, but Taron said Mr. Hawksley's mood might be because he was hungry. If that was the case, it felt cruel to ignore the issue. Drawing in a deep breath, Avery pushed to his feet and crossed to Mr. Hawksley's door, knocking quietly.

"Enter," Mr. Hawksley snapped.

When Avery poked his head in, he almost flinched. Mr. Hawksley looked... feral. He had a dark scowl pulling at his lips and his red eyes almost glowed. He said he was hungry when Avery accidentally stepped in to feed him his first day, but he didn't look nearly this bad.

"Mr. Hawksley? Are you alright?"

"I'm fine."

Avery didn't believe him, even if Mr. Hawksley had managed to get the reply out without gritting his teeth. Avery edged closer, growing more concerned the closer he got. It almost looked like Mr. Hawksley was in pain. His grip on his pen was so tight, his knuckles were white, and his lip twitched like he was fighting a scowl. This wasn't the cool, collected CEO Avery had met during his first week. Something was definitely wrong.

"I can call your feeder for you, if you're too busy. I–"

The snarl that left Mr. Hawksley's throat wasn't human in the slightest. The hair on the back of Avery's neck stood on end, and for a moment, he worried for his safety. But the longer he stood in front of Mr. Hawksley, the more he noticed how poorly he was doing. The whites around his eyes, the heavy breathing. He was close to panic.

"Mr. Hawksley?"

"He won't pick up. He hasn't for over a week. I can't–" He grimaced, curling in on himself. "It doesn't matter. I'm fine."

No, he really wasn't. And if his feeder hadn't answered his phone in a week, that meant Mr. Hawksley hadn't fed for at least that long, maybe longer. Avery last saw the feeder Wednesday during his first week. That was almost two weeks ago. How long could incubi go without feeding?

"Is there someone else I can call? A backup maybe?" Avery stepped closer, rounding the desk to at least offer some comfort.

"No!" Mr. Hawksley pushed his chair away, the panic doubled, and Avery froze where he stood. "I can handle this myself. Y-You need to leave, Avery. I–" He doubled over again, practically bent in half in his chair. Avery couldn't leave him now, not when he was starving like this. He searched his mind for someone to call, some way to help, but only one idea came to mind.

"Use me."

Mr. Hawksley's head jerked up, his eyes wide and his breathing shallow. "What?"

"Use me. I've fed you before. I don't mind doing it again. You're starving, Mr. Hawksley. We can't wait around to find your feeder. It's hurting you."

The noise that came from Mr. Hawksley's throat almost sounded like a whimper. He looked tempted, he even loosened his grip on his middle, but then he shook his head sharply.

"No. I can't. We have a contract. Exclusivity is part of it."

"Your contract is void if he can't be trusted to show up to feed you," Avery argued. "Please. Let me help you."

He didn't have time to blink before he was shoved against the wall, Mr. Hawksley pinning him there with his knee between Avery's thighs. A heavy wave of lust slammed into him so intense that he almost came instantly. He moaned loudly, his head hitting the wall as he threw it back in pleasure.

He'd thought it'd be a lot like before. Mr. Hawksley would touch him and the feeding would happen slowly. But Mr. Hawksley was too far gone to go slow. He had Avery's pants undone and his erection out in less than a breath, his grip rough as he stroked him. Avery could only hold on to Mr. Hawksley's arms, his moans the only sound in the office. When he forced his chin down, he took in Mr. Hawksley's face. His eyes were so red, they almost looked like blood. The long fangs weren't present in Avery's day-to-day interactions with his boss, and they made him shiver to look at. But it was the desperation that tugged at Avery's heart.

"I need—" Mr. Hawksley grimaced. "I need you to come."

"T-Touch me. M-My hole." If he'd had time to be embarrassed, he'd be blushing furiously, admitting to something like that. But it was too fast, too intense. Mr. Hawksley shoved his free hand down the back of Avery's pants, his fingers already slippery, though Avery had never seen him grab lube. A quick pulse of magic made him gasp, and then Mr. Hawksley's finger shoved inside, going straight for that spot that made him see stars. That's all it took to send Avery over the edge, his voice hoarse from his cries of pleasure.

Avery's eyes shut of their own volition, the pleasure too much to bear. He heard Mr. Hawksley groan, felt him lean against Avery's front, but he was so blown away, he couldn't do much more than try and catch his breath.

CHAPTER EIGHT

They both stayed quiet for a moment, and that fuzzy pleasure-filled feeling from before made Avery melt until only Mr. Hawksley's weight pressing him to the wall kept him upright.

"Are you alright?" Mr. Hawksley finally asked. His voice was gruff, still a little strained, but a lot less than before.

Avery hummed, his forehead resting against Mr. Hawksley's shoulder. "Why are handjobs so much better when someone else does it?"

His eyes flew open, and he stiffened. He did not just say that out loud. When Mr. Hawksley chuckled, Avery wanted to curl up into a ball and hide from the world. Maybe it was the sex. Everything felt just a little hazy. It destroyed the filter between his brain and his mouth.

"I believe partially due to the novelty. But you're also in the presence of an incubus. I am rather an expert on pleasure."

"You're an expert on a lot of things," Avery replied offhandedly. Again, no filter. Though that comment was less embarrassing, it still probably could've been left unsaid. He changed the subject by asking, "Are you feeling better?"

"Somewhat. I... I hate to ask, but–" He shifted far enough away to give Avery space to breathe. Avery could see the vulnerability on Mr. Hawksley's face. He was still hungry, and there wasn't a chance Avery would leave him that way.

"I'm willing to go again, but maybe not against the wall. My knees feel like jello."

Relief brought a smile to Mr. Hawksley's face for the first time in a week. "Perhaps a bed would be more appropriate."

It might, but Avery was pretty sure he'd just made a mess of his suit. His slacks had barely made it to his thighs in the rush of it all. He was going to suggest the couch when Mr. Hawksley swept him off his feet into a bridal carry, his movements fluid and effortless like Avery weighed no more than a feather. Mr. Hawksley brought him to the bookshelves behind his desk, pulling one shelf out to reveal a room behind it as it swung open.

"Woah. How did I not know this was here?"

"I prefer my feeds to occur at work. It eliminates perceived intimacy in an act that's meant to nourish me. That doesn't mean I can't treat my companions well. There's also a bathroom behind the other bookshelf, with a shower and jacuzzi tub."

It took a minute for Avery to understand the separation. "Even with a contract, they think it's more than feeding?"

Mr. Hawksley grunted, setting Avery down gently on a soft surface. "Unfortunately. It's why I struggle with finding someone more permanent. After a while, they all start pushing for more. Only once have I ever had a feeder who understood the distinction long term."

The room was dark, but he assumed he was lying on a bed. He was proven right when Mr. Hawsley turned the light on, revealing the room behind the bookshelf. Avery swallowed hard, suddenly incredibly intimidated.

Even with the low lighting of the room, Avery could see the toys on the shelves against the wall, with what looked like riding crops and paddles next to it. His eyes darted to benches, something that looked like a wooden x with straps attached to it, and even a swing. What they'd done in the office was fine, but Avery suddenly felt way out of his depth.

"Relax, firefly. Those are not a requirement. As an incubus, I cater to all appetites, but that doesn't mean everyone enjoys the same things. Besides, those items are too advanced for you."

Avery's gaze whipped back to Mr. Hawksley. "Y-You can tell?"

Mr. Hawksley dipped his chin once, his expression kind and not at all judgmental. Still, Avery cringed and felt the need to explain.

"It's not like I was saving it for something special. I just... I didn't really think about it much. I was busy with school and family and I didn't have time to think about dating, much less sex."

Mr. Hawksley sat beside him, putting a reassuring hand on Avery's knee. "You're sure you're comfortable with this? I don't want you to feel obligated. You helped enough that I should have time to contact the agency, find another feeder. I–"

"No!" Too loud. Avery cringed again. "No, I want to. I like it. I..."

Mr. Hawksley waited for Avery to continue, encouraging him when he struggled. "You should be honest, Avery. Contract or no, your consent is important, as are your feelings on the matter."

The quickie in his office seemed to melt the worst of the foul mood Mr. Hawksley had been in. Gone was the short-tempered monster and the kind and patient incubus was back. It made it easier for Avery to speak freely.

"I... I kind of like the idea of my first time being with you. You obviously know what you're doing. There aren't many guys who I could say I trust not to hurt me. I, uh, I heard that hurts. Sex with men. For the, um... receiver."

Mr. Hawksley's face softened and his smile made Avery's heart beat out of control. "I can assure you, you won't ever feel pain with me. And we're in no rush. If I may, I'd like to feed like we did on your first day. I'd like to see your face this time."

Avery's face flushed, and he could only respond with a shaky nod. He'd fed Mr. Hawksley twice now, and he was still embarrassed by his eager reactions. He was already hard, even though he'd just come recently.

His shoes came off first, followed by his socks. Avery's slacks were still undone, so it took only a quick tug to draw them down his legs. His jacket, tie, and shirt were next, Mr. Hawksley's movements methodical as he laid each item on the foot of the bed. His boxers were sticky with remnants of Avery's previous release, but Mr. Hawksley didn't comment as he dragged them off.

Avery was completely bared to the incubus's gaze, and he felt a moment of insecurity. Mr. Hawksley had probably been with some of the most beautiful people in his lifetime. Incubi were notoriously long lived, almost as long as vampires, and people clamored to experience a night with them. Avery had to wonder how he compared to the rest.

Mr. Hawksley's nostrils flared, the red in his eyes sparking anew. It'd calmed a little after earlier against the wall, but his hunger was still evident on his face. The self consciousness faded and need took its place. He knew what was going to happen next, and he wanted it more than anything. Mr. Hawksley shifted until he was lying next to Avery, his hands trailing over Avery's naked skin.

"You are a true delight. Even now, your desire tugs at my magic. I've never had such effortless feeding before."

It felt silly to be proud of that. It wasn't like he was doing anything consciously, but Avery still felt exhilaration filling his chest. He liked to do his jobs well, and apparently in this, he was succeeding.

Mr. Hawksley's lips followed the path of his hands, brushing over his chest and teasing his nipples. When he drew one into his mouth and sucked lightly, Avery moaned, his hands fisting into the bedding to stop himself from touching Mr. Hawksley. He wasn't sure he was supposed to.

Even during his self care, he never paid much attention to his nipples. He had no idea they were that sensitive, and when Mr. Hawksley nibbled on one, Avery's head flew back on a gasp.

"Mr. Hawksley..." he breathed.

The incubus lifted his head, his deep red eyes ensnaring Avery even further. "Ozen."

It felt wrong to call his boss by his first name, but Avery figured in the bedroom, he wasn't Avery's boss. Even though technically they were still in the office.

Ozen waited, his eyebrows lifted expectantly until Avery nodded in agreement. Then he went back to toying with Avery's nipples, drawing little gasps and moans from him. His cock was rock hard, the need so intense, it was almost like he hadn't come less than thirty minutes ago. And Ozen hadn't even moved lower than his chest yet. Avery squirmed, seeking friction, drawing Ozen's attention.

"Do you want more?"

"Please..."

Ozen was once again blown away at how easily Avery's desire fed him. Light teasing brought the same amount of lust as touching his cock. Perhaps it was the man's virginity. Being untouched for twenty-seven years must have made his desire more potent.

Whatever the reason, it soothed the ragged edges of Ozen's magic. He was content to play leisurely until he got his fill, but Avery's wants were just as important, and he wanted more.

Ozen skipped past Avery's dick, not wanting to rush to the finish. Quick trysts did their job, like before against the wall, but they often left Ozen feeling unsatisfied, like he'd had broth for supper instead of a proper meal. He could survive on it, but it wasn't pleasant. The longer the play lasted, the more he felt truly satisfied from it. Quick sessions also weren't easy on the feeder.

"Legs up, knees apart," Ozen commanded gently. Avery's belly still trembled with nerves, the desire in the air tinged with it, but the anxiety was missing. Anticipation warred with excitement, giving Avery's desire a more heady scent. He did asked, his feet planted on the bed, his legs falling open to bare himself to Ozen's gaze. Ozen took in the tight little bud, his own desire rearing up alongside his magic. He wanted to take everything Avery offered, but Ozen didn't trust himself with that right now. The hunger still twisted in his belly, making him feel just on the other side of feral. Two weeks was way too long between feeds. After getting what he needed from Avery, Ozen would call the agency Calvin worked through and tear them a new one.

For now, he focused on the eager man in his bed, running teasing fingers over his balls and taint. When he brushed against Avery's hole, Avery tensed automatically. Instead of using magic to relax him, Ozen placed delicate kisses along the inside of Avery's thigh, teasing the puckered entrance slowly with his thumb. Avery's moans grew louder with each pass, his body relaxed, and when he wriggled to get closer, Ozen pushed his finger inside.

"Ohh..."

Avery's noises alone could feed him for a week. He shuddered as a wave of Avery's desires washed over him. The desperation receded, and Ozen could truly enjoy what he was doing with his bed fellow. The only magic he used was to keep the connection between himself and Avery so he could feed. The rest was simple pleasure shared between men. No magic necessary.

When he switched from his thumb to his fingers, Avery's anticipation dialed higher. He knew what was coming, and yet his reaction was just as surprised as the first time. The strangled squeak melted into a loud moan, Avery's hips bucking automatically. Ozen's gaze was locked on the smaller man's face, watching the pleasure overtake him, the way his eyes squeezed shut in ecstasy, only to be forced open again moments later to look at Ozen. Warmth settled in Ozen's chest every time Avery looked at him. Most feeders spent little time looking at him. They sought their pleasure and cared for little else. Avery didn't seem to want to look away. He cared who was in bed next to him, and when Ozen's name spilled from his lips, it sounded like a prayer.

Avery's patience only lasted so long before he was pleading for release. Ozen stopped teasing, thrusting his fingers more forcefully, adding a third to increase the stretch. Avery's cries filled the room, his eyes no longer able to stay open as the pleasure overtook him. When he came, Ozen nearly followed after him. He hadn't come untouched since he was an untried youth, and yet the intensity of Avery's desire very nearly forced the issue. He groaned, dipping his head to clean up the mess with his tongue while ignoring his own erection. He'd deal with that privately later.

Avery melted into the bed as Ozen removed his fingers. After feeding him twice in less than an hour, Avery would need his rest. His eyes didn't even open as Ozen laid a blanket on top of him. He brushed a few of Avery's golden curls from his forehead, his voice low so as to not disturb him.

"Rest now, firefly. I'll wake you in an hour."

Avery's only reply was a contented hum, and his breathing evened out seconds later. Ozen took care to clean Avery's skin with a wet cloth but didn't disturb him further. The best aftercare for Avery right now was letting him rest.

CHAPTER NINE

Once he was certain Avery would stay asleep, Ozen went back to his office. He didn't close the door fully to the bedroom, worried Avery might wake up confused and alone and the dark room would frighten him. Instead, he left the door open just a crack, so he could hear if Avery woke and the light from his office would be seen from the bed.

He made a detour to his private bathroom to deal with his reaction to Avery's sweet noises first. They replayed over and over in his mind as he stroked his cock, the taste of Avery's release still on his tongue. The only consolation he had for his embarrassingly fast finish was that he was alone. It had been ages since he was at the mercy of his desire like that. He asked himself again if Avery's virginity was what made Ozen feel so wild and fulfilled at the same time.

After washing his hands, he returned to his office to officially cancel the contract with Calvin. He made a call to Mr. Martell to deal with the financial aspect of it and was about to call the agency that provided him when Taron strode into his office like he owned the place. Ozen shot him a flat look, putting the phone back in its cradle.

"You do understand the concept of knocking, correct?"

He gave Ozen a lazy grin, dropping into the chair opposite him and putting his feet on the edge of the desk.

"I'm your friend, and a little bird told me you were being difficult. I came to check on you. I'm guessing he got ahold of your feeder?"

Ozen couldn't help but scoff, his anger spiking once again when he remembered how desperate he felt to get ahold of Calvin.

"No, he didn't. I called several times myself. He refused to answer. I..." Ozen trailed off, real fear crawling across his skin. "I feared not only for myself but also for Avery, who only came in here to comfort me."

That made Taron sit up, his goofy expression turning serious. "Is Avery alright?"

Ozen nodded solemnly. "He's fine. Resting now." Before his friend could make accusations, he put his hand up and continued. "I explained what was happening and asked him to leave, but he offered to feed me instead. There was no influence from my magic. I'd been fighting it the moment he stepped into the room. I refused to make that same mistake twice, hunger be damned. Avery was fully conscious of what he was offering and knew he wasn't required to. He offered anyway, even after I tried to deny him."

Closing his eyes, Ozen remembered the struggle, the pain of holding back when he was so close to starvation he felt the icy grip of it shredding his insides. It took everything he had left not to take more from Avery than was necessary. If he had been a little younger, a little less experienced, he could've drained Avery dry in his desperation, leaving him a passionless husk for the rest of his life. Avery had no idea how close he came to truly losing himself. His risk was not something Ozen would take for granted.

"It took two couplings to bring me back from the edge, Taron. Had it been anyone else, Avery could have—" Ozen's voice cracked, betraying his emotions.

"But it wasn't anyone else," Taron interjected. "It was you, and you kept him safe. You are not a monster."

Taron always knew when Ozen had reached his worst, when he felt like the monster most humans thought him to be. In his true form, he could lure just about anyone into his bed, and that made him dangerous. Some incubi refused to hide themselves and made no efforts to hold themselves back. The amount of people drained by incubi was so significant, the government had to step in. If a feeder was fully drained of their passion or killed during the feeding, there would be severe consequences.

"Why did you wait so long? Hell, I would've volunteered if you were really that desperate. I mean, I wouldn't have let you fuck my ass, but as your friend, I wouldn't have said no to a blowjob."

Ozen snorted, the teasing doing its job to bring him out of his melancholy. Like Ozen, Taron didn't care to distinguish gender in his partners, but he was vehemently against doing things of that nature with his friends. He didn't want to muddy the waters. Ozen would never sully his friendship with sex, however, even if he saw Taron as anything other than his brother.

"Thank you for your kind offer, but I'm alright now. Thanks to Avery. As to why I waited..." His brows drew together tightly. "At first, I thought it was just a temper tantrum. Calvin was angry with me for not making Avery fetch him things like a servant. I scolded him and told him Avery was my assistant, not his. He stormed off, and when he didn't reply to my messages, I ignored his behavior because I didn't want to encourage it. After almost a week had passed, though, I considered he might be punishing me. If we hadn't signed a contract, I would've gone elsewhere for a feed, but the contract demands exclusivity on both ends."

It was safer that way. Not only for diseases, though Ozen would be able to tell before they got started, but also because in the past, enemies used feeders to poison incubi during the act. Most feeders were unaware they were being tampered with until after the incubus died. Sex magic was powerful, and incubi weren't the only supernaturals who used it. It was rare now, society had moved beyond that, but it was still a common precaution in feeder contracts.

"It wasn't until Avery pointed out that the contract was void when Calvin refused to show up that I gave myself leave to seek nourishment elsewhere. I already contacted Mr. Martell, and I was about to contact the agency before you arrived."

Taron's face had grown darker throughout the story, and by the time Ozen finished, he was so angry, he'd reverted to his true form. His skin was black as night, all identifying features absent. He looked like a shadow, and his anger made the surrounding air vibrate.

"He was going to kill you, starve you to death, because you wouldn't make your assistant cater to him? What the fuck?"

"He also took issue with me not feeding from him right away after we met. My first feeding from Avery left me quite comfortable for a few days. I didn't need to seek more. Apparently, Calvin took that personally."

"If I ever see that piece of shit again, I'll–"

Ozen interjected to stall his friend's rant. "You will do nothing, because you are not a monster either. I will make a phone call to the agency and will put in the paperwork to have Calvin blacklisted from being a feeder to another incubus. I won't let this pass, but I'm not going to let my friend end up in prison, either. Be still, my brother. I am well."

Slowly, Taron drew back into his favored form. He made minor changes here and there when he was feeling whimsical, like the larger nose he was sporting today. But every century or so, he found a new form he enjoyed and stuck with it until his next inspiration hit. His smile still hadn't returned, but Ozen was happy to see his friend's anger settle a little.

"You're sure? Twice was enough?"

Ozen tipped his head back and forth. "For now. The effects of going two weeks without feeding haven't worn off completely, but I feel closer to normal again. And I wasn't going to push for more so soon. It would endanger Avery, and I won't allow that to happen."

Taron nodded seriously. "Good. That's good. Do you think he'll sign on as your feeder? He's trustworthy and doesn't throw tantrums when he's unhappy."

Ozen sighed. He'd been avoiding asking Avery to be his feeder, not wanting to ruin their working relationship when he was so reliant on the human. But Ozen wasn't stupid. He needed a feeder, and Taron was right. Avery could be trusted to do the job, hopefully without letting feelings get involved. Thus far, he'd been the picture of professionalism.

"I'm going to ask. I don't trust the agencies anymore, and I don't enjoy going to the feeding clubs. They're not as selective in their admission process."

Taron made a face. He knew all about those clubs and had never argued with Ozen's refusal to visit them.

"Yeah, don't do that. You're better than that. Did you want me to stick around for that conversation? Maybe it'll make Avery a little more comfortable with a third party in the room?"

He fought back a smile. His friend was always conscious of other people's feelings, but he sometimes forgot his importance to those closest to him. "If Avery requires a third party, I'll ask someone a little more unbiased. Perhaps Mr. Martell. But for the initial conversation, I believe privacy is necessary. Thank you, though. I know you mean well."

After Taron left, which took too long because he needed several assurances that Ozen was well and would call him to let him know how the discussion with Avery went, Ozen finally had the time to call the company who sent Calvin. The receptionist was a peppy young woman and her voice was chipper when she answered his call.

"Wicked Delights, this is Tanya. How can I help you?"

"I need to speak with the director," Ozen replied tersely in lieu of an introduction.

"And what would this be in regards to?"

"One of your feeders tried to starve me in retaliation to an imagined slight. I want to speak to the director. Now."

His order was forceful and probably unnecessarily rude to the poor receptionist, but he needed to impress the gravity of the situation. Tanya was quick to action, though, a tremor in her voice as she responded.

"Right away. Let me transfer you. I'm so sorry."

If this was the way they ran their company, they would be. Ozen wasn't going to be satisfied until Calvin and the people who judged him sane enough to act as a feeder were jobless and blacklisted. And even then, it might not be enough.

CHAPTER TEN

Rule Number 3 - A contract between feeder and client should be well discussed and agreed upon before initiation of the client/feeder dynamic, unless in an emergency. This is for the protection of both parties.

Avery woke up feeling like he'd had the best nap of his life. His body was relaxed and there was zero tension in his muscles. It took a few moments to remember why. He felt his face flush, the memories of the encounter with his boss both thrilling him and embarrassing him at the same time. Never in his life had he ever felt so wanton. Ozen barely had to do any work to get Avery to come like a fountain. And then he had to go ahead and fall asleep before they'd even had a conversation. Avery pulled the blankets over his head, wanting to hide away for the rest of his life.

Unfortunately, his work day wasn't done. Mr. Hawksley hadn't even taken his lunch break yet. Incubi still needed regular food, as well as sex.

Ozen... It still felt wrong to use his boss's first name, but in the throes of passion, the wrongness disappeared. He was Ozen, and he played Avery's body like a fiddle.

Avery felt his cock swell and sighed heavily. That wouldn't do. He needed to get back to work, and if Ozen could tell Avery was a virgin, he was probably able to tell when Avery was aroused. He needed to reign it in and maintain professionalism while they were in the office.

"Stop thinking about it," Avery whispered to himself. "You've got work to do."

Once he was fully in control of himself, he threw the covers back and got to his feet. He'd expected a twinge or some discomfort since things got a lot rougher than the first time, but there was nothing besides a bounce to his step that hadn't been there that morning. No wonder people were so eager for sex. It put him in a fabulous mood. He found his clothes hung up neatly on a rack near the door, all evidence of his first release gone. Even his underwear was clean. Avery had been prepared to go commando the rest of the day, but the freshness of his clothes was a welcome surprise. He pulled them on, the murmur of Ozen's voice leaking into the room through the crack in the door. Avery needed a mirror to do his tie right, so he left the room to head to his desk before he fixed it.

"I'll call you back," Ozen said, hanging up the phone a moment later. "Avery? Do you have a moment?"

Spinning around, Avery fought to keep his face neutral. It was a lot more difficult looking at his boss after he made him come so hard him thought he'd gone blind. Avery wasn't sure how he was supposed to act now. Where was the line between professional and too aloof? He didn't want to make it seem like he regretted it, because he didn't in the slightest. That didn't mean he wasn't a little embarrassed. His boss had his fingers up Avery's ass earlier. The reminder made him blush deeply.

"Y-Yes, of course. I was just going to grab a mirror from my desk. I can't fix my tie without it."

Ozen stood, coming around his desk to stand in front of him. "May I?"

Avery's head bobbed in agreement, and he held his breath as Ozen readjusted the tie and started to knot it carefully. Standing this close, Avery could study every detail of his face. The red in his eyes had returned to normal and there were no fangs peeking out from between his lips. There was a hint of tension above his eyebrow, but that wasn't unusual for his boss. Usually, when Avery noticed that tension, he brought Ozen more coffee. It seemed to help.

"Would you like some coffee?"

Ozen hummed, his focus on the tie as he adjusted it closer to Avery's neck. "Perhaps, in a moment. I'd like to talk to you first. Please, have a seat."

Avery sat in the chair Ozen gestured to, fidgeting nervously as his boss sat across from him. A dozen things flashed through his mind on what this could be about. Was he angry with Avery for offering himself? Did he overstep? Was Avery going to lose his job? Or—

"I can tell you're overthinking this, so I'm going to be blunt, if you don't mind. I'd like to discuss a contract between us."

Blinking, Avery's brows drew together. "A contract?"

Ozen nodded once. "Twice now you've offered to feed me. You enjoy yourself when you do?"

He said it like a question and waited for Avery's reply, even though he was well aware of Avery's pleasure each time. Avery didn't want to leave him hanging, though, so he agreed with a sharp nod.

"That's good. Then I was wondering if you'd be interested in becoming my feeder. The compensation is agreeable, there are benefits involved, such as dental coverage and medical. The hours aren't very demanding, and there are no penalties for a conflict in schedule. Unless you ignore me for weeks," he added, a hint of exasperation over what happened with his previous feeder in his tone. "All couplings will be with your pleasure in mind, as that's what feeds me best, and your comfort levels are the priority at all times."

While Avery had daydreams since the first time he fed Ozen about becoming his feeder, he never actually thought he'd get a chance. His first instinct was to leap at the opportunity, but his analytical side was more cautious.

"I, uh... I have some questions, if that's alright."

Ozen's smile made Avery breathe a little easier. "I encourage any and all questions. I find openness and honesty are key in incubi/feeder contracts."

Avery took a deep breath, letting it out slowly as he organized his mind. He started with the easiest question.

"Would this affect the job I already have?"

Ozen tipped his head, considering it. "Your current contract? No. Having you nearby would only benefit me. Once Collette returns, I might suggest having your temp work be made strictly for my company. Unless you'd prefer to join the secretary pool?"

Avery shook his head quickly. "No, that's okay. I like the variety. I've never heard of a temp being contracted out to one company, but I can call my supervisor and ask her about it. We send a lot of temps here, so it might cut out some back and forth. Does my, uh, lack of experience pose an issue?"

"None whatsoever. And I'm happy to explore any and all of your interests during our feedings. If you'd prefer to keep it to what we've been doing, that would be fine too. It's all about what you're comfortable with."

That was encouraging. Avery hadn't been lying when he said he liked the idea of his first time being with Ozen. He felt safe to explore with him without fear of bodily harm.

"I appreciate that. And I don't think I'd limit myself to just..." He made a vague gesture with his hand. "That."

Ozen's lips twitched like he was fighting a smile, which made Avery blush. He wasn't comfortable yet talking about sex, but with Ozen being so accommodating, maybe Avery could request that he lead during exploration. It'd take some of the pressure off.

"One last question..." Avery paused, fidgeting in his seat. "Why me?"

"For a few reasons, actually," Ozen replied. "First, as you've allowed me to feed from you before, I know we're compatible. Just because I'm an incubus doesn't guarantee compatibility. Also, after the first time, you maintained professionalism, despite the intimate act we shared. I value that. As I said before, feeders often perceive more than there is to what amounts to a business relationship. I feel like I can trust you to stay professional."

True. While Avery really enjoyed the feedings, orgasms didn't equal relationships, and Avery wasn't under the illusion that more would come from the contract. It was a safe place to explore his newfound sexuality, not a romantic relationship.

"I'd also like a partnership with you because I trust you. When I was struggling, you didn't fear me, didn't panic or get upset. You took action to make things better, and when another option didn't present itself, you offered yourself instead. I haven't had a feeder that calm and thoughtful in a long while."

Avery wanted to ask about that feeder, Ozen had mentioned him before, but that felt too personal. Ozen just said he preferred professionalism in regards to his feeders, and if Avery accepted, that didn't give him access to Ozen's personal life.

"Feel free to take the afternoon to decide. After two weeks without feeding, I might need more feedings than usual to return to normal, so more than a day and I'll have to seek nourishment elsewhere."

That made Avery's head whip up. He'd been staring at the desk, thinking it through, and he hadn't realized he stopped giving eye contact.

"Wait. Are you still hungry? Do you need to feed again?"

Ozen's smile warmed and he put up his hand to stop Avery's nervous ramble. "Relax. I'm okay. Yes, I'm still hungry, but not overwhelmingly so. I can wait another day."

"But you shouldn't have to," Avery argued. "You were starved. You need to take care of yourself. I can—"

"No." Ozen's firm tone made Avery's mouth snap shut. He studied his boss, who was firm but patient when he said, "Even if you agreed to the contract today, I will not risk feeding from you again. Not today. You need more rest. Your health is just as important as mine. I am not starving anymore. I can wait."

The thought of leaving him hungry made Avery's insides squirm uncomfortably. He didn't fully understand the need to wait, but he assumed that would be explained to him if he agreed. Oh, who was he kidding?

"Yes."

Ozen frowned, tipping his head. "Yes?"

"Yes, I'll be your feeder. I still have more questions, but they're mostly logistical in nature. I'll need to contact my supervisor about your idea for being a temp here exclusively, but it won't actually change my decision. I'll just make sure to meet you before or after a job if I'm not in this building specifically."

Ozen seemed surprised, and he didn't agree right away with Avery's decision. "You don't want to take more time to think about it?"

Avery's cheeks flushed as he admitted, "I would've offered after the first time if your new feeder hadn't shown up right after we'd finished. I enjoyed feeding you, both physically and emotionally. I like feeling needed and helping others. It ticks all my boxes."

Ozen stared for a moment before he huffed out a laugh. "I'll admit, I thought it would be harder to convince you. I thought you'd need more time. I can have a contract drawn up before you leave today. I am going to insist that you read it through carefully tonight and give me your final decision in the morning. It's not a demanding job, but it is an intimate one. You should be fully aware of what you're agreeing to."

"I can agree to that," Avery said with a sharp nod. "Is there anything else you'd like to discuss? I believe we both skipped lunch, so I was going to offer to run to grab something. And I've been told you're a bear when you haven't eaten," he teased, easing the tension from their encounter earlier. Avery had been worried for Ozen, but now that he knew how to take care of the incubus better, he wasn't distressed by the interaction.

Ozen chuckled, raising an eyebrow at Avery. "You're going to be insufferable, aren't you?"

"Only when it comes to making sure you've eaten. Otherwise, I'm a joy to work with. Everyone says so," Avery responded cheekily.

"Everyone would be correct. That's all for now, Avery. Collette left you the company card for meals, correct?"

"Yes, sir."

That made Ozen pause for a moment, and Avery could've sworn he saw him shiver, but it was too quick for Avery to be sure.

"Then I agree that lunch is an excellent idea. Pick something you enjoy. I like trying new things."

So did Avery. And with Ozen, he'd be trying lots and lots and lots of new things.

CHAPTER ELEVEN

Rule Number 7- A feeder should read the entire contract before agreeing to the terms. A solid understanding of the foundation is important for a healthy client/feeder relationship.

After the feeding, the rest of the afternoon was uneventful. Ozen's mood was very much improved and Avery was smiling and relaxed even after a very rude phone call from a client who had some choice words about how long he'd had to wait to get a phone call appointment with Ozen and how he shouldn't have to be put on hold longer if Avery could do his job correctly. When Avery relayed the conversation to Ozen, he secretly enjoyed the dark look on Ozen's face. He had no doubt that man would learn to be more polite or face Ozen's wrath.

Avery went home with a feeder contract tucked under his arm and a few cookies from a satyr from account management who came to Ozen's office for a meeting. He'd been trying to teach himself to bake and no one would be a guinea pig for his creations. Only with Avery's seal of approval did the rest of the secretary pool take the offered treat. They were a little oily but still delicious, and Avery offered to be a taste tester in the future because he couldn't say no to a little sugar.

He arrived at his tiny studio apartment just before the sun fully set. His apartment was so small that it didn't have a full kitchen, so the delivery guy with his dinner met him at the door right as he arrived. Convenient timing. Avery tipped him generously and took the stairs two at a time to his fifth floor apartment, feeling much more energetic than he usually did at the end of a long work day.

His apartment was small but neat, with a kitchen that shouldn't really count as a kitchen, since it only had a sink and a small fridge, and two windows that opened to the fire escape, letting in almost zero natural light. But the bathroom was upgraded and quite nice, and the neighborhood was well lit and safe. Avery wasn't a big cook anyway, so he didn't mind. The bathroom was just off the entrance, the kitchen tucked into one corner near the windows. His desk with his computer was near the kitchen, out of direct view of the windows to discourage burglars, and his bed was across from it. There wasn't a ton of room for much else, but he had a little sitting area with a tiny tv at the foot of his bed, and plenty of storage for his things taking up what space was left. Even so, he didn't invite people over often because there wasn't a lot of breathing room.

Setting his dinner and the paperwork on the little coffee table in front of the couch, Avery stripped off his jacket and shoes, setting them neatly by the door. He hadn't felt cold all day, but he considered that maybe, possibly, that had something to do with the interaction with Ozen. He'd been warm and tingly ever since.

An almost giddy expression flashed across his face, and he slid across the floor in his socks to the rack with his suits, carefully hanging the one he wore. He couldn't afford that many, so he was careful not to get them dirty so he could re-wear them. He was thankful that Ozen had cleaned it, though he still didn't know how. After he'd stripped to his boxers, he grabbed his pajamas from where he'd left them on the foot of the bed, then headed to the bathroom to wash his hands and face. He was eager to read through the contract, so once he was comfortable, he plopped down onto the couch and set it on the arm, reading it while he pulled his dinner out of the bag.

It was pretty standard stuff in the beginning. Contract length was one year, but could be extended if the parties agreed. The exclusivity clause Ozen had mentioned with his other feeder was in plain language, and while he could see it being beneficial for both parties, Avery worried it was too vague. Ozen was determined to adhere to it, even when his life was at risk. Avery grabbed a notepad, making note of sections he thought needed a little more clarity. The contract greatly favored the feeder, and Avery didn't like the feeling that Ozen would be beholden to him to get what he needed. If he thought Ozen would go for it, he'd get rid of the contract completely and just agree to be there for him. But that was too emotional and Avery understood the need for a clear cut contract.

The compensation was a lot more than he'd expected. Granted, he was agreeing to being someone's food source, but still... He got free orgasms out of the deal. He wrinkled his nose at the pay, but chose to move past it. He doubted he could convince Ozen to lower the amount. It wasn't until they listed the risks that he understood better why feeders were paid so well.

"In the case of a feeder being incapacitated, compensation will be rewarded to the next of kin for the lifetime of the feeder," he murmured out loud. "Incapacitated?"

He didn't know enough about incubi to understand what that meant, so he put his curry down and switched to his desk to look up more information. The more he read, the more his eyebrows rose until they'd practically disappeared into his hairline.

It turned out that if an incubus wasn't careful, they could drain their feeder. It wasn't entirely like vampires, though there was mention of blood sharing that he'd have to look into more, but instead of sucking their feeder's blood dry, they sucked away their passion instead. A drained incubus feeder would never be able to feel passion or desire ever again. They'd basically become a machine.

Avery thought back to his interaction with Ozen that afternoon. He'd looked pained, desperate, and he was starved for several weeks, but he never made Avery feel unsafe. He was careful, and when Avery offered to feed him again after he mentioned still being hungry, he'd adamantly refused. Even after everything, Ozen was determined to keep Avery safe.

Avery finished reading the contract and did more research on the internet to clarify a few things he was unsure about, but in the end, he still wanted to sign it, mostly because he'd gotten to know Ozen and he cared about his well being. No one should have to wonder where their next meal was coming from.

———

When he arrived at work the following morning, contract and notes under his arm, he waved to the hydra at the front desk. She was suspicious the first week, but eventually she warmed up to him and introduced herself. Clarita was her name, and she was very proud of her position. She saw herself as the first line of defense for the company and had stopped several unruly individuals from getting past the front gates in her time here. Now that she knew Avery wasn't a threat, she nodded politely at him with two of her heads, the others busy talking to visitors and answering the phones. Avery swiped his badge on the turnstile, heading straight for the golden elevator on the right. When the doors opened, a familiar face joined him inside.

"Good morning, Mr. Martell," Avery said calmly. He'd learned through years of being a temp that not everyone was a morning person like he was. It was better to keep his voice level and his energy down until a little later in the day. Mr. Martell seemed to appreciate it, blinking up at him blearily. He seemed to question for a second how he knew Avery before his brain fully caught up.

"You're the temp."

Avery nodded. "That's right. Mr. Hawksley's temporary assistant."

The goblin nodded, his eyes shifting to the contract under Avery's arm. "That looks familiar. What is it?"

Avery hesitated. He wasn't sure if Ozen wanted their contract to be discussed in the workplace. "Um... It's for Mr. Hawksley."

Mr. Martell looked curious, but he didn't push, and when the elevator arrived on the top floor, he followed Avery to his desk. After putting his things down, he knocked on Ozen's door and poked his head in. It wasn't often that Avery beat him here, and the incubus was in his normal spot at his desk, his eyes glued to the paperwork in front of him.

"Good morning, Mr. Hawksley. Mr. Martell is here to see you. Is now a good time?"

"Now is fine," Ozen replied, his voice as calm as during Avery's first week.

Avery stepped back, opening the door farther to allow Mr. Martell to pass him. He followed, slipping the contract into the inbox on Ozen's desk as he asked, "Can I get either of you some coffee?"

Both men murmured out a polite please and he scuttled off before Ozen could ask him what he'd left on his desk. He dropped off the coffees and went straight to work, pushing the contract out of his mind until Ozen buzzed his desk to request his assistance. When he stepped inside the office, Mr. Martell was still there, flipping through the notes Avery had made on the contract. Avery came to an abrupt halt, warmth spreading through his cheeks.

"C-Can I help with something?"

Ozen gestured to the chair next to Mr. Martell and Avery hustled to obey, dropping into the seat and lacing his fingers together to stop himself from fidgeting too much.

"We've looked over your notes on the contract," Ozen began, only to be interrupted by Mr. Martell.

"I've been telling Hawksley for years that the contract was too skewed but he refused to change it. Glad someone is finally paying attention," he growled.

Ozen sighed, giving Mr. Martell a bland look. "No one would sign it otherwise."

"He would." Mr. Martell gestured to me.

"Avery is the exception, and I'm still curious as to why. You're giving me a lot of leeway to end the contract. Have you had a change of heart?" That question was directed at Avery, and he could see the real concern on the incubus's face. It made him feel like Ozen wanted this contract to work out as much as Avery did.

"No, nothing like that. I just felt like you deserved more protection. After what happened with the last feeder, I was worried people would take advantage of you. Our contract is only for a year, so unless this turns into a more long term arrangement, in the future you should have more protection."

"And the notice? That wasn't a requirement before."

Avery made a face. "It's common practice to give notice when leaving a job. The same should be done for a feeder. This is a job, after all. Besides, it's cruel not to give notice when you are literally responsible for nourishing someone."

Mr. Martell jerked his thumb at Avery, his gaze locked on Ozen. "I like him. I've got a good feeling about this." He hopped off the chair, taking the notes and the contract with him. "I'll make the changes and have it sent up in an hour. And I'll make sure the payments start as of yesterday, as you requested. I'll see myself out."

He headed out without a backward glance, looking much more refreshed after a cup of coffee. Avery turned back to Ozen, his curiosity overwhelming. "You two seem really close. Are you friends?"

He realized too late that his question was probably too familiar, but Ozen didn't seem bothered by it. He nodded, gathering a few documents and handing them to Avery. "Yes, we've been friends for a long time. He technically works for the company, but he's been my personal accountant longer than the company has been in existence. He handles all my feeder contracts because I know I can trust him." He picked up his phone, frowning at the screen. "I have meetings this morning, so I'd like you to deliver those documents to research and development, then man the phones until I get back. We should be receiving a call from Collette soon with her exact return date. After that, you should contact your supervisor about our arrangement. Even if they can't spare you to work in this build-ing, they need to be made aware of your obligations. Feeder responsibilities are often considered something like a medical appointment and are protected by law."

"Yes, sir. I've already messaged her asking when she's free to talk, and I'm just waiting on a reply." Avery hesitated after getting out of his seat, hovering by the desk. "Um... You said yesterday you were still hungry. Can I help today?"

Ozen studied him, and when his eyes flashed red for a second, Avery got the feeling he wasn't just looking surface level. He'd done some research on incubi abilities. Apparently, they could tell a lot from just a look, including lack of sexual history. Which wasn't embarrassing at all.

"Yes, I believe you are rested enough that we can schedule that. After lunch, I think. I don't want you missing meals to feed me. It's better if you're well fed and rested as well."

"Well, I slept like a baby last night, so at least on that end, I'm covered. But if I'm being totally honest, I skipped breakfast this morning. I don't like eating too early. It upsets my stomach."

Ozen's lips quirked at the sides. "Thank you for your honesty. If that is your normal routine, I think it will be alright today, but I will suggest you make use of the break room. I believe Zara keeps the snack bar stocked. You can eat when you feel it won't bother your stomach."

Avery knew about the snack bar but never partook. He didn't know if it was available for temps. Now that he was also Ozen's feeder, he felt a little less awkward. The bagels looked delicious and he'd been eyeing them for weeks.

"Understood, sir. I'll deliver these right away and update you if Collette calls." He spun on his heel, ready to get to work, when Ozen stopped him.

"Avery?"

Glancing over his shoulder, he frowned at his boss. "Yes?"

"Thank you. Truly. I agree with Mr. Martell. I have a good feeling about this."

Avery beamed. "Me too."

CHAPTER TWELVE

Rule Number 23 - A feeder is not required to leave any previous job commitments unless it is a direct conflict to their contract with their client. However, it should be discussed beforehand with all parties so accommodations can be made.

"Oh god, you're quitting, aren't you?"

Avery bit back a laugh at Morana's immediate panic. "No, I'm not quitting. It shouldn't change my schedule too much. I just thought it was important to inform you of the change."

Her relieved sigh was loud over the receiver. "Oh good. You're one of my best temps, and I would've been devastated if you left. I'd have to hire a dozen more employees to replace you. But explain it to me better. How did this happen?"

Avery wasn't sure if the warmth in his cheeks was from the praise or the idea of sharing what occurred between himself and Ozen. He chose to remain vague for privacy's sake.

"His contracted feeder was unreliable, and I volunteered to help him. It worked out well, and he asked me to replace the feeder to ensure more consistency in the future."

"And you don't feel obligated to take this position, correct?"

His boss's worry was heartwarming, and he spent some time reassuring her that his taking this job was one hundred percent consensual and without coercion.

"Well, alright. If that's what you want, I can't stop you. I appreciate you letting me know. You're scheduled to return back here in two weeks, correct?"

"Yes, that's the plan, but Mr. Hawksley has made a request about my future temp jobs. If possible, he'd like me to take the positions requested by his company so that I'm close by. He understands if this isn't an option, but I thought I'd ask anyway."

Morana hummed thoughtfully. "Well, it shouldn't be a problem. Spellbound Corps requests temps regularly enough. If there is a position available there, I can put you down as the first contact for availability. Do you only want positions from Spellbound? It might limit your workload, but with the feeder contract, you might not need to worry about the monetary aspect of it."

Avery considered it. If he only accepted contracts from Spellbound, aside from his feeder responsibilities, he'd have more time to work on his novel. But he didn't want to leave Morana down a temp either.

"How about this? For now, I'll be specifically contracted to Spellbound while I learn my duties as Mr. Hawksley's feeder. Leave me on the list for emergencies. Once I'm more comfortable with the position, we can reevaluate."

"This is why you're my favorite, Avery. You're always so conscientious. I'll write up the paperwork and make a note on your file and the Spellbound account. Make sure to send me a copy of your feeder contract. It gets added to your file so your other jobs are aware of your potential unavailability."

After saying their goodbyes, Avery wrote down a note to send a copy of the contract to the temp agency as soon as possible. Mrs. Sable called not long after, sounding much more relaxed than when they'd first met.

"I hope your vacation is going well," Avery said brightly.

"It is. I looked forward to this all year. I'd like to be able to do it more often, but with Mr. Hawksley's schedule, it isn't possible. Things are going well, I hope? Did he settle in with Calvin?"

Avery wondered if he should be discreet about what happened with the feeder Mrs. Sable chose, but she'd find out eventually when she came back.

And as Mr. Hawksley's assistant, Avery figured she needed to know who Mr. Hawksley's feeder was.

"Um... Well, it didn't work out with Calvin. He got angry with Mr. Hawksley over something, I'm not really sure what, and stopped answering his phone. It put Mr. Hawksley in a very bad position."

"Oh dear," she murmured. "Do you need me to come back early? Is he alright? He isn't starving himself, is he?"

It was easy to tell Mrs. Sable cared about Mr. Hawksley. Avery was quick to reassure her. "No, no. He's fine. I volunteered to help him again, and afterwards, he requested that I sign on as his feeder. I've spoken with my temp agency, and for now, I'll be working exclusively on the contracts with Spellbound so I can stick close until Mr. Hawksley and I are more comfortable with my new duties. I felt like it was important to give you the full picture, since you're his assistant."

She was quiet for a moment as she processed the change, but her voice was cautiously optimistic when she finally replied. "Well, I'm glad you were there to assist him. You said Calvin stopped answering his phone? How long did Mr. Hawksley go without eating? It might take a few extra sessions to get him back to full strength."

"I'm not entirely sure, but the last time I saw Calvin was the Wednesday of my first week. I thought maybe I was just missing him, but–"

"You're saying Mr. Hawksley went two weeks without feeding?" Her voice raised to almost a screeching level, making Avery flinch. He wondered if a banshee scream could still hurt him over the phone.

"You'd have to ask him to be certain on exactly how long, but Mr. Hawksley said Calvin stopped answering his phone a week ago. Either way, what he did was incredibly wrong, and Mr. Hawksley suffered from Calvin's cruelty. I am aware he needs multiple feedings to get back on his feet, and we're making accommodations for that. For now, he seems okay. He fed twice yesterday, and his mood is almost back to normal."

Mrs. Sable sighed heavily. "Of course this all had to happen while I was gone. I'm sorry you had to handle this yourself, Avery. And you're sure you don't feel obligated? It was kind of you to help him during a difficult time, but you aren't obligated to continue to do so."

"I'm sure," Avery said firmly. "We've discussed it, and I read the contract. We made a few adjustments to it, but once Mr. Martell is finished with it, I'll be signing it, and Mr. Hawksley will be well taken care of. You don't have to worry. Enjoy the rest of your vacation."

"Thank you, Avery. As of right now, my return date hasn't changed. I'll update you if it has," she confirmed, then paused. "A quick note: As a feeder, you need to monitor your energy levels. There is a healer on the third floor. If you ever feel weak or like you aren't recovering as you should, please visit her. Otherwise I'll see you in two weeks."

"See you in two weeks. Enjoy your trip."

Avery hung up the phone right as the witch secretary he'd met in the finance office pushed through the glass door. He had a calm energy, his smile soft and warm, and his tie was lavender, which Avery envied just a little.

"Mr. Martell wanted me to bring this contract to you. He said it needs to be signed in front of a notary, and I'm registered as one. Do you have time to do it now?"

That was fast. Avery took the contract from the witch, quickly flipping through it. All the changes Avery had requested were there, and there was a note on a new one that Mr. Martell added last minute. Nothing concerning, just a stipulation that if there was some sort of emergency and the feeder was unavailable, Mr. Hawksley would be able to feed elsewhere as long as the feeder was informed beforehand. Avery hoped it wouldn't come to that, but after what happened with Calvin, he could see why Mr. Martell would add it.

"Okay, I can sign this. Do I have to do anything special?" Avery had never used a notary before. He delivered documents to them from time to time, but he was usually too busy to stick around and watch them work.

"No. I just need to watch you do it, and see your ID so I can note the information. Then I use my fancy little stamp to mark it as signed with a notary present. Quick and easy," the witch reassured him.

Avery scrawled his name and initials where indicated and handed the contract to the witch, who stamped each page to mark them after adding the information from his ID. On the bottom of each stamp was a section for the notary's signature, and once it was all filled out, the witch gestured to Ozen's office.

"I'll need to have Mr. Hawksley sign it as well. Is he available?"

"He's in meetings this morning. I can call you once he gets back, if you want."

The witch bobbed his head in agreement. "Sure. I should get back to my desk. If I'm gone too long, those number heads get all fussy. I'm Morgan, by the way. Morgan Nightshade."

"Avery Whitman," Avery replied, taking the witch's outstretched hand for a shake. "I'm a temp until Mrs. Sable gets back, but I'll be taking other temp jobs around the company, so you might see me around."

"That's neat. I've heard good things about you. Hopefully you'll get at least one contract in finance so we can hang out." He paused, pursing his lips. "Just... not near tax season. It's a major dumpster fire every year, even though they are supposed to prepare for it months in advance. Spare yourself the stress if you can."

Avery snickered. He already liked Morgan and hoped he could get to know him better. There was a severe lack of friends in Avery's life. He kept himself too busy with work and his book, and he was never at a job long enough to make real connections. Hopefully by taking most, if not all, of the temp contracts for Spellbound, he'd get to know people a little better and potentially make some friends.

"I'll keep that in mind. Mr. Hawksley should be done just before lunch, but the meetings sometimes run long, so I'll keep you updated."

Avery wanted to get the contract signed before lunch, because afterward, he was supposed to feed Ozen again. While Avery was comfortable doing it without the contract, he felt Ozen would be happier if it was signed beforehand.

With his morning obligations taken care of, Avery only had to man the phones until Ozen returned and gave him more to do. He snuck into the break room and finally snagged one of the bagels he'd been drooling over for the past two weeks. He ate it at his desk so he didn't miss any calls, groaning at the soft cinnamony deliciousness. It had to be freshly baked that morning, because there was no other way it'd be that soft.

After his belly was full, Avery went looking for something to do to occupy his time. As long as he was at his desk, he could help out the other secretaries. One had made copies for a meeting in the afternoon and needed them separated and bound in plastic folders, so Avery took that task to help them out.

The morning passed steadily, and when lunch rolled around, Avery grabbed a sandwich from the deli across the street and returned to his desk to work on his novel. He took a bite every few minutes, but otherwise he lost himself in the world of his book. He was glad his monitor was at an angle so that no one could see it unless they walked around his desk behind him. He'd been writing a cheesy office romance, since he spent most of his time in an office anyway, but he admitted to himself that his spicy scenes lacked any real spice. With the memory of his afternoon with Mr. Hawksley the day before, Avery hoped to add more tension and detail to the scenes.

His face was hot as he wrote out the sensations he'd experienced the day before. The soft caresses, the teasing licks. His scenes in his book often skipped foreplay and went straight to the pounding bits. Avery knew better now. Foreplay was just as exciting as the rest of it. Maybe. He hadn't experienced the rest of it yet, but the foreplay was hot.

He crossed his legs, pushing down on his arousal to get it to subside. Maybe the office wasn't the best place to do this. He didn't normally react like this while writing. Sure, it turned him on, but it didn't normally make him feel so... needy.

He was so distracted by it, he didn't realize Ozen returned until he spoke.

"Mr. Whitman, what are you doing?"

CHAPTER THIRTEEN

Rule number 56- In cases of an incubus's feeder, clothing reimbursement should be made available in any instance that a feeder's clothing is ruined during a session. The reimbursement amount should be decided on beforehand.

Ozen's shoulders were tight as he returned to his office. The hunger was a subtle gnawing, a distraction that usually occurred after several days without feeding, not twenty four hours. Two weeks without feeding had done him in, and he felt on edge because of it. He was beyond grateful that he could count on Avery to be there once lunch was over. Unlike Calvin, Avery could be trusted to show up for the job.

He had lunch with Taron again, reassuring him that he was feeding as often as was safe, and that Avery had agreed to the contract so he wouldn't be without a feeder. He was touched by his friend's concern and did his best to mask his foul mood around him. His mood was entirely because of his need to feed, and he didn't want to take it out on Taron.

Ozen could see Avery at his desk through the glass doorway when he returned. He was concentrating hard on something, the remains of a sandwich and chips resting by his elbow. At least Avery listened about eating before assisting him. He was going to praise him for that when he pushed into the office, only to be hit face first with Avery's desire.

Ozen blew out a harsh breath, his magic and his cock responding immediately.

"Mr. Whitman, what are you doing?"

Avery jumped, his face turning dark red with his embarrassment. "I, uh– Nothing," he squeaked.

He found it hard to imagine Avery was doing something against the rules, like indulging in pornography in the office. Curiosity warred with his hunger, but the hunger won in the end.

"My office, if you please."

Avery shut off his monitor and launched to his feet, opening the door for Ozen before scurrying inside after him. If Ozen had more time, he'd move them to the bedroom, but the intensity of Avery's desire made it difficult for Ozen to concentrate.

"My desk. Pants off."

Avery's desire spiked again and Ozen nearly stumbled over his feet. His magic surged, the tethers latching onto Avery even before he could reach Ozen's desk. The force of it made Avery wobble and moan, using the edge of the desk to keep himself upright. Ozen drew his magic back until only the tethers remained, dropping into his desk chair next to Avery.

"A-Are you that hungry?" Avery asked, his hands shaking as he opened his belt. Ozen didn't answer at first, watching as Avery undid his slacks and the material fell, revealing pale legs with a light dusting of hair. Avery's boxer briefs went next, and Ozen's mouth filled with saliva as he was faced with Avery's rounded behind.

"Starving," he finally replied, grabbing Avery by his hips. Avery's hands shot out, keeping himself upright on Ozen's desk as Ozen tugged his hips back. He released one hand, sliding it up Avery's back and gently pushing between his shoulder blades. Avery lowered his chest down to the desk, his breath quickening in anticipation.

The air was heavy with Avery's desire, and Ozen hadn't even started yet. It was intoxicating, and his fangs lengthened automatically. Ozen wouldn't use them; blood sharing was only meant for mates and lovers, not feeders, but that didn't stop his body from reacting. He cupped Avery's rounded cheeks, spreading them apart to reveal Avery's rosy pucker.

The first lick made Avery squeak, his body jolting in surprise. Ozen was supposed to take it slow, to guide Avery into new experiences, but his hunger made him reckless, and the first taste drove him to distraction. He dove onto Avery's ass, feasting off him like a starving man. Avery's shocked noises melted into moans, his knuckles turning white as he clutched the edge of Ozen's desk. Avery's desire skyrocketed, but before he could succumb to his release, Ozen pulled back.

"I'm sorry, firefly, but if this is too quick, I won't get everything I need. I understand you're new at this, but try to hold back until I say so. I promise to let you come. Eventually."

––––––

Avery thought he might cry. The first twenty minutes or so was pure bliss. He'd never thought about anyone using their mouth on that part of his body, but it lit up nerves he didn't realize existed, and he'd almost come in under a minute. He understood Ozen asking him to wait, and he wanted to hold out for him, but it felt like they'd been doing this for hours, and Avery didn't know how much more he could take. Every swipe of Ozen's tongue made Avery cry out. His legs trembled, his hands clammy on the desk's edge. He squeezed his thighs together, trying desperately to stave off his release. He'd given up hope for his slacks, his cock leaking like a fountain onto the material at his ankles and the carpet beneath his feet.

He learned something new about incubi that day that the internet decided not to warn him about. Ozen wasn't lying when he said incubi were built for pleasure. Including, apparently, the ability to lengthen their tongue. It had shocked Avery when Ozen managed to reach far enough to lick his prostate. And now, minutes or hours later, Avery wasn't sure, the pleasure was almost unbearable. At first, he held out for at least a few minutes at a time before Ozen had to give him a break, alternating between light kisses on his cheeks and nipping bites. But the longer they were at it, the less time Avery was able to last before he got too close again and Ozen had to pull back. Ozen's tongue speared him again and Avery's stomach tightened in warning.

"O-Ozen, I–"

One more firm lick over his gland was all it took for Avery to lose it completely. He came with a sob, pleasure and relief coursing through his system, followed closely by regret. Ozen told him not to come until he said so. Avery tried desperately to follow that order, but he couldn't stop it. The force of his release ripped through him like fire and left him raw and shaking. He slumped heavily against the desk, unsure if he'd be able to keep himself upright if he stood fully.

"I-I'm sorry..."

Ozen groaned, and when Avery's trembling eased enough to look over his shoulder, his eyes widened in surprise. Ozen's head was tipped back, his hand rubbing against his erection through his slacks, his eyes closed. Avery moaned at the visual, his cock twitching despite just experiencing the most intense climax of his life. His arousal at the image only seemed to set Ozen off, his teeth clenched as he rubbed a little faster.

Avery's desire was turning him on.

It became a vicious cycle. Avery was aroused by watching Ozen, which made Avery's desire spiral higher and Ozen's reactions grew more intense. Avery couldn't imagine the friction being very pleasant after this long. To spare his boss, he pushed away from the desk and reached for him, touching his free hand to get his attention. He was going to offer to go to the bedroom so Ozen could get some relief, but Avery was surprised when Ozen's face twisted and he then let out a surprised shout.

Ozen's hips lifted and his back arched as he came. Avery couldn't look away, his breath caught in his chest as his gaze flicked between the wet spot forming in Ozen's lap and his pleasure filled expression. Avery was hard again just from watching Ozen stroking himself through his slacks. He'd be embarrassed if he was with anyone else. Since Ozen knew about his inexperience, Avery figured he would forgive him for his reaction.

The room went quiet aside from their choppy breathing. Avery was frozen, his mouth hanging open and his cock throbbing between his legs. From what Ozen had explained, he didn't generally get off during feeding sessions, so Avery was a little confused. He wasn't opposed to it, if anything he enjoyed it immensely, but it did leave him with a lot of questions.

When Ozen finally opened his eyes, Avery wasn't sure what to say. They both just kind of stared at one another until Ozen's phone started ringing, breaking the awkward tension. Ozen blinked a few times, his gaze shifting between Avery and the phone. Avery gestured to it with an awkward laugh.

"You should get that. I'll just, um…"

He wasn't sure what to do, honestly. His clothes were a mess, but that was his fault for not removing them completely. He couldn't just stand around half naked for the rest of the day. While Ozen picked up the phone, Avery pulled up his slacks with a grimace. Note to self: Remove all clothes unless you want to spend the afternoon with cum stained slacks.

"Hawksley," Ozen muttered gruffly into the phone, seizing Avery's wrist before he could walk away. He listened to the other end while pointing at the spot next to him. Avery took that to mean Ozen wanted him to stay put, so he clasped his hands in front of his lap to hide the mess and waited. He wasn't sure why he felt so embarrassed, Ozen was in the same predicament as him, but this was all new to him and he felt his ears burn waiting for Ozen to dismiss him.

"I'll be in my office. No, I don't think that's necessary. Give me fifteen minutes."

He hung up without saying goodbye, setting the phone back in its cradle. When he turned to face Avery again, his expression was a bit remorseful.

"I wanted to apologize before you left. I don't normally participate beyond bringing my feeder pleasure. It helps maintain professionalism. I just…" He drew in a slow breath, his brows drawing together tightly. "I find myself quite sensitive to your desire. It normally takes a great deal more to feed me. Usually full penetration is necessary for me to feel satisfied."

Avery's eyebrows shot up. "You don't need to do that with me? If you're holding back on my account, I promise I can handle it."

Ozen lifted a hand to stall out his rambling before he could truly get going. "That wasn't a complaint. It's merely a curiosity. I don't need more. I'm actually quite satisfied with what we've been doing. My magic is strengthened greatly, and the hunger tempered much more than I'd expected after two weeks without feeding. I was apologizing because I'd planned to handle my arousal privately. You didn't consent to my participation outside of feeding, and I shouldn't have subjected you to that."

That surprised a laugh out of Avery, though he tried quickly to muffle it, his hands slapping over his mouth. He winced when Ozen raised an eyebrow at him. "Sorry. I guess I don't see it as a big deal. I don't know if you noticed, but I liked watching you. I've never seen someone do that before outside of porn. It was... hot."

His face flamed and he averted eye contact. He really needed to get a handle on the lack of filter he seemed to have after sex.

Ozen's chuckle was warm and he drew Avery's eyes back to him with a gentle hand on his chin. "Then instead of dwelling on it, I'll say thank you. I enjoyed our session together. How are you feeling? Tired? Do you need any rest? Water, perhaps?"

His immediate response would have been to dismiss Ozen's concern. Avery took care of others, not the other way around. But Ozen said he wanted open communication and honesty, so Avery took a second to really consider how he felt.

"Um... Not tired, no. More... dreamy? Is that normal?"

Ozen nodded once. "It can be. Increased serotonin makes your body relaxed after release. What else?"

"Maybe a little embarrassed," Avery grimaced, gesturing to his messy clothes. "I, uh, should've probably taken more care to remove my clothes."

"That's my fault," Ozen argued with a shake of his head. "I was hungry and demanding, and I apologize for that. Luckily, it's an easy fix."

He waved his hand over Avery's clothes and all traces of bodily fluids vanished. Ozen's clothes were pristine as well, the wet spot gone. Even the carpet was clean.

"So that's why my clothes were so clean last time. I thought you'd sent them out while I was asleep or something."

"Perks of being an incubus," Ozen commented with a grin, but his face fell again after a moment. "You are sure you're alright? I pushed you a little far today. I wasn't lying when I said the longer the session, the better I felt, but I didn't mean to extend it so long that you'd lose control. I hope I didn't upset you."

A shiver rolled up Avery's spine at the memory. It wasn't easy, holding his orgasm back for so long, and he had been frustrated, but it was so worth it in the end. His orgasm was so intense, he felt his soul leave his body.

Ozen drew in a sharp breath, the red in his eyes glowing a little. "I can tell by your reaction that you're not upset with me. I will still take care in the future not to push you past your threshold. Do you feel able to return to your work or would you like to head home for the day? As my feeder, you're allowed to tap out early if you're too tired."

"No, thank you. I'm alright. I'm just going to pop into the break room really quick before I return to work. I'm craving something sweet. Did you want anything?"

Ozen tipped his head thoughtfully. "Something sweet sounds good to me. Surprise me. And a coffee, please. Did Mr. Martell finish the contract?"

"He did. I signed it and Morgan notarized it. I can call him when you're ready and have him bring it for you to sign as well."

"After your snack. Thank you, Avery."

CHAPTER FOURTEEN

They fell into a routine of sorts, with Avery meeting Ozen after lunch each day. It wasn't necessary for an incubus to feed daily, and Ozen would have been satisfied for a few days with the way he reacted to Avery's desires, but he was proceeding with caution. He felt healed from the two weeks of starvation, but he didn't want to reach that point again. He'd nearly gone feral, and the results would have been disastrous. Especially for Avery when he came to assist him.

The question of his reaction to Avery nagged at him. Not only could Avery feed his magic to bursting, Avery didn't seem as affected to the frequent feedings as Ozen would have thought. Ozen made sure to check before each coupling, and each time, Avery's energy and well being was pristine. It was almost like Ozen's feedings had no effect on him whatsoever, aside from the pleasure. Most feeders need a day or two to recover afterward.

A knock on his office door interrupted his thoughts, and Avery popped in a moment later. It was a point in Avery's favor that his professionalism never wavered, despite such frequent couplings. He was quick to return to work and always greeted Ozen with a smile at the start of each day.

"Good morning, Mr. Hawksley. There were a few deliveries at the front desk for you, and Mr. Cunningham asked to reschedule lunch. He's meeting a thunderbird outside of the city to potentially help with research. He didn't want you to wait for him."

Ozen hummed, taking the offered documents from Avery. "When did he tell you this?"

"Just now. He stopped me as I was waiting for the elevator. He looked like he was already on his way out."

Ozen nodded. Either Taron forgot to tell him, or the meeting was set last minute. Taron didn't adhere to schedules as strictly as Ozen did and could be forgetful at times. His own assistant had said several times that she deserved permanent overtime pay for keeping up with him. She got a significant bonus every year.

Avery was a bundle of energy already, listing off the meetings Ozen had and the projects he needed to approve. He disappeared long enough to get Ozen a cup of coffee, his hair still a little tousled from the wind. Ozen's office was darker than usual thanks to the gray weather, and Avery set about turning on more than just Ozen's desk light to brighten the room.

Ozen looked over the documents he'd received while listening, nodding along to show he heard Avery. It wasn't until he opened the manilla envelope on the bottom of the stack that he stopped listening. He made a tsk sound, flipping through the papers with a scowl.

"Mr. Hawksley? Is everything alright?"

"It's fine." If you could call being sued by your former feeder for breach of contract and defamation fine. He picked up his phone, dialed the legal department, and asked to be connected to his lawyer.

"Van Buren," a gruff voice answered.

"Mav. I need you in my office."

Maverick was quiet for a moment before he sighed heavily. "Who's suing you now?"

"The man who tried to kill me," was Ozen's terse reply. Avery had been about to leave to return to his own desk but he froze at the doorway at the mention of Calvin.

"This will be a story," Maverick grumbled. "I'll be right up."

After he hung up, he turned his attention to Avery. "This may take a while. Please reschedule my morning meeting for after lunch."

It meant he'd miss their scheduled session, and with how busy he was today, he probably couldn't reschedule it before the end of the work day.

He'd probably end up working late. Three days without feeding was possible. He'd enjoyed the daily feedings, but it couldn't be helped. He had to deal with this before Calvin got any traction.

Avery didn't argue, hustling out the door to make the appropriate phone calls. Ozen sighed wearily. Things had just started to settle. Less than a full week with Avery as his feeder, and his magic was stronger than it ever had been. The company was doing well, he'd finally convinced Taron he wasn't about to keel over, and he just acquired an item he'd been hoping to attain for years for his personal collection. Ozen wished things could remain on a high note for longer than a few days.

Maverick didn't bother knocking, striding into his office with a single minded purpose. Ozen had the papers in his hand and waiting because the dragon shifter wasn't known for his patience. He was known, however, for hoarding office supplies, so while Maverick looked over the lawsuit, Ozen cleared his desk of anything that wasn't paperwork. His favorite pen was locked away in his desk drawer because Maverick had been eyeing it for quite some time.

"He says you ended the contract without cause."

Ozen scoffed, scrolling through his email for anything important he had to attend to that day. "I ended the contract because he refused to pick up his phone or meet me. He was trying to starve me."

Maverick's low growl filled the room. Calvin would regret suing him. Maverick was one of the most cut throat lawyers in the country. He was also licensed to practice law almost everywhere in the world. When you live for hundreds of years, you pick up licenses and hobbies like candies. Like Maverick, Ozen was fluent in most supernatural languages and a few human ones as well. He had businesses on almost every continent and was an advocate for minority supernaturals at the government council level. He also had an affinity for painting in his spare time. All Supes who lived as long as he did were the same.

"What's this about negligence of duties?" Maverick queried.

Ozen rolled his eyes. "Of course he'd add that. I didn't feed from Calvin. I'd fed from someone else the day we met and didn't need to until a few days later. He started ignoring me before I had the chance."

"A few days? Did you dislike him that much?"

"It had nothing to do with like," Ozen replied, though he could admit,

the idea didn't thrill him. It had been a long time since he enjoyed his feedings. Not like his sessions with Avery. Those he actually looked forward to.
"The feeding I had before we met was very satisfying. I didn't need to feed,
and I wasn't going to do it just to appease him. I'm not there to provide
him pleasure at his beck and call. I wasn't hungry."

Maverick's eyes narrowed for a moment before he waved his hand
dismissively. "We'll come back to that later. So to my understanding, he
refused to answer when summoned for a feeding, and he was angry with
you when you didn't give into his demands for sex? That's a contradiction."

"I'm well aware," Ozen growled. He went through the timeline,
growing more annoyed as he laid out all the facts. Three days. That's how
long it took for Calvin to decide to starve him. Had he waited even a few
hours, he would've gotten what he wanted and Ozen's suffering could've
been avoided.

Maverick grunted, pacing by the window as he looked over the papers.
He did that when he was thinking. The smoke that seemed to hover
around him only appeared when he was in a bad mood and his dragon was
close to the surface.

"So he's an idiot, then?"

"More a petulant child. I didn't know him well enough to comment on
his intelligence."

"And he says you defamed him? How?"

"I had him blacklisted," Ozen replied. "I didn't want history to repeat
itself with a less controlled incubus. Had it been anyone else, the results
could have been disastrous. I was lucky that my assistant volunteered to
feed me. Any longer and I worried I'd go feral."

The unnatural green of Maverick's eyes began to glow and the smoke
grew denser. Like Taron, Maverick had been Ozen's friend for years. He
was a little standoffish, he liked his isolation, but he was insanely protective of those he considered friends, Ozen included.

"Why didn't you tell me?"

"I didn't think it was relevant."

"Ozen..." Maverick growled.

He sighed. "The issue was resolved on its own and the agency took full
responsibility. Calvin and the person who hired him were fired and blacklisted. It should have ended there."

"And your feeder?"

Ozen gestured to the doorway. "You passed him on the way in. He's diligent and professional. I am fully healed from the event, and it's been less than a week. I couldn't ask for anyone better."

Maverick grunted, which was as much acceptance as Ozen was going to get on the matter, though he considered warning Avery that Maverick might question him. If Maverick was worried about him, he'd interrogate anyone involved in Ozen's life to make sure they were to be trusted. Colette had been on the receiving end of that behavior more than once, despite her loyalty to the company.

Returning to the subject at hand, Ozen gave a significant look to the papers in Maverick's hand. "So? Do I have something to worry about?"

Maverick scoffed. "No. It's a frivolous lawsuit. I'll need to get statements from anyone who'd seen you during the weeks where you went unfed. And I want copies of all attempts you made to contact him. Did he ever reply when you asked him to come in?"

"Yes. For the first week, he'd say he was busy. If he was hoping that behavior would change anything, he was sorely mistaken, and by ten days under contract, he stopped responding entirely."

"So then he was the one who breached the contract, not you. It's his job to show up. The whole purpose of the contract is to ensure that. Have you gotten him to pay back the money he was given? He didn't earn it."

"I wasn't going to waste my time with that," Ozen admitted. "This is already more than I wanted to deal with."

He'd hoped Calvin would be smart enough to understand what was wrong with his behavior. Things were never that easy, though. Ozen rubbed his temples to ease some of the tension.

A warm hand settled on his shoulder, and when he looked up, Maverick's stoicism warmed just enough to pull off reassurance. The man really wasn't good at expressing himself at the office. He only ever relaxed around his friends.

"I'll handle the twerp. Have your assistant start gathering the things I'll need. I also want to see the contract. I helped Martell write it, but you've been recycling the same one for years. I can't remember everything that went into it. Your new feeder should have a copy, yes?"

"Yes. Wait– No. Avery's contract isn't the same. He updated it."

Maverick's eyes narrowed in suspicion. "Why would he do that?"

Ozen felt a smile pull at his lips. "Why don't you read it and find out?"

The easiest way to prove to Maverick that Avery was a good choice was to show him the demands Avery made on his contract. None of them were to his benefit; they were all to protect Ozen. His chest warmed as he remembered reading through the notes for the first time. No feeder ever went to such lengths to protect him like that. Not even Tristan.

CHAPTER FIFTEEN

Rule Number 20 - A feeder should treat people with respect independent of their status or despite disagreement with them, especially with those in close contact with their clients.

Avery left his desk long enough to get copies printed for Ozen's meeting with finance that afternoon. Projections for the costs of Taron's project, from what it looked like. Avery had never seen numbers that large attached to money before. The company really was worth billions. He was counting out the copies to make sure he didn't miss one when he stepped back into his office and collided with a massive figure. Avery startled hard and would have landed on his butt if the person he'd collided with hadn't steadied him with strong hands around his biceps.

"Do you always walk around without looking?"

Avery had to tip his chin up to look the enormous man in the eyes. Silky jet black hair, wide shoulders, and a deep scowl on his face. He was the one who Ozen was meeting with before. Avery had only gotten a brief look at him when he came in earlier. The man didn't even stop to acknowledge him, heading straight into Ozen's office without a word.

Realizing he'd yet to answer the man's question, Avery stepped back to give them some breathing room. "Not often, no. I'm sorry I wasn't paying attention. Are you alright?"

The man's dark eyebrows twitched slightly, like he was surprised Avery was asking. He didn't answer the question, asking one of his own instead.

"You're the new feeder?"

Avery's gaze flicked momentarily to Ozen's office door and back to the man. Ozen hadn't mentioned in the contract or out loud about keeping things under wraps. If the man was asking, Ozen must've told him already.

"Yes... I'm Avery Whitman. And you are?"

The man stared at him long and hard for a few painstaking moments before he responded. "Maverick Van Buren. I'm Ozen's friend. And his lawyer."

That last sentence was said a little ominously and Avery had to wonder if he'd done something wrong. He shifted uneasily, the hairs on the back of his neck standing on end. For some reason, this man made him nervous, which meant he probably wasn't a man at all. Shifters looked human, but if their animals were dangerous, humans often felt a little like prey in their presence.

"Is there something I can help you with?"

Maverick's stare continued to bore into Avery. His pauses were long and made Avery nervous. The door to Ozen's office opened and Avery nearly sagged with relief when Ozen came out and frowned at them. He sighed.

"Maverick, stop intimidating him. If you make him change his mind about the contract, I'll make you my feeder instead."

A sharp grin cut across the stoic man's face for a split second as he looked over his shoulder, which only made him look more intimidating in Avery's opinion.

"We've done that before. You didn't like it."

Ozen scoffed, crossing his arms. "It has nothing to do with like. And you were so pissed about my needing help that the smoke filling the room was oppressive. Who could enjoy themselves like that? Back up. You're making him nervous."

Maverick did as Ozen asked and Avery was quick to dart past him. He didn't like being intimidated, and he liked feeling like prey even less. He was going to put his desk between him and the glaring man, but Ozen took his arm before he could pass and put a hand on his cheek.

"Deep breath. You're safe here."

A small amount of Ozen's magic tickled Avery's senses. Not enough to arouse him, just to relax him. Avery did as Ozen asked, taking a few deep breaths, and once the panic receded a little, Ozen moved until he was in front of Avery and between him and Maverick.

"You like him," Maverick commented gruffly.

Avery couldn't see Ozen's face, but he could hear the exasperation in his voice. "We have a good working relationship, and I don't want you to ruin that. Did you want to ask him something, or were you just planning to intimidate him?"

"I want to see the contract," was the terse reply.

Glancing over his shoulder, Ozen's scowl softened. "Do you have a copy of our contract, Avery?"

"Yes. I keep it in my bag. Why?"

"Maverick is my lawyer. He just wants to check it. Do you mind?"

Avery shook his head, but hesitated to move. He was uncomfortable leaving the safety of Ozen's back, but he didn't want to keep Ozen waiting. His eyes darted to his bag, which was on the coat rack. Behind Maverick. Right now would be a perfect time to have magical abilities. Summoning spells would help immensely.

"Maverick, hand me that bag behind you, please," Ozen asked politely. He must've seen what Avery was looking at.

Maverick did as Ozen asked, handing over Avery's bag with a grunt. It became a weird game of pass along, where Maverick handed over the bag to Ozen, who handed it to Avery, who then gave the contract to Ozen to give to Maverick. It was a little ridiculous, and the fact that Ozen looked like he was trying not to smile eased some of the tightness in Avery's chest.

While Maverick read through the contract, Ozen turned to face Avery. "I'm going to need you to write down everything that happened the weeks after Calvin started. Spare no details about my behavior. It's important. Can you do that?"

Avery nodded quickly. "Yes. Is something wrong?"

"No. Calvin is just causing trouble. If you can think of anyone else who might have witnessed the effects of Calvin's behavior on me, I'd like them to do the same."

Avery thought about it before replying. "The secretary pool could probably describe a little. Everyone could feel the energy up here when it got bad. They were avoiding your office like the plague."

A muscle in Ozen's jaw twitched. "Well, I'll need to apologize for that. Thank you for letting me know. Please ask them to write down what they can. It will help. I'll need Collette to give her account on hiring him. Did she say anything before she left?"

"She said something about being worried that Calvin was acting during his interview. He acted differently with her than he did when he met you."

"Different how?" Maverick demanded. He was finally looking up from the contract and he seemed to be exuding some kind of smoke.

"Uh... Well, I'm not sure exactly, she only commented on it for a moment. She said she vetted him before introducing him to Mr. Hawksley, but when he got upstairs, he was a little cold to her."

Maverick grunted again, his eyes dropping back onto the contract. The smoke hadn't thinned and it smelled like a smoldering fire while camping. Avery's eyes burned from it and he blinked rapidly to stop them from watering.

Abruptly, Maverick handed Ozen back the contract. "It's good. I agree with the changes. Martell has a copy of the old one, correct?"

Ozen nodded, and Maverick left without another word. Avery sighed in relief.

"He's not that bad, once you get to know him. Fiercely protective, but not a bad man. Once this is settled, I'll introduce you properly. He can be a good ally if he likes you."

"What if he doesn't like me? It kind of seemed like he wanted to hurt me before."

"I wouldn't allow that," Ozen growled. "No harm will come to you while under my care."

He said it with such intensity that it startled Avery. His heart did a little leap in his chest and Avery felt his cheeks warm. He quickly pushed the feeling aside. Avery wasn't going to let himself feel anything but professionalism toward his boss. Ozen had enough trouble with feeders making more out of their relationships. Avery wouldn't be one of them.

Sucking in a sharp breath, Avery started coughing immediately. Ozen sighed, opening the doors to his office and Avery's to help expel the smoke.

"I apologize. It happens when he's angry and his dragon is close to the surface. I almost made a rule that we could only meet up on the ground floor where we could open the windows. Unfortunately, I don't always have time to go down there when I need to meet with him."

Avery felt like he swallowed his tongue. "D-Dragon?"

Apparently Avery needed to do more research on supernaturals. He didn't know dragons actually existed.

———

It was nearing the end of the work day when Avery grew concerned. He and Ozen usually met after lunch for his feeding. That had to be pushed because of his meeting with Maverick, but Ozen was still busy hours later and there didn't seem to be a break in his schedule coming any time soon. If it were any other day of the week, Avery would let it pass. He'd just feed him the following day. But it was Friday, and Avery wouldn't see Ozen again until Monday. Three days without feeding sounded awful, and probably not very safe. Avery considered offering to come to his house on the weekend, but then he remembered Ozen's preference to feed here at the office to keep things professional.

There was only an hour left in the work day, and Avery didn't want to accidentally work overtime by putting this off for too long. He worried about overstepping, but his worries for Ozen's wellbeing outweighed his nerves, so he brushed them away and stood, heading into Ozen's office after a quick knock.

Ozen's desk was messy, paperwork scattered everywhere. Some days were busier than others. Today just happened to be a busy one, and Avery would probably come to work on Monday and need to spend time cleaning up the mess before starting on his usual tasks.

There was a crease between Ozen's brow as he read through whatever he was working on. He only looked up when he noticed Avery waiting.

"Avery. Is there something you need?"

Avery considered his words carefully. He didn't want to come off as needy, or as if his request was about him wanting sex. Avery heard Ozen's complaints about his previous feeders and he never wanted to act like them.

"I was just wondering if you had a moment? You haven't fed yet and I don't want you to go hungry over the weekend because we skipped it."

Ozen sighed, rubbing at his temples. "I'm afraid not. This needs to get done, and if I don't want to be here all night, I can't stop. I've gone weekends without feeding before. I'll be fine."

Avery wavered between accepting Ozen's words at face value and arguing his point. He'd never been passive when it came to his work, so he leaned heavily on the latter.

"With all due respect, sir, I think that's unwise. You were recently hurt pretty severely. I don't think it's a good idea to test your continence so soon after that event. And a fifteen minute break shouldn't put you too far behind. Or I can stay late and wait for you to finish. Whichever you prefer."

Ozen's eyes narrowed slightly. "You're not normally so pushy about this. Why now?"

"I..." Avery frowned down at his feet. His reasoning was probably too emotional. He didn't want Ozen to think it was anything aside from professional. But he didn't have another excuse available. Avery sighed and decided honesty was best. "I saw how hard it was on you after what Calvin did. I don't want you to have to experience that again. I'd worry about you all weekend if I went home without feeding you. No one should have to starve themselves that long."

Ozen took Avery's hand, drawing his focus off the floor. Avery worried he'd be angry, since Avery was being emotional, but Ozen's smile was warm and there was no underlying tension.

"I appreciate your concern. You're right. Fifteen minutes wouldn't hurt. We've stuck to simple things for now. Is there anything you'd like to explore?"

Avery's stomach flipped and he sucked in a breath. There were a great many things he wanted to explore. He'd spent an embarrassing amount of time on the internet looking up sex between men to get ideas of what he could try with Ozen. It felt safe to try them with someone with so much experience. But most of the things he looked up would probably take more than fifteen minutes. It usually required both men to be fully naked. There was only one thing he could think of that would be quick.

"I... I'd like to suck you, if that's alright."

CHAPTER SIXTEEN

Ozen found himself momentarily speechless. He'd wanted to reward Avery for his thoughtfulness by giving him the option to try something new. He never expected his request to include Ozen's pleasure. After the incident earlier in the week where he'd lost control of himself, Ozen was careful not to let it get that far. Avery said he didn't mind, but Ozen preferred to keep his pleasure separate. Now Avery was asking to focus on him.

"I... I think I might have misunderstood you. You want to suck me? Not the other way around?"

Avery nodded quickly, bouncing on his toes. He looked nervous and his face was bright red as he explained, "I've seen videos online and I was curious what it'd be like. You don't have to if it makes you uncomfortable. I'm fine with what we've done so far. You can just ignore me."

Ozen almost agreed to pretend like the request hadn't happened. He wasn't sure he wanted to include his pleasure in the process. But he'd offered to let Avery explore, and it felt rude to deny him immediately. Besides, Avery was the picture of professionalism. If anyone could keep feelings out of it, it would be him.

"If that's what you want to try, then that's what we'll do. If you don't enjoy it, we'll stop immediately, understand? There is never a time when we start something that you can't stop whenever you need to."

Ozen wanted to remind Avery of this, because the last time they explored something new, Ozen went a little far. Avery said he enjoyed it, but edging him for an hour was cruel for a beginner, and Ozen was determined not to let that happen again.

"Yes, sir." Avery's reply was a little breathless, and when he sank to his knees between Ozen's spread thighs, his pupils were blown out. The desire was thick in the air and Ozen's magic latched on immediately. Very few feeders wanted to do this with him. They enjoyed it when he performed the act, but they got little pleasure from doing it themselves. Avery was just as excited as if Ozen was doing the act himself, and they hadn't even started yet.

"Whenever you're ready, then."

Ozen actually felt nervous. It wasn't as if this was the first time he'd received oral, but he'd admit it'd been a while. He had to ask himself when it was that he stopped enjoying sex. After thousands of years, it lost its excitement and became a chore he had to perform to feed himself. Only with Avery had he started to feel that excitement again.

Avery's hands trembled as he drew Ozen's zipper down. His movements were a little timid, but Ozen didn't think it had anything to do with Avery changing his mind. This was the first time Ozen was letting Avery lead, and nerves were normal, especially for someone's first time. He tried to be patient, only letting out a small grunt when Avery drew his erection from his slacks.

It was the first time Avery was seeing his cock as well, and his wide-eyed wonder was flattering. There were differences between a human's anatomy and an incubus's, but not enough to be a deterrent for Avery. He stroked Ozen slowly, feeling the ridges under his palm while Ozen could only watch reverently.

Avery licked his lips when precum welled on the tip of Ozen's cock, and Ozen had to bite back a groan. He looked hungry, and Ozen's cock twitched with need. He was starting to worry he wouldn't last very long, not with the desire soaking the air and the burning hunger in Avery's eyes.

The first tentative lick over Ozen's cockhead made him hiss, his fingers tightening around the arms of his desk chair. Avery paused, a little uncertainty tainting that delicious desire.

"Am I doing something wrong? Did I hurt you?"

Ozen huffed out a strained laugh, shaking his head. "No, firefly. You didn't hurt me. It will take effort on my part not to fuck your mouth. I don't want to choke you."

"Oh." The desire kicked up a notch and Ozen had to close his eyes. Avery had barely touched him, and he was nearly to the point of begging. There had to be some magic in Avery's family line, something that gave him this much power over Ozen's desires.

Soft lips wrapped around his cock and Ozen gritted his teeth to silence himself. He choked on a gasp as Avery lowered his head, taking more of his length into his mouth. Wet suction made him shiver, and he had to start going over business facts in his head to not reach completion too quickly. This weekend, he was going to figure out why Avery had such an effect on him. If this blowjob didn't kill him first.

———

Avery didn't think he'd enjoy this as much as he was. In a lot of the videos he'd seen online, the men in them made these awful gagging and choking noises during the act. Only a few looked like they truly enjoyed it. It was those videos that made Avery curious enough to try it.

Ozen wasn't like those actors on the internet, though. He let Avery explore his limits without pushing for more. Avery could tell it wasn't easy for him. Ozen kept shifting restlessly, and his attempts to silence his gasps and groans were failing the longer they were here. When Avery prodded at the slit at the top with his tongue, Ozen groaned out loud and the armrests under his hands creaked.

Touching Ozen was just as exciting as Ozen touching him. Avery's dick throbbed in his slacks, and he had to push down on it more than once in an attempt to ease the ache. But the more noises Ozen made, the more insistent the ache grew, until Ozen finally noticed his struggle.

"Take it out. Let me see you touch yourself."

Avery moaned around the cock on his tongue, bobbing his head a little faster. Ozen's breathing picked up considerably, and when Avery glanced at him through his lashes, Ozen's eyes were squeezed shut, his head thrown back and his mouth hanging open in pleasure. That image alone spurred Avery into action. His fingers were clumsy as he opened his slacks, most of his focus on the heady weight on his tongue. When he finally freed his erection and stroked, he moaned in relief and Ozen's hips jumped in surprise.

"Yes, that's it. Get yourself off. Let me feel your desire."

Avery's already clumsy blowjob turned sloppy as he split his focus between sucking and stroking himself. If Ozen noticed, he didn't seem to mind. His hips lifted in micro thrusts, not deep enough to gag Avery, but Ozen couldn't seem to sit still either. He lost the ability to hold back his groans, one hand carding through Avery's curls almost affectionately. Each sound only made Avery feel hotter, until he was jerking himself off at warp speed. He moaned around Ozen's cock, sucking him down farther, his eyes watering as he fought the urge to gag. It didn't turn him off like he thought it might. He was so lost to the pleasure, he would be pleading for more if he could speak.

When Ozen's cock brushed the back of Avery's throat, Ozen let out a helpless sound.

"Ah! Fuck. Relax your throat. Yes, like that. I– Shit!" His head flew back, and the first pulse of Ozen's cock on Avery's tongue set Avery off. He moaned as his release slammed into him, cum coating his fist and the carpet. Ozen shouted through his release, his hips arching off the chair. Avery tried his best to swallow all of it, but some dribbled down his chin despite his best efforts.

Avery kept sucking until Ozen stopped him, gently guiding Avery off his cock with a hand on his chin. That grip was the only thing keeping Avery upright, his body getting that floaty jello-like feeling despite the fact that Ozen didn't touch him. Avery never felt this way when he was alone with his right hand. Ozen's presence was intoxicating.

Ozen's thumb brushed over Avery's bottom lip, his deep red gaze penetrating Avery's very soul.

"Are you sure you're human?"

Avery blinked in surprise. "Uh... Pretty sure. Why?" His voice was a little hoarse, and the reminder of the reason why made his cock twitch. Ozen groaned, releasing Avery's chin to sit back in his chair.

"No reason. Scoot back. I'm going to get a cloth to clean you up."

Avery did as he was told, falling back onto his behind after Ozen walked away. He stepped into the bathroom Avery had yet to explore, hidden behind another bookshelf. Must've been nice to have his own private bathroom he didn't have to share with anyone. Ozen never had to follow after a troll coworker and have to clean up to be able to sit down. Avery was jealous.

Ozen came back with a warm washcloth, kneeling in front of Avery to gently clean his face. It felt... intimate, and made Avery's stomach tighten. To distract himself from it, he focused on Ozen instead.

"I'm surprised you didn't just–" he waved his hand like Ozen had when he cleaned Avery up earlier in the week. Ozen chuckled.

"It's called aftercare, firefly. You worked hard to feed me, and you deserve to be pampered for your efforts. How are you feeling? Did I hurt you at all?"

Avery smiled at his concern. "No. I'm fine. How about you? Did you get enough to tide you over for the weekend?"

"Yes, thanks to you. I appreciate your diligence, Avery. You're right, it would have been difficult to not eat for three days."

"And two isn't too long?" Avery asked. "I couldn't imagine going that long without eating. I get grouchy if I skip a meal."

Ozen chuckled, helping Avery to his feet. He magicked away the mess Avery's release made while Avery tucked himself away again.

"I can handle it. Incubi don't need to eat daily. It keeps us strong if we do, but it won't kill me if I skip a day or two. I'll be fine to wait until Monday." Before Avery could protest, Ozen lifted a finger to stop him. "I have your number, and if I'm concerned about the length of time, I'll contact you to meet me. Otherwise, I want you to enjoy your weekend."

Well, that was better than nothing. And Avery trusted Ozen to call him if he needed him. He let the concern go and smiled brightly.

"Alright, Mr. Hawksley. I'm going to finish up my work and head home. Let me know if you need anything from me before I go."

Ozen's gaze shifted to his desk and he sifted through the mess until he found a manilla folder in the pile. "These can go down to legal on your way out. Floor 52. Maverick should still be there to receive them."

Avery fought off a grimace. He didn't want to face the dragon shifter twice in one day, but it couldn't be helped.

"Right away, sir. Have a nice weekend."

"You as well. I'll see you on Monday."

CHAPTER SEVENTEEN

Rule Number 8 - A contract between a feeder and a client should not be affected by outside influence. The terms should be set between the feeder and the client alone.

Avery did one last check of next week's schedule, making sure there would be time on Monday for another session. He didn't want Ozen going hungry because he was too busy. After he was done, he gathered his things and shut down his computer. They'd taken longer than fifteen minutes, but Ozen didn't seem upset about it, and Avery certainly wasn't going to complain. It took a lot of effort not to replay the session in his head on repeat as he waited for the elevator, but he didn't want to walk around with an erection on display. He held his jacket in front of his lap and thought about work instead. Next week would be his last week as Ozen's assistant. He hoped the transition to him temping in different departments in the company would be smooth and painless.

Since it was the end of the day right before a weekend, the office was mostly empty by the time Avery left. The elevator wasn't crowded for once, and he didn't have to squish himself into it to get where he needed to go. He preferred the gold elevator when he could take it, since it was rarely crowded, but it only went from the top floor to the main floor. It didn't stop along the way.

The legal floor was quiet and the reception desk empty when Avery approached. He'd never been on this floor before, and he wasn't sure where Maverick's office was until a gruff voice called out from the hallway on the right.

"Over here."

Avery followed the sound to the office on the end, which was a corner office with a great view of the city and lots of natural light. It even had a doorway to the roof of the building next to it, which surprised Avery. Then he remembered what kind of shifter Maverick was. He probably flew to his destinations a lot. It would be tedious to have to go all the way downstairs and find a big enough space to shift every day.

"Mr. Van Buren? Mr. Hawksley asked me to bring this to you on my way out. Can I come in?"

After years of working with supernaturals, Avery knew better than to enter an office without express permission, even if Maverick called out to him. Shifters especially were territorial.

"Come in," Maverick growled.

Avery crept into Maverick's office, finally finding the dragon shifter in one corner next to a bookshelf, his face practically buried in a book. He wasn't shrouded in smoke anymore, so that was a positive, and he barely paid any attention to Avery. Putting the file on his desk, Avery debated on if leaving quietly was polite so as not to interrupt him, or rude by not at least saying goodbye. He decided on the former, since Maverick hadn't even looked in his direction yet, but before he could leave Maverick stopped him.

"Why did you change the contract?"

Avery froze, turning slowly to face the stoic dragon shifter. Maverick was finally looking his way, his unnaturally green eyes unblinking as he stared at Avery. Still incredibly intimidating. Fun. Avery spit out his answer in hopes of escaping sooner.

"It felt wrong to take advantage of him like that, like Ozen was being punished for needing to feed. If I was going to be working with him, I wanted things on more equal ground. He needed a few failsafes so he wouldn't have a repeat incident."

"Ozen?" Maverick quirked an eyebrow.

Avery's face flushed. He only ever called his boss by his first name during a session. It was a slip of the tongue, and Avery felt like the dragon shifter was the last person he wanted to slip in front of.

"Ah, um... Sorry. I–"

"You like him," Maverick commented. He'd said the same thing to Ozen earlier. It lacked any judgment, sounding more curious instead. Avery lifted a shoulder uneasily.

"I think he's a good person. He works hard to make marginalized supernaturals feel equal in a world that wasn't built for them. And he's kind. He doesn't deserve to be taken advantage of."

Something like approval flashed across Maverick's face. It was gone in an instant but he dipped his chin to acknowledge Avery before turning back to his book. Since they already spoke, Avery felt awkward not saying goodbye, so he quickly mumbled, "Have a nice weekend," before scurrying out the door.

He couldn't be certain, but he might've heard Maverick reply with a simple, "You too."

CHAPTER EIGHTEEN

Ozen hadn't found the time to research his reactions to Avery before his friends requested that he join them for a drink the following evening, and it wasn't so important that he felt it needed to be addressed immediately. It felt more like a constant nagging in the back of his mind, a curiosity that he wouldn't be able to let go of until he figured out what made Avery so special.

Maverick and Taron were waiting, along with Dorian, who ran the technology division of Spellbound in the building adjacent to the main one. Ozen was the last to arrive, which meant only one thing.

"Drinks are on you, my friend," Taron said with a gleeful expression. Ozen nearly rolled his eyes.

"Yes, I'm aware of the rules. Don't gloat."

Taron's grin never wavered, and he wiggled his eyebrows just to taunt Ozen. His bright red eyebrows. Not copper, like natural hair, but red like the primary color. They matched his hair, which was oddly spiky and short.

"Strange addition this time," Ozen commented.

Maverick snorted and took a healthy swallow of his whiskey before agreeing. "I told him that when we got here. He refuses to see reason."

"My niece chose it. She's into these cartoon shows and the characters all have wild hair. I am nothing if not a doting uncle who doesn't mind playing a guinea pig," Taron defended himself.

"How did she blackmail you?" Dorian asked. He was the only one without a drink. The alcohol would go straight through him, which as he'd explained, wasn't pleasant. Therefore, Dorian didn't drink often. Vampires were some of the few supernatural species that couldn't consume regular food. Their sustenance only came from blood. His feeder was a spoiled little man, but at least he was diligent in showing up for feedings and cared enough about his paycheck to be on time.

The waitress came to get Ozen's drink order while Taron tried to pretend he wasn't being forced to keep his hair that way. Taron liked to experiment and would sometimes choose odd additions just to get attention, but this was out of the norm for him. He wanted attention, not embarrassment.

"Maybe we should start inviting Brennus to these little get-togethers. That way, you won't be so tempted to lie to us," Maverick threatened.

"You wouldn't," Taron gasped.

Brennus wasn't a bad person. However, it was impossible to lie in front of a griffin, which could make some conversations tedious. It did make him the best person to run the supernatural resources department. If there was conflict, he'd get to the bottom of it faster than anyone else.

"I might. Unless there is something you'd like to tell us," Ozen offered.

Taron's shoulders slumped, defeated. "Alright, fine. She found some pictures on my phone. If I don't want the entire world, namely my mother, to find out, I had to agree to be her doll for the week. And that's as much as I'll tell you."

He crossed his arms over his chest, and Ozen knew the conversation would go no further. Taron was stubborn when he wanted to be. But it wouldn't stop Ozen from asking later when they were alone. They were each other's confidants since childhood. Some things they only shared with each other.

"Changing the subject," Taron said petulantly before turning to face Ozen. "How is it going with Avery? You're looking much better."

Ozen nodded once, accepting his wine from the waitress. "It is going well. He is professional, courteous, and incredibly diligent."

"Diligent, how?" Taron asked, waggling his eyebrows suggestively.

Ozen gave him a flat look. "I have no interest in sharing details with you. But that wasn't what I was referring to. Our session was pushed on Friday because of the Calvin business, and Avery made sure I was fed before the weekend. He genuinely cares for my well being, which is far more than I could say for any of my other feeders. Not since Tristan."

"Finding a good feeder is difficult. You have been unlucky lately. It's about time you found someone decent," Dorian said.

Ozen agreed. His luck very nearly got him killed. Or worse, made him feral. It felt worse to lose your mind to the bloodlust than to succumb to death. Ozen didn't want to hurt people, even by accident.

"What's this Calvin business?" Dorian asked after a moment.

Annoyance made Ozen scowl, but he explained the details to his friend anyway. It was important that Dorian knew the story in case it was a new tactic amongst feeders to get their way. Some of them gathered in groups to gossip and discuss their contracts. Ozen thought those groups were more trouble than they were worth.

Dorian bared his fangs in a hiss when Ozen described his brush with starvation. He, more than any of their other friends, understood what it was like to be reliant on another to survive.

"Is he still alive?"

"Alive and causing trouble," Maverick answered with a growl. "He's trying to sue Ozen for having him blacklisted."

Just the memory of what Calvin did made Ozen's stomach clench. He almost considered calling Avery for a quick feed. He wouldn't. It wasn't professional to bother him on weekends, but the weekend felt too long now that he'd had regular feedings. He hadn't had daily feedings in years. He tried to stretch it out a few days with his other feeders, since the task had become tedious.

"How did you get out of the contract in time?" Dorian asked. "I would think he would draw it out to continue your punishment."

"Avery," Ozen answered. "He pointed out that the contract was voided when Calvin refused to show up to do his job. I never once fed from Calvin. It was also Avery who fed me and saved my life."

Dorian whistled, and Taron nodded. "That's how I responded, too. If Ozen let Avery leave without asking him to be a feeder, I would have approached him myself. You can't buy that kind of loyalty."

Maverick grunted his own agreement. "He is a good match. He changed the contract to make the playing field more equal. It included several fail-safes in case Avery wasn't around to feed Ozen in time."

"You've hit the jackpot, my friend," Dorian exclaimed. "Do what you can to keep him. I've never met a feeder willing to even the playing field. It was always skewed in their favor."

Ozen wasn't going to argue. He would do his level best to keep Avery happy and in his employ. The idea of losing him... Ozen almost wanted to panic at the thought. He needed Avery. No one else fed him as well as Avery could.

When Maverick stepped outside to answer a call and Taron went to the bathroom, Ozen decided it was a good opportunity to ask Dorian about his experiences with Avery. Vampires didn't need desire to feed, but there might be some similarities in his experiences with feeders.

"Dorian. Have you ever had a feeder who felt more... potent than the others?"

Dorian frowned, considering him. "Potent how?"

"It takes considerably less for Avery to feed me. With my other feeders, it took longer, and there had to be full penetration for me to feel satisfied."

"And you don't need to do this with Avery?"

Ozen shook his head. "No. He's inexperienced, so we've been taking it slow. We haven't moved to full penetration. And yet, I'm better fed than I ever have been before. I don't understand it. Do you think his lack of experience has something to do with it?"

"Well... it doesn't with vampires," he replied thoughtfully. "There was once the belief that virgins were better to feed from, but that was proved to be a myth centuries ago. I'm not sure if it's different for incubi. Have you ever fed from a virgin before?"

Over the years, those who fed him started to blur together. It was hard to pick out just one. "I'm sure it happened a time or two in my past. I can't be certain. I never kept track."

"Well, let's assume for the time being that you have. You weren't as picky when you were younger, so I'm sure it's occurred before. If you can't remember a time where a feeder felt more potent, it's safe to say Avery's inexperience has nothing to do with it. What is his species? Is it something new for you?"

"He's human," Ozen answered. "No magic, to my knowledge, but I haven't looked into his family line. There hasn't been a new species for me in generations, and I've fed from humans before. They were nothing special."

Dorian listened and nodded, his brow furrowed as he considered Ozen's puzzlement.

"Are you worried it's a spell? Something intended to harm you?"

"No," Ozen said quickly. "I check before each session. He hasn't been influenced in any way. Nothing jumps out at me that makes him different from any other human, so I don't understand why being with him feels so intense."

Dorian leaned back in his chair, his arms crossed over his chest, his eyes squinted in concentration. "I've never heard of such a thing, either. Have you done any research?"

"Not yet. Things have been busy, and this Calvin issue only makes things worse."

Dorian scowled at the reminder. "Well, I would do some research. It might be species specific. Either on your side or his. I'll help, since you're overloaded. I always liked puzzles."

Ozen gave him a flat look. He didn't appreciate his personal troubles being used as a source of entertainment for his friends. It's why he hadn't brought it up to Taron. The shapeshifter would never let it go.

Taron returned before they could discuss it any more, and Dorian didn't seem inclined to share the conversation, which Ozen appreciated. They moved on to more neutral topics. Taron's consideration to gender swap was given suggestions, like trying it out for a few days before making the commitment to expend that kind of magical energy. Maverick's continued troubles with smoke damage in his home. Dorian's mother's demand that he settle down within the next century. It was nice to speak with his friends without the stress of work. They shared a few drinks, helped each other with troubles, and just enjoyed each other's company.

When the night ended, Ozen was feeling relaxed. Relaxed and, unfortunately, hungry. He tried to brush it off, choosing to walk home instead of calling his driver to pick him up. The distraction only worked long enough for Ozen to figure out which direction he needed to go before his mind wandered back to his hunger.

He'd thought the effects of his two-week starvation were gone. Perhaps he'd been too hasty. Daily feedings helped considerably, but they also masked the damage. His body still needed more time to recover. At least, that was the excuse he was giving himself as he called the number Avery had given him on his first day in the office.

"Hello?"

"Avery. Are you free?"

"Free for what?" he asked. Avery sounded a little distracted, and Ozen thought perhaps it wasn't a good time, but now that he had Avery on the phone, he was reluctant to give up on the venture.

"For a session. I thought perhaps I would be back to normal by now, but–"

"Oh!" There was a clatter on the other line, and Avery sounded more alert now that Ozen had his attention. "Absolutely, Mr. Hawksley! Sorry, I thought– Nevermind, I was distracted. Yes, I'm free. Is there somewhere you'd like to meet? I know you said your home was off limits to maintain professionalism. Is my place under that same rule?"

His eagerness made Ozen smile. Normally, if he wasn't in the office, he preferred to rent a room at a hotel. However, curiosity burned at him and Ozen found himself saying, "Your place is fine. Send me the address."

Avery lived far enough away that Ozen had to call his driver. While he waited, he considered the situation. It wasn't the first time he'd gone to a feeder's home for a session, but it wasn't the norm for him, especially in the last few hundred years. He established his rules a long time ago to better protect himself. His only excuse for ignoring them for Avery was because he hoped to better understand Avery's potency if he got to know him better. Perhaps his apartment held some sort of clue.

CHAPTER NINETEEN

Rule Number 19 - After Hours - A feeder can be called upon in cases of dire need after hours. However, those instances should be kept at a minimum to better care for the feeder's needs. If a feeder's health is compromised, action should be taken with the local feeder protection agency.

Avery had been so distracted with the scene in his book that he hadn't fully clued in to who had called him until Ozen mentioned a session. He felt embarrassed for his mistake, and once Ozen hung up and Avery sent him the address, the panic set in. He turned, wide eyed, to look at his apartment. His very messy apartment. Avery had been so entranced by his book, he'd completely ignored regular cleanliness. He'd at least had the mind to shower, but his apartment was in a poor state, which was unacceptable with his boss coming over.

Leaping into action, Avery hustled to clean up. Take out containers were tossed in the trash, clothes put in the hamper and when the hamper turned out to be too full to close properly, the entire thing was hidden in the kitchen. He did a quick scrub down of the bathroom and made his bed. It was only when there was a knock on the door that Avery looked down at his outfit. He whimpered. He didn't have time to change, and he was in sweats and a hoodie. His comfort clothes while writing. Avery hung his head, dismayed, and dragged his feet to answer the door.

Ozen, of course, looked perfect as always. He was dressed more casually than when he was at the office, his suit jacket and tie gone and the top few buttons of his shirt undone. Somehow, it made him look even more mind numbingly gorgeous than before. Avery ogled for just a little too long. Ozen had to clear his throat to get Avery's attention.

"May I come in?"

Face bright red, Avery leapt back to make room. "Of course, of course. Sorry, I—" Avery didn't know how to finish that sentence. *I was too busy checking you out to let you in?* He'd die from embarrassment.

Ozen looked amused as he stepped inside. Avery's gaze darted around the room, checking to make sure he hadn't missed anything in his haste. Satisfied with his quick clean up, he turned back to Ozen to find him frowning at the room. Avery looked around again, trying to figure out what bothered him so he could fix it.

"Is... everything okay?"

Ozen blinked a few times before he masked the frown, his face softening as he turned to Avery. "Yes. I appreciate you making time for this. I thought I'd returned to normal, but I fear I was too optimistic."

"I was worried about that. I'm glad you called. I'd much rather you do that than starve yourself for even a few days."

Avery's sincerity seemed to surprise Ozen a lot. Avery had to wonder if his experience with his last feeder wasn't as out of the norm as Avery thought. Which begged the question yet again, who would choose to be anywhere else when Ozen was offering to pleasure them?

Anticipation kicked up as he looked over his boss again. He doubted there would ever come a time where he would choose something or someone over being with Ozen. Thankfully, with the contract, he knew he wasn't going anywhere any time soon.

Ozen drew in a deep breath and a smile pulled at his lips. "I'm glad you're as eager as I am. I prefer not to use magic to get my partners in the mood. It defeats the purpose."

It still made Avery blush that Ozen could so easily tell when he was aroused, and it wasn't just the outline of his erection, since that was mostly hidden by his sweatshirt. He bought them too large on purpose because he liked the way they fit better. Ozen picked up on the desire Avery felt first. Desire that Avery had no control over the moment he was in the same room as Ozen.

When Ozen stepped up to him, Avery's breath stuttered a little. There was always the question of what they'd be doing to feed Ozen. Avery had no complaints so far, though he was kind of hoping to suck him again. Watching Ozen's face, hearing his groans of pleasure, the whole experience played in his mind when he was alone in the shower. Only the reminder that he would be taken care of during the next session kept his hand off his cock, though it was a very difficult thing to resist.

Ozen growled low, pulling Avery flush against him. "What are you thinking about, firefly?"

"O-Our Friday session," Avery admitted shyly. His cock twitched at the thought of tasting Ozen again, and he let out a needy whimper when Ozen's magic latched on to him. Ozen hummed, his free hand gripping Avery's jaw and tipping his head to the side. It gave him full access to Avery's neck, and when the incubus nipped lightly on the sensitive skin, Avery's knees went weak.

"Perhaps I should return the favor. I haven't gotten to enjoy your taste in a while."

All the breath left Avery at once and he swayed, his fingers clutching Ozen's shirt to keep himself upright. Ozen didn't give him oral often. Unless rimming counted. He seemed to prefer to attack Avery's ass instead. Not that Avery was complaining. Just thinking of Ozen tonguing his ass could get Avery off. Avery wanted so much for Ozen to suck him, but he also wanted a repeat of Friday.

"Can we both do it?"

Ozen's smile grew and he pushed lightly on Avery's shoulder until they crossed the minimal space of the room and he dropped back onto the bed. "Yes. Is that what you want to do?"

Avery nodded quickly, his eyes glued to Ozen's hands while he undressed slowly. Another thing Ozen didn't do was get undressed during their sessions. His focus was solely on Avery. Friday was the first time Avery had seen his cock, which was a shame. It was a gorgeous cock. It wasn't smooth like a human's but more bumpy, sort of like a ribbed condom. The thought of those ridges teasing Avery's hole as Ozen fucked him sent Avery's desire into overload, and Ozen groaned in response.

"A part of me wishes I could read your thoughts to know what was turning you on so much," Ozen purred. "Clothes off, firefly. Let me see you."

Without buttons or belts to get in his way, Avery was naked in five seconds flat. He pulled himself higher on the full sized mattress to give them more room. His dick was so hard, it was already leaking onto his belly, and he couldn't resist giving it a stroke. He never expected Ozen to bare his teeth, showing off those sharp fangs.

"Don't touch what's mine, firefly," he growled. "I won't hesitate to tie you to the bed."

A small mischievous part of him wanted to keep stroking until Ozen followed through on his promise. It was only when Ozen dropped his pants and revealed that delicious cock that Avery made up his mind to behave. He wanted another taste. He needed it.

Ozen crawled onto the bed, completely naked and so gorgeous Avery could cry. Every inch of him was flawless, his muscles lean and not overly bulky, his skin soft and without a single blemish or scar, and surprisingly no hair aside from on his head. Avery wanted to run his hands over every inch of it, but Ozen's threat still rang in his ears. He kept his hands to himself so he could reach the end goal.

When Ozen loomed over him, Avery's stomach fluttered with anticipation. His gaze dropped to Ozen's lips and he wondered for a moment what they would feel like against his own. That, actually, *was* in the contract. No kissing. Ozen didn't want his feeders getting the wrong idea. Kissing was too relationship-y. Avery kept that desire carefully under wraps.

With a quick movement that Avery didn't see coming, he had suddenly switched positions with Ozen. Desire spiked at how easily Ozen manhandled him, and Ozen grinned wickedly in response.

"Turn around, firefly. And remember, no quick finishes. If it gets to be too much, tell me."

Overeager, Avery wasn't as graceful as Ozen was in maneuvering himself. He was careful not to knee Ozen in the face, but getting into position wasn't a sexy single movement. He didn't have time to be embarrassed about it though. Once his cock lined up with Ozen's mouth, the incubus sucked on the head, ripping a surprised cry from Avery. He had to fight the urge to thrust into the hot wet suction. He distracted himself by giving Ozen's cock the same attention, contorting when Ozen's groan vibrated around his cock. Holding off his release was going to be excruciating.

Avery spent half the time trying to think of anything other than the feel of Ozen's mouth on his dick. His treatment of Ozen's erection was sloppy in comparison, spit dripping down his chin and over Ozen's cock. If Ozen was bothered by it, he never let on. He groaned, his hands on Avery's hips, drawing him farther down the incubi's throat. More than once, Avery had to pull off Ozen's dick to ask for a reprieve. Ozen gave him breaks to draw out the session, letting Avery focus on Ozen's cock while his blood cooled a little. Then Ozen picked the task back up and had Avery squirming all over again.

It wasn't nearly as long as Avery had hoped before he'd reached his limit and had to beg for mercy. His need to come bordered on painful. Any longer and it'd start to hurt. He released Ozen's dick, moaning into the man's thigh as Ozen sucked lazily at Avery's cockhead.

"O-Ozen... please..."

Ozen hummed his acknowledgement, startling Avery with a smack on his ass. "On your back, firefly. If I do my job right, you won't be able to hold yourself up after this."

Avery could barely hold himself up now. Half his weight was held up by Ozen's hand on his hip. He flopped to the side and onto his back, again far less gracefully than the incubus in his bed. He was too turned on to worry about it. Anticipation lit in his belly as Ozen got more comfortable between Avery's legs. He almost wished he knew more about sex to be able to predict what was coming. Then again, not knowing was part of the fun.

Avery's back arched and his mouth fell open in surprise when Ozen sucked him down again. That strange tongue of his wrapped a few times around Avery's cock, stroking him while Ozen sucked hard. The combined sensations ripped Avery's release from him, and he screamed so loud, his neighbor started pounding on the wall. Avery might have blacked out for a minute, and when he came to, Ozen looked smug.

"You too..." Avery murmured, but his limbs were too heavy to lift to draw Ozen closer. "I want you to finish."

Ozen's smug grin fell and his brow furrowed slightly. "You don't have to—"

"I want to," Avery assured him. He wriggled his fingers which was about as much energy as he could muster to get Ozen to come closer. Thankfully, Ozen didn't argue. He crawled over Avery's sated body, straddling his shoulders, and when Avery opened his mouth eagerly, he groaned, fisting his cock.

"Your eagerness to assure my pleasure is a true delight. I hope you understand that it's not required."

"I know. I still want to."

From the look on his face, Ozen couldn't resist any more. He fed Avery his dick, stroking what Avery couldn't suck down at this angle. It didn't take long before Ozen came. He grunted, his cock pulsing on Avery's tongue, and Avery's dick twitched in response. If he had the energy, he'd be begging for round two, but Ozen had wiped him out. Avery would have to be patient for tomorrow.

CHAPTER TWENTY

Given the late hour, Ozen wasn't surprised when Avery started drifting off. He was sated and comfortable in his bed. With very little mess to clean up, Ozen chose to hold Avery as a form of aftercare. He rearranged them on the bed, tucking the covers around his sleeping assistant. He felt tired as well, but figured a few moments to ensure Avery didn't feel used by a quick escape was best. Ozen wanted to keep Avery as his feeder for a long time, and he knew to do that, he had to take care of him.

Propping his head up with his hand, he took in Avery's sleeping form. He was beautiful. Even when he answered the door in sweats and a sweatshirt that absolutely swallowed him, he was beautiful. Raw eagerness and joy lit up his features whenever they started a session, followed quickly by that heated look that drove Ozen mad.

Ozen would need to speak with Dorian again about his reactions to Avery. He had something new to add. Feeding from Avery without participating had left Ozen satisfied for days. Avery's increased interest in giving Ozen pleasure only seemed to heighten his desire. Avery got pleasure from giving pleasure, and in turn, he fed Ozen so well, he felt almost drunk. He was almost worried about the effect of full penetration. The shared experience might overwhelm his magic entirely. Ozen had never heard of an incubus with too much magic, but he felt full to bursting after each session with Avery. Perhaps joining the research team for some spells might dissipate some of the excess.

While contemplating the research he could assist with, his eyes drifted closed. He tried to force them back open, but Avery was warm against his chest and Ozen was worn out and sated from their shared pleasure. He figured a few minutes of closing his eyes wouldn't hurt, and then he'd head home for the night.

When he opened his eyes again, his brain felt foggy. Perhaps it wasn't a good idea to meet with Avery right after drinking with his friends. The buzz from the alcohol plus the drunk feeling from feeding from Avery knocked him on his behind. He didn't even remember going home last night. He'd have to apologize to his driver for making him come back to pick him up so late.

Something rustled beside him, and it took a few moments for Ozen's brain to wake up. The warmth against his side was pleasant and the sunlight wasn't hitting the bed enough and blinding him like usual.

Suddenly he stiffened and his eyes flew open. The reason the sun wasn't blinding him was because he wasn't in his own bed. He was still in Avery's tiny apartment. Ozen didn't do sleepovers. It was too intimate. Feeders got the wrong idea. The thought of losing Avery because Ozen's lack of professionalism made fear spike in his veins. He didn't want to lead Avery on. That was cruel. He should have left as soon as they were finished.

Avery was curled against his side, using Ozen's shoulder as a pillow. Ozen had even wrapped his arm around Avery's slim form to keep him close. The position was romantic and panic made Ozen want to rip away. Ozen's rapid breathing didn't wake Avery, but running would. Perhaps Ozen could get out before Avery woke up. He didn't have to know.

He was easing himself away from Avery when an alarm went off. Avery grumbled, snuggling more closely to Ozen's side, his brow furrowed in irritation. Ozen held his breath, but it was too much to hope that Avery would sleep through it. His gorgeous blue eyes blinked open slowly, and like Ozen, it took Avery a moment to process his surroundings. His reactions were so much like Ozen's, it would have been comical if the situation wasn't so unfortunate. Avery stiffened, sucking in a sharp breath. He seemed to follow Ozen's first instinct, ripping himself away with a yelp.

"Oh my gods. I'm so sorry! I didn't mean to fall asleep on you! I hope you didn't feel obligated to stay! That was so unprofessional of me!" Avery scrambled out of the bed, flushing bright red when he realized he still had no clothes on. He looked around anxiously, snatching his sweats off the ground and yanking them on, nearly tripping over them in his haste.

Avery's immediate reaction to take the blame on himself surprised Ozen. He hadn't been the one to act unprofessionally. It was Ozen who failed to follow the contract to the letter and leave after the session was over. Cuddling with the person sharing your bed was not uncalled for.

"Avery. Avery!"

Ozen tried to get Avery's attention by calling his name, but Avery was babbling in his panic and didn't hear him. Ozen had to use his magic to capture his attention, soothing the panic enough for him to heed Ozen's words.

"Avery, this wasn't your fault. It was mine."

"What?" Avery croaked. His hands shook with adrenaline and his pulse was much too high. Ozen's magic continued to soothe him, his words soft so as not to increase Avery's panic.

"I apologize. I had only meant to lie with you for a minute as a form of aftercare. I didn't mean to fall asleep. You did absolutely nothing wrong."

To Ozen's surprise, Avery's chin trembled and his eyes turned misty with unshed tears. Ozen had dealt with tearful feeders in the past, but it was usually in regards to an imagined slight or a temper tantrum. He very rarely gave it the attention the feeders were hoping for. But Avery's reaction was unexpected and Ozen found himself rolling out of the bed to draw Avery into his arms.

"I am truly sorry, firefly. I didn't mean to upset you. I crossed a line by staying the night. If you wish to end our contract, I will understand."

Avery stiffened and jerked his head up to look at him. "Is that what you want?"

Not in the slightest. Losing Avery as his feeder was abhorrent, but Ozen had obviously made Avery uncomfortable, and he didn't want him to feel obligated to continue working with Ozen. Finding a new feeder would be... dreadful, but Ozen was prepared to face the consequences.

"It's not about what I want. I upset you. I didn't respect the terms of the contract, and therefore, you're allowed to break it. I don't want you to feel obligated to continue our working relationship after I made you uncomfortable."

Avery's brows drew together and he shook his head quickly. "I– You didn't!" he blurted.

It was Ozen's turn to frown. "I clearly did. You looked close to tears. You don't have to lie to–"

"No! I–" Avery sighed heavily, a frustrated look taking over his face. "That wasn't– Ugh. That wasn't about you. Sort of. I mean, it was, but not because I was uncomfortable. I thought you were going to fire me and I got upset before you said it was your fault, but the emotions didn't just disappear after you said I wasn't in trouble, so they just kind of came out. Humans are emotional and I don't think that should be held against me, and–"

He was babbling again. Ozen was admittedly not as familiar with humans as he was with supernaturals. He didn't spend much time around them. But it wasn't the first time someone mentioned them being emotional. Avery's reaction was simply an adrenaline induced reaction that needed to run its course. The relief was dizzying and Ozen's own emotions got the best of him. He yanked Avery into his arms, hugging him tightly against his chest. Avery made an *ooph* sound, but the surprise stalled out his nervous rambles and he was quick to hug Ozen back.

"I am sorry," Ozen murmured against the top of Avery's head. "I believe I need to refrain in the future from indulging in alcohol before a session. The combination left me drowsy, and I only intended to close my eyes for a moment."

For a moment, Avery didn't respond, but when his shoulders started to shake, Ozen leaned back to see Avery fighting back laughter. He had his lips pressed together tightly and his eyes danced with mirth. His convulsions were entertaining and Ozen found himself joining him in his laughter.

Once Ozen chuckled, Avery's attempts at holding back failed completely. He burst out laughing, his hands hugging his sides. Ozen didn't share many light hearted moments with his feeders. They were only interested in one thing. Laughing with Avery made Ozen's heart feel full and the self loathing and fear from the morning faded away. If they were both able to laugh about it, then it was unlikely that either of them wished to end the contract.

They parted on much better terms, and Ozen promised to call if he needed to feed again. He felt certain he could last until Monday morning at the latest. Ozen planned to meet with a healer as soon as possible to see how long he'd need to continue daily feedings. He wasn't complaining about them, but Avery would begin temping elsewhere in the building starting next week, and Ozen didn't want to make Avery's life more difficult by demanding his assistance on a daily basis.

Avery's laughter had been appreciated. Taron's was less so. Ozen found him waiting outside Ozen's door when he got home. Taron wouldn't let it go until Ozen finally told him where he'd been the night before. His friend was still laughing several minutes later and showed no signs of stopping.

"Are you through yet?" Ozen growled.

Taron's attempt to stop lasted maybe a few seconds before he howled again, slapping his knee with mirth. Ozen's irritation got the better of him and he shoved Taron off the couch. It didn't do much to stop his laughing. Instead, he was rolling on the floor.

"You got drunk and passed out at your feeder's place! You! Mr. Professionalism! Mr. Iron-Clad contracts and strict feeding locations! Got drunk and went to your feeder's apartment! Oh gods, I might pass out!"

"If you could hurry along with that, I'd appreciate it," Ozen drawled sarcastically. He didn't appreciate his flaws being held against him like this. He knew he could sometimes be considered rigid, but Taron knew why his contracts were so strict. He was only getting so much enjoyment out of this because it ended well.

When he didn't look to be stopping any time soon, Ozen let his magic swell and smacked his friend in the face with it. Taron's amusement died immediately, and he groaned in response.

"What was that for?"

"Maybe a case of blue balls will make you a more sympathetic companion."

Taron glared at him. "Dick move, man. Here I was, happy that you finally had a feeder you trusted enough to be that vulnerable with, and you treat me this way. Rude. Just rude."

Ozen rolled his eyes. "Yes. That's why you were laughing yourself silly. Did you show up here for a reason, or did you just plan to torment me?"

"Tormenting sounds good," Taron replied with a grin. "I'm bored. An afternoon of tormenting my best friend sounds like the perfect way to fix that. After I use your restroom. I'm not spending the whole day like this." He gestured to his crotch, where the outline of his erection could clearly be seen.

"I should just make you come so you'll have to leave to change."

Taron hightailed it to the bathroom before Ozen could finish the sentence. "Mercy! Mercy! I'll be good!"

Ozen shook his head with a smirk, heading for his bedroom to change his clothes. He was still in the outfit he'd worn last night. While he changed, he thought about what Taron had said. Last night was a series of poor decisions, but it struck him that Taron was right. He had allowed himself to be vulnerable with Avery. Anything could have happened while he was asleep, and yet Avery never took advantage of that fact. The worst he accomplished was cuddling, something that Ozen had to admit he enjoyed quite a bit.

What in the world made Avery so special? Why was he so enraptured by him? And what was he going to do about it?

CHAPTER TWENTY-ONE

Rule Number 7 - Performance Evaluations - Performance evaluations should be provided on an as needed basis to better give the feeder an understanding of how they are doing with their client and where they could stand to improve.

Avery's last week as Ozen's assistant ran smoother than the rest. Avery and Ozen continued their daily feeding schedule, and during his work hours as Ozen's assistant, Avery prepared for Mrs. Sable's return. He wrote up a report of everything that had happened and the things she would need to accomplish first when she got back. He also got word from Morana about his next assignment. The research floor needed a secretary while theirs was out sick. It would be a quick assignment, only a week long unless the illness turned out to be complicated, but Avery didn't mind a quick turn over.

The phone on his desk rang and Avery picked it up immediately. "Mr. Hawksley's office, Avery speaking. How can I help you?"

"Good morning," a craggy voice said. "I'm calling from Doctor Chapman's office to confirm Mr. Hawksley's appointment."

Avery's brows drew together tightly. He hadn't been told of any appointments.

"Okay... What time?"

"Friday at 3 P.M."

Avery pulled up Ozen's calendar. He thought he knew the thing front to back, but when he looked up the time of the appointment, there was a stretch of time blocked out that hadn't been there before. It was labeled personal and gave no other indication of what it was referring to.

"Uh... I see the schedule blocked off for that time, but I'm having trouble getting the details. Do you mind if I put you on hold and ask Mr. Hawksley directly?"

"If you don't mind. Supernaturals like him aren't inclined to visit a physician. If he asked for an appointment, it would be important."

Important, indeed. Avery had made a few appointments for long-lived supernaturals, usually at the request of someone close to them. Immortal or near immortal supernaturals didn't like to see physicians. They figured they'd been alive long enough that they would just get over whatever ailed them with enough time.

Placing the caller on hold, Avery popped out of his seat and knocked on Ozen's door. Thankfully, Ozen was working in his office this morning and Avery didn't need to chase him down or interrupt him from something important. Ozen's 'enter' was a lot more polite now that he was no longer affected by starvation. Avery poked his head in, giving Ozen an apologetic smile.

"Good morning, sir. I have a call on the line to confirm your Friday appointment at 3 P.M. Is that correct?"

"Yes, that's correct. Thank you for checking."

A dozen questions whirled through Avery's mind, but he had a job to do. He hurried back to his desk, quickly confirming that Ozen was aware of the scheduled appointment and would be there. After he hung up, Avery went back and forth on whether to ask Ozen what the appointment was for. On one hand, it wasn't his business what he did in his personal time. On the other hand, he was Ozen's feeder and if it was medical, it might affect him as well. Not that he believed Ozen would do anything to put Avery at risk. But was it too personal to ask?

Avery chewed on the problem for a while, frowning at his computer screen, when a familiar face popped into the office. Pushing his thoughts on the matter aside, he smiled.

"Good morning, Taron. I–" Avery paused, nearly swallowing his tongue when he finally took in Taron's appearance. The shapeshifter still had masculine features and a five o'clock shadow, but he had augmented his usual appearance with absolutely enormous breasts. They were comically large, and the shirt he wore strained to contain them. Avery could only gape.

"Uh..."

Concerned for Taron's mental well being, Avery reached for his phone without looking away, buzzing Ozen's office. It wasn't often that Avery had to buzz him, usually just an appointment reminder if he was in the middle of a meeting, so Ozen was confused when he opened his door.

"Avery, what– Oh, good gods. Really, Taron?"

Taron spun around and the giant knockers nearly threw him off balance with the motion. He beamed at his friend.

"What? I'm just following your advice."

Ozen rolled his eyes hard. "You couldn't manifest something a little more appropriate for the office? Your shirt is bursting at the seams."

And in the front, but Avery wasn't going to say that out loud. He'd seen Taron change little parts of his appearance. Different nose, different hair color, that kind of thing. It was amusing to pick out what new thing had changed since the last time they ran into each other. This was... a bit much.

"Yeah," Taron agreed, his nose wrinkled. "I didn't have anything that fit right. And, I didn't know this, but these things are killer for your back. I've been aching all morning. I manifested them last night and I struggled to get comfortable to sleep. At one point I thought they might smother me."

Avery tried so, so hard, but the snicker escaped without his say-so. He hunched over, keeping his head ducked to hide his laughter, but it just wouldn't stop.

"Your assistant enjoys my pain," Taron said dryly.

Ozen chuckled. "Good. I do too. Fix those things, will you? You're going to hurt someone."

That wasn't helping. Avery covered his mouth with his hands, his shoulders shaking with suppressed laughter.

"You know we can see you, right? You're not very subtle," Taron complained.

Another laugh slipped out and it seemed to set off Ozen. He started laughing too, which made Avery laugh harder. Even Taron joined in after a minute. Tears pricked Avery's eyes from laughing so hard, and when he swayed in his chair, Ozen came to stand beside him to keep him off the floor.

"Well, I'm sad I missed the party. What's going on in here?"

Avery sucked in a sharp breath, whipping his head up. "Mrs. Sable! You're back early."

Mrs. Sable smiled at him. She looked a lot more relaxed than the last time he'd seen her, with no tension around her eyes and a healthy glow to her skin. "Not officially. I'll be back on Friday for the trade off. I just thought I'd stop in and check on things. Last time we spoke, things were a little hectic."

True. The office had settled considerably since then. And while Avery was prepared to vacate his position as Ozen's assistant, he couldn't help but feel a certain amount of dread. He enjoyed working here. He liked being close to Ozen. It made it easier for him to notice if Ozen was hungry and needed him earlier than planned. He knew he wouldn't be far, the research department he was needed at was only about ten floors down, but it felt too far for him.

The thought process made Avery hesitate. Maybe being separated from Ozen would be a good thing. He was getting attached. He wanted to say it was just because he cared about Ozen's wellbeing, but that felt like a lie on his tongue. It was more than that. Avery was usually diligent about focusing on his work. He wasn't easily distracted, but he was distracted by Ozen. His thoughts were constantly on his boss, on what he was doing and what he might need to make his day better. He thought about their next session and had to fight the urge to go to him early.

The separation was good. Avery needed to clear his head. He assured Ozen left and right that he could keep his emotions out of it. He was determined for their relationship to remain professional for Ozen's sake. He needed a feeder he could rely on. Avery wasn't going to let his feelings get in the way of his work.

———

Normally, when Collette returned from her vacation, Ozen was overjoyed to see her. She was an excellent assistant and she was missed every time she was gone. However, this time was different. As Collette caught up with Taron and Avery, Ozen's gaze flicked to the man beside him.

Avery might have Collette beat on the best assistant title. Not only was he efficient and well liked in the office, his loyalty was something to admire. He'd gone above and beyond for Ozen since the day he arrived. Colette was diligent and a good worker, but she wasn't Avery.

Ozen realized his train of thought was dangerous. There was nothing wrong with Collette. He had no reason to favor Avery over her, aside from the man's position as his feeder. His need to keep Avery close was merely a result of that. Perhaps because of the Calvin ordeal, he was feeling more anxious than usual about the whereabouts of his feeder. He'd need to ask Doctor Chapman about that come Friday afternoon. Ozen was unaware of the effects of starvation on an incubus, or the recovery. He assumed his feelings on the matter correlated somehow.

Brushing that aside, Ozen gave his focus back to the room. "Collette, did you receive my request for your account of Calvin's behavior?"

"Yes, Mr. Hawksley. I stopped by Mr. Van Buren's office on my way up. It was one of the reasons I came here before my return date. I didn't want to drag the process out any longer than necessary."

"I appreciate that. Thank you. Avery, could you please set up a phone meeting with Maverick some time today? I want to check on his progress on the lawsuit."

"Yes, sir. Right away."

Avery still didn't know the effect his words had on Ozen. Every time Avery called him sir, Ozen wanted to shiver. It didn't help that during their sessions, Avery was quick to follow directions. Ozen wasn't going to introduce that kind of dynamic while Avery was still exploring. He needed to experience the basics before they added kinks into the mix. And while Ozen's were relatively tame for an incubus, they were still more than Avery needed to deal with right now.

Taron joined him in his office after Collette left. Avery was still on the phone with Maverick, his gaze locked on the calendar as he found a time in his and Maverick's schedule for a meeting. Ozen left him to it and closed the door to give himself and Taron privacy.

"I'm assuming you didn't come upstairs for a visit."

"Unfortunately, no," Taron agreed. The air shimmered and his new appendages disappeared. All his extras disappeared as well, leaving Taron looking a little worn and a lot exhausted. Ozen's chest filled with concern and he gestured for Taron to join him on the couch.

"What's the matter, my friend?"

Taron sighed, scrubbing his hands over his face. "I'm feeling... out of balance lately. Nothing makes me feel comfortable in my own skin. No changes I make help the issue. It's why I've been so fixated on gender swapping. I was playing with something new that might not fundamentally change things. And while tits are great fun, they didn't do a thing to make the feeling go away."

Ozen put his hand on Taron's shoulder, his smile patient. "It's time, isn't it?"

Taron grimaced. "I guess. I don't want to, though. I like this form."

Usually, Taron changed his permanent form on his own. But if he liked a particular form, he'd try to stick with it for a while. Unfortunately, his body wasn't capable of keeping it forever. Like your favorite suit, you could mend it when it was damaged and take good care of it, but eventually, it would become threadbear and need replacing. Taron had this current form for over a hundred years. It was one of his longest, and no amount of simple augmentation was going to fix it.

"When are you leaving?"

Taron sighed, his head drooping forward. He had to return home to get the magic he needed. It only took about a week for major form changes, but Taron dreaded it every time. His home life wasn't... pleasant.

"I think I can stretch it out another week. Maybe. Any chance you trust Avery to take over as VP?"

Ozen chuckled. "I trust Avery's judgment on a great many things, but I don't think he would be qualified for that. Don't worry. I'll cover your work. Collette will be back and Avery will be around to help if necessary. Go home, my friend. I look forward to seeing the form you choose next."

CHAPTER TWENTY-TWO

Leaving early was almost unheard of for Ozen, but he had an appointment to keep. It was Avery's last day as his assistant, and he hated the thought of leaving him to head out alone on his last day, but it couldn't be helped. Ozen needed this appointment. There were too many questions he needed answered. Too many unknowns. He didn't often seek a physician, and when he did, it was always for something important.

His desk phone buzzed as he was pulling on his jacket, a reminder from Avery that he had an appointment. Since he was leaving anyway, he didn't answer, instead heading out of his office to where Avery sat waiting. He smiled brightly, still ever professional, despite the last two weeks as Ozen's feeder. By now, the red flags would usually make themselves known with Ozen's feeders. Avery had none. Not even Ozen's reactions to him were off-putting. They were more of a curiosity. Ozen was grateful that it was Avery that showed up in his office a month ago.

"Have a nice evening, Mr. Hawksley. Did you need anything else from me before I leave?"

"No, nothing important. You've set up for Collette's return, correct?"

He bobbed his head in acknowledgement. "Yes, sir. Everything is ready and I'll be reporting to the research floor Monday morning to temp for their secretary who's out sick. Did we want to keep our sessions after lunch? I'm not sure how different my schedule will be downstairs."

"It shouldn't affect you. Like I said, feeders get certain accommodations to make their sessions a priority. If you feel another time would be easier on you, just let me know. You've been an excellent assistant. I'm sure you can make it work."

Avery's smile only brightened further with the compliment. A feeling, almost like dread, hit Ozen in the gut. He wasn't looking forward to not seeing Avery every morning. He almost wished he could bring Avery with him to his appointment to drag out their time together. After all, it was Avery who was healing the effects of his starvation.

Ozen shook off the stray through and sighed. "I appreciate your help over the last month, Avery. And no matter your position in the company, if you need anything, please come to me. Let me know if after lunch still works for you on Monday. I'll see you later."

Ozen wasn't going to delude himself that he could go an entire weekend without seeing Avery. He would try, for Avery's sake and for his own need to keep things professional, but he wouldn't let himself get upset if he needed to see his feeder again at least once this weekend.

"Thank you, Mr. Hawksley. I'll wrap things up here. A few of the other secretaries are taking me out for dinner tonight, so if you need anything, I'll have my phone on me."

Always so diligent. Ozen dipped his chin to acknowledge him and left, stopping himself from looking over his shoulder to see if Avery watched him go.

There had to be some reason why he was so attached to the human. He was sure the starvation had something to do with it. Or maybe Avery's inexperience. He needed to prioritize doing research if Doctor Chapman didn't have any answers for him.

———

Supernatural physicians were druids more often than not. Their connections with earth magic gave them more control over the body's natural processes. They were mostly human, aside from their magic. Only the elders looked different, growing horns like antlers made of wood once they reached a certain age.

Doctor Chapman was an elder, his horns massive and a little intimidating. One quick turn and he could take an eye out with those things. He seemed aware of them, though, and he was careful with them as he examined Ozen with a scrutinizing eye.

"You said you were starved. For how long?"

"Two weeks," Ozen reported. "I felt quite close to going feral before my assistant stepped in to help."

The doctor hummed, his head tipped and his eyes narrowed. He was looking at Ozen, but it didn't look like he was seeing him, more like seeing through him. It was always disconcerting to Ozen when people did that.

"From what I can tell, the effects of starvation were not long term. I'm seeing no residual effects plaguing you now."

Ozen's brows furrowed. "Then why do I still require frequent feedings? I've tried to go without. I prefer sticking to the work week to keep things professional, but I still needed to see my feeder on the weekend."

Doctor Chapman pursed his lips thoughtfully. "It could be a mental block. Facing starvation and nearly going feral would make anyone overcautious. Health wise, you're doing quite well. Your magic feels strong to me, and your body is well fed. Have you experienced any other symptoms other than frequent hunger? Headaches? Brittle nails? That sort of thing?"

Ozen shook his head. "No. Nothing like that. The only other unusual experience I have is in regards to my feeder's potency."

"What about it?" Doctor Chapman asked curiously.

"My newest feeder has been significantly more potent than the others. I don't need to go nearly as far to feel well fed. At first, I believed it had something to do with his inexperience, that perhaps going so long without sex made his desire more robust. But while I don't remember every feeder I've ever had, I doubt I went this long without ever feeding from a virgin before. It doesn't make any sense."

The doctor bobbed his head in agreement, his expression thoughtful. "That is strange. I've never heard of one feeder being more potent than others. I'm seeing no signs of poisoning or magic tampering, so I doubt it's a bad thing. Even with their potency, you still need frequent feeding?"

"Not at first. The first time I fed from him, I went three days without needing to feed again. And even while I was starved, I still didn't require full penetration to bring myself back from the brink. Several weeks later, and we still haven't gone that far yet. But going more than twenty-four hours feels... impossible."

Chapman's eyebrows shot up significantly. "Really? That's interesting. I'll admit, my incubus background is lacking. You lot tend to avoid physicians like the plague. I'll have to do some research on why you're reacting like that. All I can say for now is health wise, you're fine. There are no lingering effects of the starvation. Your frequent feedings are most likely an emotional response to the events."

That wasn't what Ozen wanted to hear. He wanted an answer. Maybe he should have brought Avery along and had the doctor look at him as well. Even now, despite having fed from Avery only a few hours before, Ozen felt a distinct need to be close to him. It was inexplicable and a little irritating. He did not get attached to his feeders. If the relationship was a little less perfect, Ozen might be looking for a replacement for Avery. He didn't like feeling this needy.

On his way out, Doctor Chapman's voice made him pause. "Just a moment. You never said what species your feeder is. I'm curious if that could be related."

"He's human," Ozen replied.

"Oh. So not related then. Humans don't have magic to contend with. Alright, I'll do some digging, see if there are any articles about incubi and potent feeders. I'm sure there's an answer out there somewhere."

"Thank you, Doctor."

Ozen left the doctor's office more frustrated than when he arrived. He'd been hoping at least part of his issue was him still healing from two weeks of starvation. But apparently, he was well. His continued need to feed frequently had nothing to do with it, which meant it had something to do with Avery. Ozen was quite sure that there wasn't magic involved. He checked before each session. But the lack of explanations was irritating.

There was only one other person he knew he could call to ask these questions. But if Ozen avoided physicians like the plague, his avoidance of this particular person was even more extensive. He refused to pick up the phone unless it was life or death.

Instead, Ozen decided to push himself to go longer without feeding.

Doctor Chapman said it was a mental block after the trauma of starvation. Avery was still as potent as ever, and Ozen knew he was well at hand for now. He would strive to return to his work day feeding schedule. That way, he would avoid mishaps like sleeping over at Avery's house again.

The reminder of his mistake made him grimace, but it also reminded him of another issue. Avery lived in a shoe box. It took considerable work not to let his displeasure show on his face when he visited Avery the weekend prior. There wasn't even a proper kitchen, and everything was crammed into one room. Avery made good money as a feeder, plus the money he made as a temp. He didn't need to live in such squalor, and the idea of leaving him in that place was deplorable to Ozen.

Normally, he would have Collette deal with issues like these. She was an excellent assistant and would have several options for new housing for Avery in a matter of hours, but she wouldn't be returning to work until Monday. Checking his watch, he realized that Avery had probably gone home for the night, so that option was out. Avery was no longer his assistant, and he told Ozen about his plans for the evening. It would be unfair of Ozen to drag him back to work for something like this.

Instead, he decided to look for a place for Avery himself. He didn't often take on tasks such as these, but for some reason, the thought of finding a place for Avery pleased him. Avery did so much to take care of him, so it was only right that Ozen did this for him. And that was the only reason for it. It had nothing to do with Ozen's growing affection for his feeder, or some foolish need to make Avery happy. This was a professional courtesy. His feeder needed to be healthy, including having things like a safe and comfortable place to rest and a kitchen to feed himself. Avery's building didn't strike Ozen as safe, either. A doorman was necessary to protect his asset.

Maybe if he said it enough, he'd sound more convincing to others, because Ozen refused to admit that he couldn't even convince himself.

CHAPTER TWENTY-THREE

Rule number 75 - Training - A feeder should be provided with adequate training to better support their client. This includes the client's likes and dislikes, as well as what to expect in the event of an emergency.

Avery was surprised when he heard nothing from Ozen all weekend. And he could admit, he was a little disappointed. He'd deep cleaned his apartment in hopes of Ozen coming to visit again, but Avery's phone was quiet, and no one came knocking. He attempted to work on his book, but he was too distracted and got nothing decent done with it. By the time Monday rolled around, Avery was worried. Instead of heading to the research floor like he was supposed to, he went to Ozen's office first to see if he needed to feed earlier, since he skipped all weekend.

Mrs. Sable was already there, working diligently at her desk. She smiled when Avery stepped into the office, her relaxed disposition still visible after a month of vacation.

"Good morning, Avery. How was your weekend?"

"Fine, thank you. I, uh... I came to check in with Mr. Hawksley. He hasn't fed since Friday, and—"

The office door jerked open without warning and a seething Ozen glared at them both. Avery's mouth fell open in surprise, but he didn't get a moment to ask what was wrong before Ozen stepped back and gave him a pointed look. Avery jumped to follow orders, scurrying into Ozen's office. He didn't have time to blink before Ozen grabbed his arm and spun him, shoving his back against the door the second it closed fully.

"O-Ozen, what—"

Ozen cut him off with his teeth on Avery's neck. The sting was sharp, but it was right on the spot that made Avery melt. He moaned, tipping his head to give Ozen more room. It was like a switch was flipped and all Avery could think about was sex. He lost all sense of himself, completely at Ozen's mercy as he fumbled with Avery's clothes until he could reach Avery's cock. Avery cried out in surprise at the rough treatment, his fingers digging into Ozen's arms. It didn't hurt, Ozen wouldn't hurt him, but it was more rough than usual, almost like the first day that Avery noticed Ozen was starving.

Avery forced his eyes open, looking at Ozen's face. The fangs were back, and his eyes were blood red and wild. Avery watched as Ozen tore open his own zipper, releasing his cock. His movements weren't normally so uncontrolled. Avery opened his mouth to ask, but then Ozen fisted both their cocks together and Avery could only make a strangled sound, his eyes rolling into his head at the first stroke.

Avery could always feel when Ozen's magic latched onto him. It usually happened right away, as Avery's eagerness seemed to feed Ozen just as much as his arousal did. This time it took a minute. Ozen was too distracted. When he finally latched on, the pleasure that slammed into him was too much, and Avery came without warning. His cock pulsed in Ozen's hand and the incubus groaned, thrusting more forcefully into the ring of his hand, his ribbed cock massaging Avery's oversensitive skin. It bordered on painful, and Avery whimpered in response.

Without warning, Ozen spun him around, shoving Avery's front against the door. When he jerked Avery's hips back, Avery's breath stuttered in his chest. They hadn't gotten to full penetration yet, and Avery wasn't sure he was comfortable with the idea of his first time being up against the door. Thankfully, Ozen was coherent enough to not push the issue. Instead, he thrust his cock against Avery's ass, rubbing through his cheeks as he got himself off. It felt good, really good, and Avery's fingers fisted against the door as he moaned and writhed.

Ozen's growl grew louder with each thrust, and the hairs on the back of Avery's neck stood on end. It sounded almost threatening. When his arousal faltered a little, Ozen reached around him, stroking his cock in time with his thrusts. Avery groaned, losing himself in the pleasure, and he quickly returned to full hardness with Ozen's fierce attention.

"O-Ozen, I–"

The warmth of Ozen's release splashed across Avery's cheeks, surprising him, and Avery's entire body lit up in response. The knowledge that he sent the incubus over the edge before Avery could finish the second time like Ozen wanted was heady, and it took only a few more strokes of Ozen's hand for Avery to follow after him, his cum splashing on the door.

Avery barely stayed on his own two feet, being trapped between the door and Ozen's body the only reason he was upright. The mixture of shock, pleasure, and confusion swirled in his mind as he fought for breath. It wasn't until Ozen started kissing along Avery's neck that Avery felt brave enough to speak.

"A-Are you okay? That was–"

"Unexpected. I know. I apologize." Ozen shifted, pulling Avery's back against his front to support his weight as he moved Avery away from the door. "My doctor says I'm healthy and no longer suffering from the effects of starvation, but my attempt to go back to how things were backfired. I was starved by the time you showed up this morning, and I couldn't control myself." He looked Avery over with a worried frown. "Are you alright? Did I hurt you?"

"No, no. You didn't hurt me. Just surprised me."

He said that, but he was more tired than usual after a feeding, his body like jello, unable to support itself. Ozen picked up on that and carefully scooped Avery into his arms, moving him to the couch. He used his magic to clean Avery up and situated Avery's clothes for him, since Avery's arms felt like dead weights.

Now that Avery could see his face, Ozen looked a little better. Less dangerous, at least. His eyebrows were pinched in concern, and his mood didn't seem much better, but the fangs were gone and his eyes were back to normal again. He did seem distracted, though.

"I'm afraid I have a meeting to get to. I'll have Collette bring you a snack. It'll help get your energy back."

When Ozen stood, Avery was surprised. He reached out, gripping the corner of Ozen's sleeve, confusion swirling through his muddled senses.

"W-Wait... You said quick sessions didn't give you what you needed. Are you sure you'll be alright? If you're hungry, you really should eat."

For a moment, Ozen's tight expression softened before he brushed Avery's hand away. "I appreciate your concern, but unfortunately, I'm too busy. Taron is away this week, and I'm picking up the slack of his absence. Quick sessions are better than nothing. I'll be fine."

He gave Avery no room to argue and marched out the door before he could even open his mouth. Avery's mind felt turbulent. He was obviously dismissed, and he didn't want to come off as pushy or demanding, but Ozen told him multiple times that the longer the session, the stronger he felt afterwards. Their session this morning wasn't even five minutes long. Yes, Avery came twice, but was it truly enough? Especially if Ozen said he was starving over the weekend? He'd thought once the frenzy was over that they'd go back to the feeding room like before.

He wasn't sure what to do. He was a temp, he knew how to adapt to new situations, but being a feeder was outside his realm of expertise. He didn't know where the line was and how best to do his job when Ozen was telling him to leave it be. Did he push? Did he ignore the fact that Ozen was basically starving this morning? He didn't even know who he could ask.

A sharp knock on the door made him look up and Mrs. Sable bustled in with a tray of snacks and a bottle of water. Her smile was warm, and she offered him a hand to help him sit up better before sitting next to him and handing him the bottle.

"How are you feeling?"

"Tired," Avery answered honestly. "I'm not usually this tired afterwards."

It felt awkward to talk about in front of her, but she didn't seem disturbed by the conversation. She nodded in understanding, offering him a cookie from the tray she brought in.

"Sugar will help. Quick sessions can often be exhausting for the feeder. If Mr. Hawksley is in a rush, he'll draw out energy too quickly, and your body will suffer the effects of it. It's why he doesn't like to rush. It's safer for you if he takes his time. Unfortunately, this week is going to be difficult for you both. His schedule is hectic when Taron is gone, and he will be working late most nights to keep up. A few minutes here and there is all he'll have time for."

Avery blinked a few times. Ozen told him that longer sessions were to make sure Ozen got what he needed. He never said anything about it being for Avery's benefit. It was almost as if he knew Avery would protest taking up too much of his time just to keep his energy levels up when Ozen was busy.

"How long will Mr. Cunningham be gone?"

"At least a week. He had to return home. Many supernaturals return to their home realms when something regarding their magic comes up. I do it every few years for a boost. That's why you were covering for me."

He knew that part, at least. He felt like he was constantly playing catch up with supernaturals and their abilities, but he never complained about that. He enjoyed learning new things, and he didn't hold it against himself for being different. It's just who he was born to be.

"Is there anything I can do to help? I'm temping in research right now, but I can call my work and find someone to cover me if you need me up here instead."

Mrs. Sable smiled. "You're a good man, Avery. I'm glad Mr. Hawksley can rely on you as his feeder. Right now, the best thing you can do is your job. If the research team is floundering and not getting the work done in time, the fallback will be on Mr. Hawksley. You doing your job will keep some stress off him at least. And showing up for your sessions on time will help. I understand you normally meet after lunch?"

"Yes, but if he's that busy, it might be better to meet first thing. I can come in before my work day starts so I don't interrupt his schedule." Avery's brows drew together. "Though, if I'm this exhausted after each session, it might make doing my job a little difficult. I'm supposed to be downstairs soon, but I'm not sure my knees can support me yet."

She patted his knee reassuringly and nudged the cookie in his hand to get him to take another bite. "I already called down and let them know where you were. They understand. Your job as a feeder supersedes your job as a temp. They have to accommodate you since you're literally feeding someone else. With a little sugar, we can get you back on your feet again. As for tomorrow, let me look at the schedule. If necessary, we can plan your sessions during lunch and I'll have something waiting for you when you're finished. That way, you can recuperate while you eat."

"Mr. Hawklsey prefers if I eat before," Avery argued. "He said it will keep my energy up."

It would take some finagling to get the right timing for a session now that Avery didn't work upstairs. If he was still Ozen's assistant, he'd be able to initiate a session whenever Ozen had an opening. Now that they had to work around both their schedules, it was more difficult. Mrs. Sable promised she'd help him figure it out and sat with him until he felt like he could move on his own again. It was a little disconcerting to be that exhausted after a session. Avery wished Ozen would've warned him about that particular side effect.

CHAPTER TWENTY-FOUR

Rule Number 36 - It is important to be on time to meet with your client. If being late is consistent, it may be cause for a dropped contract.

Avery made it downstairs thirty minutes late, which irked him. He considered having words with Ozen later for not warning him what quick sessions would do to him. Their first session had been quick, but that was over a month ago, and at the time, Avery had been thrown for a loop as it was just by being mistaken as Ozen's feeder. Had he known what would happen, he might have asked Ozen to slow down a little, at least enough that Avery could make it to his desk on his own power on time. Avery detested being late.

The research level he was going to be working on was the largest level of the building. It spanned two floors and was the only level that you could get to each tower from without having to go all the way down to the lobby and switching elevators. The reception desk where Avery would be working was close to the elevator bank, and someone was already there waiting for him. He sat behind the desk, a pair of half-moon glasses balanced on his beak. Avery had never seen a griffin use glasses before. He glanced up when Avery approached, and his eyes warmed in greeting. Kind of hard to smile with a beak.

"Good morning, you must be Avery."

"Yes, good morning to you. Sorry I'm late, I was... feeding Ozen." Avery slapped his hand over his mouth. He hadn't meant to say that. His intention was to be more discrete.

The griffin looked amused, dismissing Avery's embarrassment with a wave of his claw. "Don't worry. People are compelled to be honest around me. You get used to it. I'm Brennus Brightbeak. I'm the head of Supernatural Resources. Normally, one of my subordinates would be doing this, but I felt it prudent to introduce myself since you'll be working around the building more often. Because you are a temp, you weren't hired through me, and I like to get to know the people working in the building before they start."

Ah. That explained why the head of Supernatural Resources was here to train him for a simple receptionist job. Avery was only originally supposed to be here for a month. Now that they changed things up so that he could be nearby if Ozen needed him, introducing himself to Supernatural Resources wasn't the worst idea.

"That makes sense. And I promise, I'm not normally late." He considered his wording carefully so the griffin's magic wouldn't make him say anything embarrassing. "I usually react better to sessions, but today was... difficult."

Brennus frowned, studying him carefully. "Are you well enough to start today?"

"Oh, yeah, definitely. I was just tired. Mr. Hawksley didn't warn me about the effects of quick feedings. Mrs. Sable helped me afterwards, since Mr. Hawksley had a meeting to get to."

Again, too much information, but Avery was in a hurry to reassure the griffin and didn't think things through. He pinched his lips together and resisted the urge to cover his mouth again. Brennus seemed understanding, though.

"Ah. Yes, I've heard those can be difficult. Not many feeders hold two jobs, since they need rest afterwards. But I've been told you continued to work the last month as Mr. Hawksley's assistant, despite your feeder duties. That went well?"

"Yes, really well. We had a specific time each day that we met for his feedings, set in his calendar like a meeting so we weren't in a rush. I usually feel fine afterwards and can do my job without issue. Today was a special circumstance. He was in a hurry."

And starving, but Avery didn't mention that. He pressed his lips together to stop himself from saying something he shouldn't. Ozen's condition wasn't anyone's business but Ozen's and Avery's.

"Well, alright. I've heard good things about you, so I'm sure you can make it work. Your job here is simple. Answer and transfer phone calls, deliver faxes and, on rare occasions, you'll escort volunteers from the lobby up here for their appointments. They don't do that every day, so it might not come up. The usual assistant, Dakota, made an emergency booklet with all the extensions and a few notes. She should only be out until the end of the week, but I'll let you know if that changes. Do you have any questions?"

"No, thank you. I can handle it."

The griffin studied him before nodding once. "I believe you can. If you have any problems, don't hesitate to reach out. I'm here to support all the staff, humans included. It may be called Supernatural Resources, but that doesn't exclude you."

That was nice to hear. Some companies, despite allowing humans as temps, didn't much care for them and had no interest in fair treatment. Since this was Ozen's company, Avery didn't doubt there would be support, but it was good to know he wasn't assuming anything.

After Brennus left, Avery settled into his new desk. He never minded not having a desk that was truly his own. Avery was an extrovert by nature and enjoyed meeting new people, so he didn't have trouble introducing himself to people as they passed the reception desk. Most were curious and polite. A few seemed wary. That was to be expected. Since humans were minorities and often kept to themselves, supernaturals weren't always sure how to handle them. There were old stories about how humans used to be the majority and started a war with supernaturals to gain control. According to the stories, the humans failed miserably but still managed to cause a lot of damage before they were subdued. Avery wanted to believe those stories were myths, but some supernaturals still believed them.

He dragged a little through the morning, still recovering from the session with Ozen, but he perked back up after lunch. A decent meal and a cat nap with his head on the table in the break room did him wonders, and he arrived back at his desk energetic and upbeat. He smiled brightly at everyone as they came off the elevator back from their lunch breaks.

He was just finishing up a phone call when a group of supernaturals in suits exited the elevator. Most ignored him, which was fine, but a group of three shifters broke off, the middle one sneering at him.

"Ugh. What's a human doing here? Have we really fallen that far?"

The friend on his right smirked, enjoying the commentary, but the one on the left elbowed him, shaking his head.

"Don't. That's Hawksley's feeder," he murmured in warning.

If anything, that only made it worse. The middle one looked downright disgusted, staring at Avery like he was a piece of crap on the bottom of his shoe. "No. That can't be right. There's no way Hawksley would sink so low as to feed from one of *them*."

It was moments like these where Avery wished he could speak his mind. He didn't appreciate being belittled, but they were clever. They weren't speaking directly to him, just about him close enough for him to hear. It wouldn't quite be considered harassment, since they could say it was his fault for eavesdropping. Avery just had to deal with it until they finally brought him into the conversation or left.

He usually had a thicker skin about these things, but a month working in Ozen's office under Ozen's protection left him a little unprepared. He gritted his teeth, ignoring the group as best he could, but apparently they didn't like that. They got closer, their comments growing harsher and more targeted.

"I've heard humans are riddled with diseases. I'm surprised Hawksley hasn't caught anything."

"Maybe he has. It's not like he'd ever admit it. Mighty incubus wouldn't bother interacting with those beneath him."

Avery's fists were clenched tightly on the desk. He could handle people talking about him. Discrimination against humans, unfortunately, wasn't a rare occurrence. But he couldn't tolerate people trash talking Ozen. He was a good person. He built an entire company, striving to help marginalized supernaturals. He never acted superior or treated his subordinates poorly. Even when Calvin was starving him, he was careful in his interactions with others and apologized to everyone who felt uncomfortable around him once he was well again.

"Maybe he's off his rocker. Why else would he stoop so low?"

"Could be. Or the human is manipulating him. I've never heard of a human feeder before. He probably is on his knees every night to get that cushy job."

Cheeks flushed, Avery's careful control of his tongue was slipping. Any longer and he'd lose his cool. There was only so much he could take.

Thankfully, someone called out to the group, and they wandered away, snickering to themselves. Avery felt tears burn the back of his eyes. He was used to this, but the humiliation was never any easier to bear. He wished often that he had been born a supernatural. Even the weakest supernaturals were respected more than humans were. Avery was belittled and gossiped about merely because of his species, something he had no control of. There were even some who thought themselves so far above him that they made demands and threatened to hurt him if he didn't obey. In jobs like those, he was quick to report them to Morana and move on to another job, but he couldn't do that here. He needed to stay close to Ozen. Complaining and causing a ruckus on his first day outside of Ozen's office wouldn't look good for him.

The bullies didn't bother him again. They passed by with their group and entered the elevators with only a few sneers in his direction at the end of the day. Avery waited for a while to make sure they weren't going to bump into each other before heading home on his own. He kept his head down, eyes on his shoes, all the way home. He couldn't stomach seeing another judgmental supernatural looking down at him.

Usually, he got home and immediately started working on his book. It was a hobby as much as it was a dream for a future job. But he bypassed his desk entirely, dropping face first onto his mattress.

For a little while, he let himself be sad. It wasn't pleasant when he had run-ins like that, and he hadn't been expecting it after working upstairs, but he could get over it. It was most likely a one-time event, and he would have a better experience tomorrow.

———

He did not, in fact, have a better experience the following day. Or the one after that. Most of the week was pretty awful, if he was being honest with himself. He never realized how much protection he was getting by working upstairs with Ozen until he started this new job. The shifters who talked badly about him stopped by at least once a day. Avery got complaints from a few researchers when he had to leave for a session with Ozen and berated him almost constantly for being sluggish afterwards. Ozen didn't have time to do longer sessions, so Avery was wiped out afterwards every day that week. More than once, he wanted to take Ozen up on his offer to go home for the day, but they had no one else to cover for the receptionist on the research floor, and he didn't want to cause more trouble for Ozen.

By the time Friday rolled around, he was exhausted to the point of tears and so tense his whole body hurt. He had a sore in his mouth from biting the inside of his cheek so often to keep himself from talking back, and several times he found his lunch tossed in the trash, so he didn't get to eat as much as he should have been. He hid his upset as best he could from Ozen, who was in too much of a hurry to notice, but after he left, he couldn't hold back the tears any longer. He wrapped his arms around his middle, choking on sobs. This wasn't him. He wasn't this person, to let things like this slide. But what other choice did he have?

CHAPTER TWENTY-FIVE

Ozen felt a little like he was swimming against the current. He knew the week would be long with Taron away. He just forgot how much his friend took off his plate. He would need to send Taron a gift once he was back, because Ozen wouldn't be able to run this company without him.

He was so busy, he was forgetting things. Usually, he had to get Collette to bring him whatever he left behind, but thankfully this time, he remembered before he got into the elevator. He went back for his phone, grumbling to himself. It was something he couldn't leave behind. Collette looked amused, raising an eyebrow at him.

"Forget something again?"

"Taron's return can't come quick enough," he said tersely in reply.

She chuckled, turning back to her computer as he stepped into his office. He came to an abrupt halt, his eyes landing on Avery. His feeder was scrubbing at his face, trying desperately to hide the fact that he had been crying. All thoughts of meetings were wiped away in an instant, and Ozen hurried to his side, kneeling by the couch.

"What is it? What's wrong?"

"Nothing," Avery insisted, though his chin trembled and he couldn't stop the tears from slipping down his cheeks. His continence broke, and he sobbed again, dropping his face into his hands.

Ozen was unsure of what to do. Avery seemed fine when he left. Tired, but that was to be expected. It was unfortunate how many quick feeds he'd needed this week. No matter how many times he tried to make himself stretch out the time between when he saw Avery, it never seemed to work. It wasn't easy on the feeder when quick feeds happened, but Avery didn't let on that it was bothering him. Ozen didn't realize he was putting on a brave face.

"Is everything alright?" Collette asked from the door. Ozen had been in such a rush, he hadn't closed it behind him. Good, that would make this easier.

"Cancel my meetings for the rest of the afternoon."

"N-No!" Avery wailed. "I-I-I-I'm fine!"

Ozen ignored him, scooping him off the couch and into his arms. He headed for the bedroom so he could at least get Avery more comfortable. Now that he was paying attention, he could see how low Avery's energy levels were. He was exhausted, and Ozen was at least partially, if not fully, to blame for that. He would never forgive himself for upsetting such a beautiful soul.

Inside the dark room, Ozen set Avery on the bed, combing his fingers through Avery's golden curls. His body shook with his sobs and his breath came out in sharp gasps. He wanted to push Avery to talk to him, but now was not the time. Not while he was so upset.

He waited a few moments for Avery to calm down, but his poor feeder seemed beside himself. He sobbed into his hands, hiding his face, until a hiccuping plea finally gave Ozen a clue of what to do.

"I-I can't stop!"

Ozen climbed into bed, pulling Avery against his chest. He tried using his magic to soothe Avery, but it only set him off more.

"N-No! You just ate! You shouldn't waste it–"

"Avery... Your comfort is not a waste. Hush now. Let me help you."

He shook his head rapidly, refusing. Ozen's chest ached, watching Avery fall apart. He couldn't handle seeing someone usually so bright and happy falling to pieces like that. It felt wrong. Especially because Avery was his to protect. He promised he wouldn't let Avery get hurt.

Using the smallest amount of his magic possible, since he knew it'd only upset Avery if he used too much, he soothed Avery's mind little by little. The sobs slowed and the hiccuping breaths evened out, and eventually, Avery fell asleep with his head pillowed on Ozen's chest. Ozen got them more comfortable, cuddling Avery close, and he refused to move an inch until Avery woke up. He was disgusted with himself for letting it get this bad. He should have paid more attention. Quick feeds were exhausting, he knew that. He had hoped Avery would rest afterward, but knowing him, he went back to work the moment he was strong enough to stand.

While he waited for Avery to wake up, Ozen watched him sleep, taking in the little details he'd missed this past week. The light from the open doorway was enough that Ozen could see the dark circles under Avery's eyes, his normally pristine suit rumpled and his tie crooked. How much of that was just from the feeding, Ozen wasn't sure. He didn't even think about it. Avery was always quick to tell Ozen he was fine and for him to return to work, and Ozen didn't question him. He'd been grateful that Avery had understood and rushed out without a backwards glance. Idiot, idiot, idiot.

Trailing his knuckles down Avery's tear stained cheek, he silently vowed to do better. A busy week was no excuse to treat his feeder so poorly. Avery was the best feeder Ozen had ever had. If he didn't want to lose him, he had to do better.

———

Avery was out for several hours. Ozen expected that and didn't begrudge him. His energy levels were still severely low when he opened his eyes. He woke up with a sharp gasp, so Ozen knew he didn't wake up because he was refreshed. More likely, Avery woke himself up because he was dedicated to his job.

When he tried to sit up, Ozen pushed him back down with a gentle hand on his chest. "Shh... You're not needed anywhere. Relax."

Avery looked confused, his eyes darting around. "But–"

"No buts. You're exhausted, Avery. There is nothing more important than you getting your rest."

From the look on his face, Avery didn't agree. Now wasn't the time to argue, Ozen knew that, but he had to ask, "Why didn't you tell me? I never wanted to hurt you. You should have told me I was being too demanding on you."

Avery's brow furrowed as he frowned up at Ozen. "What are you talking about?"

"I've been demanding too much of you. Quick feeds are rough on a feeder. I should have insisted you take the week off when I knew Taron would be out."

"But–" Avery protested again.

"No, Avery. I understand you want to continue to be a temp, but you can't do both jobs effectively, not all the time. Had it been a normal week, I know you would have been just fine, but because I was too busy to care for you properly, you suffered, and for that, I'm sorry. It won't happen again. However, I have to insist that if I have a need for a quick feed that you take the day to rest and recover. Feedings take a toll on you and I don't want you wearing yourself out."

"I..." Avery sucked in a shaky breath, his chin trembling ever so slightly like he was fighting back tears again. "I don't blame you. I just... Things would've been easier if I was up here this week. I..." He trailed off, turning his face away. Something about his sentence made Ozen pause, and he frowned, catching Avery's chin to force him to face Ozen again.

"What do you mean by that? Why would it have been easier up here? Did something happen?"

Avery's expression shuttered, and he tucked his chin, defiance barely masking the underlying pain. It wasn't just the feedings then. Something else had contributed to Avery's breakdown.

"Avery. I told you, if you ever needed me then–"

"There was nothing you could have done. I'm fine."

"You're lying," Ozen snapped. His brusque response startled Avery enough that his gaze finally lifted, locking eyes with Ozen. His eyes swam with unshed tears, and his face was pale. Whatever upset him, it was bad enough that he was hiding it from Ozen, and that irritated him.

"Either you can tell me, or I can go down to the research floor and find out for myself. What happened that upset you so much?"

Avery looked away again, and a few tears slipped out. Ozen brushed them away gently. He would be patient–for now–and give Avery the chance to explain himself, but the fury was already building. Ozen was already angry at himself for the way he treated Avery. To realize that he had missed something troubling his feeder right under his nose was unimaginable.

"I... I guess I got used to being up here where everyone accepted me. Comments and gossip are par for the course as a human, but... a few people took issue with me being a feeder too. They yelled at me for showing up late, or taking a long lunch, and got frustrated when I didn't move as quickly as they would have liked. I was trying my best, but between the exhaustion and the comments, I guess I just got overwhelmed. I promise I'll do better next week. I haven't had time to figure out my next assignment yet, but I'll manage my time better and–"

A snarl ripped through Ozen. He felt his control slip, and with it his grip on his glamor. Avery's eyes went wide, locked on the horns on Ozen's head. His focus was diverted when Ozen's tail lashed around, giving away his mood entirely. His skin took on an unnatural hue, and he knew he glowed whenever he released his glamor. Incubi were made to draw people in, especially in their looks. Like moths to a flame.

"You're beautiful..." Avery breathed.

The compliment drew Ozen's attention away from his violent mood. He looked down at the man still wrapped in his arms, forcing himself to take a breath. He would not be taking his mood out on Avery. He didn't deserve that for being honest. Cupping Avery's cheek, Ozen leaned until he could press their foreheads together, giving himself a moment to deal with his emotions. Once he felt more stable, he opened his eyes, smiling at the dazed look on Avery's face. He effortlessly brought his glamor back up, tucking away that part of himself that he didn't show often. He didn't like it. It felt less like consent when people threw themselves at you because of your magic.

Avery blinked a few times, surprised. "Uh... What just happened?"

"An incubus's true form is... dangerous, in my opinion. It's like my magic in physical form and can lead to people making questionable decisions to get close to me. I try not to drop the glamor often."

"But you had wings. And a tail," Avery pointed out. "Doesn't it get uncomfortable to hide them all the time?"

He paused. No one had ever asked him that before, and he wasn't sure how to respond. "How much do you know about glamors?"

"Not much. Most of the supernaturals I know who use them do it to avoid discrimination or hide the things that people might target them for."

He nodded. That was mostly true. There were only a few minute details he was missing. "They are also used to block certain kinds of magic. Like mine. There are regulations on incubi and their true forms. There are some who assert that an incubus's true form removes the ability to provide consent. They tried to make laws banning our true forms entirely, but they never passed. There were too many nuances that made the laws difficult to enforce and easy to bypass. It is understood that a true form should only be used sparingly, and most incubi choose to hide it unless they're somewhere they're comfortable and all parties involved consented beforehand to its usage. I use my glamor for that reason. But no, it isn't uncomfortable. I've been using the magic for so long, I don't even notice it anymore."

Avery looked curious but not at all judgmental. And Ozen's outburst provided enough distraction for the both of them that their moods settled a little. Ozen chose to take the win for what it was, and for a little while, he laid with Avery and answered the questions he had about magic he wasn't familiar with. It was a simple thing, cuddling and taking part in pillow talk, but while desire fed his magic, it felt to Ozen that moments like this fed his soul.

CHAPTER TWENTY-SIX

Rule number 27 - Sick leave - A feeder is allowed to request sick leave at any time and is encouraged to take this leave if it directly affects their ability to do their job.

Avery was still tired when Ozen finally pulled him out of bed. He honestly dreaded the trip home, but he couldn't stay in the office forever. It was a Friday evening. He had an entire weekend to recuperate before he was back on Monday.

He needed to check his email before he left. He didn't know where his next assignment was yet, but while he was thinking about where to check it so he could avoid the research floor, he missed Ozen speaking to him.

"Avery?"

Jerking his head up, he grimaced. "Yes?"

"So you're amenable to the plan, then?"

"Uh..." Avery didn't want to admit he hadn't been listening. Ozen just spent hours comforting and cuddling him. He didn't want to appear rude or ungrateful. So he just went with it. "Yes."

Ozen nodded once. "Then we will stop by your apartment to grab you some things. For tonight, I think we will order in. You've proven incapable of resting without assistance, and I'm not sure I trust you to relax if I'm in the kitchen."

Avery wasn't sure which thread to follow. For one thing, he resented the idea that he didn't know how to relax. He knew plenty. He just hadn't had the time this week. But he didn't know why that was relevant, either. And what was this about stopping by his apartment? What exactly had he agreed to do?

He was too tired to argue or question what was going on. He trusted Ozen. He let the incubus lead him downstairs and out of the building, nudging him into the back of Ozen's town car. They didn't even pull away from the curb before Avery was asleep.

He woke up again to Ozen's fingers carding through his hair. "Avery. You need to wake up."

He groaned, burying his face farther into the pillow. "Five more minutes."

Someone made a poor attempt to cough to cover their laugh, and Ozen chuckled. "I'm afraid I must insist. At least until you get out of the car. I'll carry you inside if you're too tired to remain upright."

Avery's brain felt fuzzy, and he didn't really know what was happening. He assumed Ozen was nice enough to drive him home. It spared Avery a train ride, which was a win in his book. But then, where did Ozen get a pillow for his head?

Forcing his eyes open took considerable effort, and it took a second for him to figure out what was happening. Apparently, in his sleep, he decided Ozen's lap was the perfect resting place. The pillow in question was actually Ozen's thigh. He was warm under Ozen's jacket, too. A blush stole up his cheeks, and he sat up abruptly.

"Oh crap. I'm so sorry."

Ozen chuckled again. "Relax, firefly. You needed the rest. Come. You need to eat something. It will help."

"Okay..." He didn't want to point out that there was probably no decent food in his apartment. Avery had been neglectful of keeping the place clean, and the fridge probably needed to be cleared out. He doubted there was anything safe to eat in there.

But when Avery looked around, they weren't parked in front of his apartment. Instead, they were in front of a row of brownstones several stories high and covered in ivy. The one they were parked in front of looked a little like a castle with its fancy facade and big stone fence in front. Ozen's hand on Avery's back guided him forward, and Avery was startled to realize they were going inside.

"W-Where are we?"

"My home," Ozen replied evenly. "Do you not remember our conversation earlier?"

Avery was suddenly glad Brennus wasn't around. He played up the fatigue because, no, he had no idea what Ozen was talking about. As far as he knew, Ozen's home was off limits to feeders. Avery rubbed his eyes, trying to make his brain work while emphasizing his exhaustion.

"Uh, no. Not really. I'm really tired. Why are we here?"

Ozen's expression softened and turned sympathetic. "You're staying with me this weekend. I overdid it, and you need to be taken care of. Food should be delivered momentarily, so let's head inside and you can change into something more comfortable."

Avery felt like his eyes were going to bug out of his head. "But... I thought feeders weren't allowed here."

"I trust you to maintain professionalism. You have never given me any reason to doubt that," was Ozen's smooth reply as he guided Avery inside. Avery felt a little proud of himself that he had Ozen's trust, but he was also freaking out on the inside. Avery did his best to keep things professional, but if Ozen spent the entire weekend taking care of him, it might blur the lines a little. Or a lot.

He felt his ears pop as they stepped through the wards surrounding the building. It wasn't Avery's first experience with wards, but it was disconcerting each time. They stepped into the foyer, and Avery looked around while Ozen gave him a quick tour.

"This is the formal living room. Just past it is the dining room and at the end of the hall is the kitchen." Avery got a peek into each room before they moved on. Ozen seemed to have a nice balance between vintage and renovated. He kept the things that made a brownstone special, like the crown molding and the intricate designs in the wood of the handrails and around the doors and windows, but the paint was fresh, the chandeliers looked well maintained, and there were definite upgrades like a redone kitchen that chefs would drool over. The bathrooms were all renovated as well.

The second floor had Ozen's home office, a media room, and a freaking library. Avery might have drooled a little when he saw that.

The top two floors were all bedrooms. Three on the third floor, two on the fourth. The master took up half the fourth floor, and the master bath took up another quarter of it. The guest room next to it was small in comparison, but still lavish and beautiful. That was where Ozen said Avery would sleep. He tried not to get too caught on the fact that Ozen was going to be just down the hall. Be professional, be professional, be professional.

The tour ended with the rooftop terrace. It wasn't as fancy as the rest of the house. Ozen obviously didn't spend much time up here. Avery loved it, though. There was an amazing view of the city and plenty of room for plants and comfortable seating if Ozen ever wanted to have outdoor parties. He let his imagination run away with him as he followed Ozen back downstairs, imagining fancy parties with hor d'oeuvres and champagne and twinkle lights. Maybe one day, if Avery ever got the nerve to publish his book, he might be invited to parties like that.

The doorbell rang and Ozen answered it, taking the food from the teenage kitsune delivery girl. Her tails swayed happily when Ozen handed her a big tip, and she gave him a small bow before scurrying away. Ozen locked the door behind her, gesturing to the stairs with his chin as he handed Avery the bag of food.

"I usually eat in the den or the media room. I'll grab us some drinks."

Avery nodded quickly and headed back up the stairs. It still felt surreal, being in Ozen's home, and Avery's nerves were doing a little tap dance as he set the food on the coffee table in front of the absolutely massive couch in the media room. He was certain a troll could sit comfortably on it without scrunching themselves up even a little. It could be a bed all on its own. It sat in front of a tv that took up an entire wall. There was a bar behind the couch, and a popcorn maker in the corner that didn't look like a decoration. Avery had to muffle a snicker at the thought of Ozen making popcorn for himself and his guests on movie night.

"What's so funny?"

Avery spun around, putting on his most innocent expression. "Nothing!"

Ozen raised an eyebrow. He had divested himself of his suit jacket at some point, his tie was missing, and the top two buttons of his dress shirt were undone. He was rolling up his sleeves, and Avery had to work hard not to stare. He had yet to see a version of the incubus he didn't think was drool-worthy.

"Feel free to get comfortable. You're not working tonight."

"Well, if I'm working after hours, I'm usually naked, so–" Avery cut himself off with a squeak. Where had that come from? He was not usually so devil-may-care around Ozen. His boss. Several times over. He was more tired than he thought if his mouth was running away from him.

Ozen's smirk said he didn't mind the joke. "If that's truly how you wish to spend the evening, I'm not going to say no. However, you won't be feeding me tonight, so it might not be as beneficial as you'd hoped."

Avery blushed hard, shaking his head quickly. "N-Nope. I'm good. I just, uh... I say weird things when I'm tired. Or I've been drinking. Or after a session, sometimes. Just ignore me."

"I have no interest in doing that. I find your rambling amusing. Come sit down. I ordered sushi and a few appetizers from a friend's restaurant." He paused, frowning down at the food. "I realize now I should have asked first. Do you even like sushi?"

"When I can afford it, yes, I like it. Thank you. I really appreciate it."

Ozen's shoulders loosened a little, and Avery fought off a grin. Ozen taking care of him outside of aftercare was going to be interesting, that was for sure. Avery was used to being in the caretaker roll, so he was uncomfortable letting people take care of him. Meanwhile, Ozen was accustomed to people caring for him, bringing him the things he needed and making sure he was comfortable. The role reversal was disconcerting, and they were both a little out of sorts.

Dinner was amazing. Avery had never had fresh made sushi delivered before. He groaned with every bite and earned more than a few heated looks from Ozen in response. He couldn't help himself. It was just that good. While they ate, they watched a popular cooking show that Ozen followed. Avery didn't watch much tv, preferring to read and work on his book, but it was interesting. He couldn't cook, so he didn't know half the words they were using, but Ozen made comments now and then about flavor profiles and recipes he'd tried to mimic, and Avery loved to hear him talk. He had such a nice voice.

The awkward tension faded eventually, and when Avery's head ended up pillowed in Ozen's lap for the second time that night, Ozen helped Avery up to his room and gave him some spare pajamas to change into. Because Avery passed out before they could reach his apartment, Ozen hadn't had the heart to wake him to pick up his things. He promised he'd send someone to pick him up some clothes the following morning so he had something to change into. Avery tried to protest, his apartment was a mess, but Ozen was determined to make up for the rough week Avery had endured, which seemed to include keeping Avery with him at all times. Unless he was willing to let Ozen see his destroyed apartment, it was better to let someone else pick him up some clothes. Maybe he could just buy something new to avoid both scenarios.

CHAPTER TWENTY-SEVEN

Ozen found it difficult to sleep that night. Knowing Avery was just down the hall was distracting. He found himself getting up more than once to check if Avery was doing alright. He slept soundly and never stirred, but Ozen couldn't seem to settle. He ended up falling into a fitful sleep well past midnight and woke up only a few hours later, rising with the sun as usual. The fatigue made him grouchy, and he headed to the kitchen, grumbling to himself, eyes barely open enough to press the buttons on his coffee machine. Only after his second cup was he awake enough to function. He went back upstairs to shower and get dressed, resisted the urge to check on Avery again, and distracted himself by making breakfast. He made a plate for Avery and put it on a tray, intent on bringing his breakfast upstairs, but Avery came down before Ozen had the chance.

"Morning," Avery mumbled, rubbing his eyes. He looked adorable, his hair a mess of curls and his eyes barely open. It did something to Ozen's insides to see Avery in his clothes, even something as simple as his pajamas, and Ozen had to look away to get himself together.

"Good morning. I made breakfast. Do you want to eat at the table or upstairs?"

"Here is fine," Avery said, slipping onto a stool at the kitchen island. "Thank you."

He liked that Avery wanted to stick close to him and took the stool next to him after Avery's food was settled in front of him. He also had a cup of coffee and some juice for Avery to drink, and Ozen gave him a pointed look when Avery frowned at them.

"You can't exist off of caffeine. You're recovering. You'll drink both cups and then plenty of water throughout the day. You need to get your energy back before you can even think of doing either of your jobs."

Avery's mouth fell open in surprise and he choked out a few jumbled words like he wanted to argue, but wasn't sure what to say. "But– I need– You can't–"

"You'll find I very well can. You're my feeder. Like it's your job to feed me, it's my job to make sure you're well enough to do it. I neglected that this week, and for that, I'm sorry. I won't let it happen again. But until I'm sure you're well enough, I won't be feeding from you again."

It almost looked like fear flashed across Avery's face, which made Ozen frown. "What's wrong?"

"I just... It doesn't seem fair. I'm a little tired. You'll literally starve yourself while you're waiting for me to get better. That doesn't seem right."

For the dozenth time, Ozen was grateful that Avery was his feeder. He was determined to keep him well fed, even after the week he'd had.

He didn't think refusing Avery outright would get him the results he wanted. He'd need a compromise of sorts.

"Very well. If you listen and do as you're told for the rest of the day, I'll consider a small feeding. Not too much, I can handle a day without a full feeding, but I wouldn't want to add to your stress by going without entirely. Does that work for you?"

Avery nodded quickly. "Yes. I just don't want you to hurt yourself. Last weekend you went without eating and by the time Monday rolled around, you were so hungry, you looked almost feral."

He winced at the reminder. He'd been so desperate to believe his issue was a mental block like Doctor Chapman had said that he'd bullied himself into staying away from Avery even though he felt out of control with hunger by the time Monday rolled around. What worried him the most wasn't how hungry he was, but how much it bothered him that he hadn't seen Avery in days. That alone set him on edge.

None of his research could explain what was happening to him. There were no articles about the potency of different species or special feeders. Not much was written on starvation effects on incubi either. Everything that was written about it said a week or two of consistent feeding was enough to handle most cases, except for the truly extreme cases, such as incubus who went feral. Since that wasn't the case for him, it wasn't relevant and he skipped past it. Doctor Chapman hadn't called with any more information either, and Dorian had even less luck than Ozen had. There was nothing written about what was happening with regards to Avery, and unless Ozen was willing to contact his father, he doubted he'd find anything else on the matter. Ozen would rather eat dirt than call that man, so he was resigned to going with the flow for now. Not a favorite way to handle things for Ozen.

"I apologize for that. Perhaps next week, once Taron is back and things are a little less hectic, we can sit down and discuss a weekend schedule. I don't want to take up too much of your time. I'm sure you have other things you'd rather be doing."

Avery raised an eyebrow, his lips twitching like he was holding back a laugh. "Other things I'd rather be doing than spending time in bed with you? With all due respect, sir, have you seen you?"

Ozen snorted, warmth spreading through his chest at the roundabout compliment. Avery was never subtle about his interests, but he did maintain professionalism at the office, so he only ever showed his desire during their sessions. It was nice to know he found Ozen attractive, and not just the pleasure he could provide. Avery's desire tinged the air, and Ozen pursed his lips against a smile.

"First rule for the day. No seducing me into bed. Your energy levels are still much too low. You'll finish your breakfast and go straight back to bed. While you rest, I'll go to your apartment to pick you up some–"

"No!" Avery cried out, his eyes as wide as dinner plates. He slapped his hands over his mouth, mumbling a quick apology. The mood shift was so fast, it gave Ozen whiplash. Avery shook his head wildly. "No, thank you. I can go by myself. Or... I'm sure there's a store nearby where I can pick something up. We don't need to go all the way to my apartment. I'm fine."

Ozen's eyes narrowed with suspicion. "Is there a reason you don't want me to go to your apartment?"

He normally wouldn't push this kind of thing, but considering the week

Avery had, Ozen figured having a few of his own things would be comforting. And it made no sense that Avery was comfortable with Ozen at his house before this last week and suddenly changed his mind.

Avery's face was flushed with embarrassment and he whimpered when Ozen guided his face up to look him in the eye.

"Avery. Is there something you need to tell me?"

If Avery was seeing someone and hiding the evidence, then–

"I, uh... I didn't have time to clean up this week, is all. It's nothing... Just... Maybe I should spend the weekend resting at home. You shouldn't have to take care of me just because I had a bad week."

Well, that was a relief. And perfectly understandable. Ozen shook his head. "When that awful week was my fault, I do. And I'm not sending you home to clean. That's not resting." He put up a finger when Avery began to protest. "I've known you long enough now to know you won't be able to help yourself. I'll have my housekeeper stop by your apartment this weekend instead of mine. In the meantime, I'll give you some of my clothes. They might be a little big, but we're not going out, so it should be fine."

Ozen was a firm believer in clothes being washed before wearing them, and new clothes weren't often as comfortable as clothes that were worn a few times. He wasn't at all thinking that he preferred Avery in his clothes anyway and him being too embarrassed to show Ozen his messy apartment was a convenient excuse to keep him in them. Though there was nothing wrong with his feeder wearing something attractive, even though Ozen wouldn't consider his clothes attractive. Not unless they were on Avery, of course.

———

Avery did as he was told and went upstairs for a nap after breakfast. Ozen almost wanted to join him to make sure he actually rested, but he talked himself out of that. His behavior was concerning, and he had to make a few phone calls, starting with a phone call to Taron.

The phone barely rang once, and Ozen could hear Taron's muffled voice shouting, "It's company business. Very important. You know how it is. I need to take this upstairs. Yes, I'll be back down in a minute."

Ozen chuckled, listening to his friend's heavy breathing as he no doubt ran up the stairs to avoid his family. Ozen understood the urge, since he avoided his own family like the plague, but he couldn't hold back his amusement when Taron finally whispered harshly, "Please tell me you need me to come back. Please!"

"Are you not having a pleasant vacation?"

"Screw you. This was not a vacation and you know it," Taron hissed. "I don't care if you have to make it up, but there needs to be an emergency. I need to get out of here!"

"Did you accomplish what you went there for?"

"It only took three days," Taron grumbled. "She won't let me leave. She's trying to demand I move home. Help. Me."

Ozen chuckled, letting Taron stew just long enough for him to whimper before giving him the excuse he needed. "I do actually need you back. I've been so busy that I've only managed quick feeds all week. It's taking its toll on Avery. I don't want to lose my feeder because I don't have the time to tend to him like I should."

"Shit. Is he okay?"

Taron knew how important Avery was to him. Finding a good feeder was difficult, and Avery was the best. While the excuse wasn't entirely business related, even Taron's family knew how important feeders were. They wouldn't keep him there if it meant Avery would suffer for it.

"He's alright. Resting in my guest room right now."

Taron was silent for a long moment. So long that Ozen thought perhaps the call was dropped. It happened between realms from time to time. He was lucky that he had pulled the phone away from his ear to check when Taron started shouting.

"He's where?! You brought a feeder to your home? Where is my friend and what did you do with him?"

Ozen's expression went dark, and he glared at the wall, his voice terse. "You didn't see him, Taron. He was so exhausted and upset that he couldn't stop crying. Not only was he subject to my terrible schedule, he was also being mistreated on the research floor. He didn't get into much detail, but he made comments about people being unhappy with his job as my feeder and his species."

It was something Ozen planned to address Monday morning. Discrimination wasn't allowed in his company, especially against feeders. Their jobs were important in keeping people alive. Ozen would not stop until he found whoever hurt Avery and dealt with them. Taron seemed to feel the same way, because his response was a dark growl.

"What the hell did they say to him?"

"I intend to find out. For now, he's with me, so I can be sure he's resting as he should be. And I would appreciate your return as soon as you're able to prevent another week like the last one. Working two jobs while attending to my needs during a week without you is too much to ask of anyone. Avery deserves to be taken care of."

"You're right. I don't want you losing him because of me. I'll be home no later than tomorrow."

CHAPTER TWENTY-EIGHT

Rule Number 11- A feeder's health should be monitored both by the feeder and by the client, to ensure a feeder's wellbeing is maintained.

Avery wasn't really a nap person. There was always too much to do, and it was hard to settle. He knew he needed to. Not only was he still exhausted, but Ozen wouldn't feed until he was better. Avery didn't want him starving himself waiting for Avery to get better, but napping wasn't working and Avery gave up after a while.

The night prior, the exhaustion had been so overwhelming that he couldn't keep his eyes open. Now that he was a little more awake, he was hyper aware he was in Ozen's home. Technically, Ozen wasn't wrong that he wouldn't be able to help himself from cleaning up or working on his book if he were at home. But he kind of doubted he'd get much more rest here.

It smelled like Ozen.

He was trying so hard to maintain professionalism, but being surrounded by Ozen wasn't helping.

He paced the room, lecturing himself about professionalism. Ozen needed him. He needed a feeder he could trust would show up for him. Avery made a commitment to be that person. He needed to keep his ever-growing crush out of it. People had sex every day without getting feelings involved. Avery could do that, too. Maybe. He'd try his best anyway. He'd keep his crush to himself at the very least.

A quiet knock on the door stalled his movements, and he sucked in a breath, steeling himself to be close to Ozen again. One reason he agreed to go take a nap, like Ozen suggested, was because he wanted a chance to get his head on straight. Being in Ozen's space, seeing him so relaxed and casual, it was doing things to Avery's libido. Ozen being who he was, he'd be able to tell in an instant, and Avery was determined to follow the rules and keep his lusty desires out of the air. Though, in his defense, Ozen in casual slacks and a sweater that clung to every inch of him was cruel. Or maybe perfect. Or a little bit of both.

He opened the door a few inches, and when Ozen raised his eyebrows, Avery gave him a sheepish look. "I'm trying, I swear."

"I can hear you pacing, Avery. What's wrong?"

Opening the door enough to let Ozen in, Avery sighed. "I don't actually nap that often. The only time I have since I was a kid was after sessions. I tried to lie down for a while, but I just ended up tossing and turning a lot. I'm sorry. I promise I'm trying."

Ozen hummed, leaning against the door jamb. "How about a movie instead? As long as you're resting, I believe it will have the same effect. Pacing isn't helping, though."

A movie was better than staring at the ceiling, overthinking everything. Avery nodded quickly.

"Alright. I'll set something up. Let me grab you a change of clothes. My housekeeper will be by soon to grab your keys. She can pick you up some of your own clothes when she's there if you want."

The embarrassment over the state of his apartment still made Avery blush. In his defense, he'd been so exhausted all week that he could barely manage to shower. He stripped when he got home and fell into bed, only to wake up bleary eyed the following morning like he hadn't slept at all. He took a shower to try and wake up his brain, but he couldn't muster the energy to clean up after himself. Clothes were strewn everywhere, wet towels on the bathroom floor, empty containers of take out from nights where he had just enough energy to remind himself to eat something. His fridge was full of old take out, his trash can was probably overflowing, and the smell probably wasn't pleasant. Avery didn't want anyone anywhere near his apartment, but he knew from one look that Ozen wouldn't let it go. At least the housekeeper might be discreet. Hopefully anyway.

Like he could see the shame on his face, Ozen's eyes softened, and he cupped Avery's cheek reassuringly. "Miriam loves a project and will enjoy the challenge. There will be no judgment from her. I promise."

Avery gave in to the urge to lean into Ozen's palm, soaking in his comfort for a moment until his brain so helpfully reminded him that he was being inappropriate and not at all professional. He drew away, sucking in a breath to steady himself a little. This weekend was going to drag on. He wasn't sure yet if that was a good thing or a bad thing.

He did manage to nap at least once. He had a sneaking suspicion that Ozen set him up. During the first movie, Ozen had left him alone and made a few phone calls in his office. But during the second, he joined Avery and urged him to put his head in Ozen's lap. With Ozen's fingers gently carding through his hair, Avery didn't stand a chance. He woke up drowsy a few hours later, the movie over and Ozen scrolling through emails on his phone.

Lunch was simple but healthy. Gourmet sandwiches with toasted bread, tons of vegetables, meat that was probably more expensive than Avery's rent, and sauce that was to die for. Avery had to work incredibly hard to keep his noises to himself, since he didn't want Ozen to think he was trying to seduce him into bed. It was just that good.

In the afternoon, Ozen let him explore the library while he got some work done. Avery wanted to point out that he was just as bad as Avery was when it came to relaxing, but Ozen wasn't the one who worked himself into exhaustion, so he kept his mouth shut. Picking out a book was the hard part, since there were so many great options that Avery couldn't decide. Once he'd finally settled on one, he got comfortable on one of the vintage couches by the unlit fireplace and immersed himself into a fantasy world for a few hours.

"So that's how I get you to relax," Ozen commented. Avery blinked a few times, looking around. He'd lost track of time, and the sun was going down now. Ozen had a small smile on his face, one hand tucked casually into his pocket as he studied Avery. Avery wasn't sure what he was looking for, and he was a little self conscious. He'd found a blanket at one point and made himself into a burrito, melting into the cushions. The only time he moved was to take sips from the reusable water bottle Ozen had insisted he take with him. He probably looked like a child.

"I, uh..."

He didn't know what to say, his face burning with embarrassment. Ozen either didn't notice or chose to ignore it for Avery's sake, instead asking, "I'm going downstairs to make dinner. Did you want to join me?"

Using the little ribbon on the spine to save his spot in the book, Avery wriggled free of his blanket burrito. "Okay. Do I get to help?"

Ozen's mouth twitched like he was holding back a smirk. "I'm not sure I would consider that resting."

"It's probably more restful than letting me stress about not being allowed to help," Avery pointed out.

Ozen's lips pressed together in a thin line, and he narrowed his eyes slightly. "Yes, I considered that as well. Fine. You can help, but only a little. You're supposed to be resting."

———

Ozen was glad Avery didn't seem to be aware of how often he checked on him that afternoon. At least once an hour, Ozen found himself drawn to the library to check on his guest. He didn't have to sneak around. Avery didn't seem to notice his surroundings when he was immersed in a book. Ozen refilled his water bottle and set out a blanket when he noticed Avery was cold, and still Avery didn't look up. It was endearing, and Ozen wished he could join him. It was that urge that sent Ozen back to his office time and time again. He didn't understand it. He'd had never been this attached to his feeders before. Not even Tristan.

He lost the fight to stay away from Avery by the time dinner rolled around. His invitation for Avery to join him was entirely selfish. Ozen wanted his company, even though he knew he should leave Avery alone. Avery's energy levels were quickly returning to normal now that he was truly resting. Ozen should have left him alone until dinner was ready. He just couldn't seem to help himself.

Avery didn't seem to mind the interruption to his reading, and he smiled brightly when Ozen handed him some vegetables to chop. Since

Avery was recovering, Ozen felt it was important to make him healthy meals to resettle his system. From what he'd read online while Avery was napping, humans needed plenty of vitamins to maintain their equilibrium. With that in mind, Ozen set to making a dinner that was both healthy and of high quality. He was not showing off for his feeder. He merely wanted to take care of him. Avery needed to be healthy to continue their working relationship.

The lie felt stale even to him. Ozen was getting too attached. It was normally the other way around. He would need to distance himself from his feeders because they were too clingy and saw the arrangement as more than business. This time, it was Ozen who was the one who was unprofessional. There was no other feeder he would've willingly brought to his home and insisted on caring for the entire weekend. If they had been distraught like Avery had been, he would have sent them home to recover on their own and avoided feeding for a time. He couldn't do that with Avery. The more time they spent together, the more necessary the daily feedings felt.

He was at a loss on how to handle the situation. He was never the unprofessional one. He'd never even considered being on the other side of the equation. He reminded himself almost daily to be professional, but one smile from Avery had him abandoning any rules he made for himself in favor of fishing for more of Avery's attention. The couch was large enough to give them both plenty of space, but once they went upstairs to enjoy their meal in front of the television, Ozen couldn't stop himself from sitting right beside Avery. And once their meals were finished, Ozen tempted himself further by pulling Avery against his side. He made the excuse to himself that he was trying to get Avery comfortable enough to sleep, but even that felt flimsy. And when Avery's desire made itself known, Ozen didn't put in an ounce of effort to deny him. He pinned Avery to the couch and ground their hips together until they both came with a shout.

Avery paused just inside the door to his room after Ozen insisted he get some rest, frowning.

"What is it?"

"I just... I know you said you'd only take a little, since I'm still recovering, but you got enough, right? I didn't even feel your magic that time."

Ozen stiffened and his voice was hoarse as he replied, "I'm fine. Get some rest."

He didn't wait for Avery to reply before he nearly ran for his room. He leaned against the door after it shut behind him, his eyes wide and horror filled. Magic. He'd forgotten completely about the magic. That was the whole point. He said he'd only feed a little, to not affect Avery's energy levels. But he had been so lost in the pleasure, he forgot entirely.

For the first time in his life, Ozen indulged in sex without actively feeding. Purely for the pleasure of it. And he did it without Avery's informed consent.

What the hell had he done?

CHAPTER TWENTY-NINE

Rule Number 19 - A feeder should make wise decisions despite ambiguity. It is not the client's job to walk the feeder through every decision in their life. This is a work contract, not a relationship.

The Saturday with Ozen had been amazing, but Avery had to return to his apartment eventually. He was surprised that Ozen didn't put up more of a fight when he mentioned it the following morning. Avery was hoping to distance himself a little, to better hide the ever-growing crush he had on his boss, but with the way Ozen had been so demanding about taking care of Avery, he thought Ozen would argue at least a little. He tried his best not to be disappointed. It was harder to mask his disappointment when Ozen wouldn't even accompany him home. He called his driver to pick Avery up and instructed him to relax at home for the rest of the day before sending him on his way.

Avery figured he'd overstayed his welcome, and that was why Ozen was so dismissive of him, but when he showed up to work on Monday, Ozen was nowhere to be found. When he asked Mrs. Sable where he was, she only said he wouldn't be in the office today. It worried him. Ozen hadn't fed from him the day before, and he had no idea if Ozen would contact him sometime that day to feed. Avery wasn't sure if it was appropriate for him to call to find out, either. He felt out of sorts and barely followed the conversation when Mrs. Sable told him to report to Mr. Van Buren's office for the week.

The legal floor was quiet when Avery headed downstairs. He had shown up early to feed Ozen, so most of the office hadn't arrived yet. Mr. Van Buren's office door was open, however, and he invited Avery inside when he knocked.

"Mrs. Sable said to report to you this week."

"She was correct. Our normal legal assistant is incompetent, and I don't trust her to help me. I've heard good things about you, so I requested your assistance."

He must not have spoken to anyone from the research floor then. Avery was dreading when that came to light. He'd done his absolute best with what was in front of him, but he had to acknowledge that last week wasn't his best work. He wouldn't have been surprised if there were several complaints about him waiting on Brennus's or Ozen's desks this morning. Perhaps Avery beat them since he arrived early, and Mr. Van Buren would find out later.

Avery's mood sank lower and lower throughout the day. He did his job and gave no reason for Mr. Van Buren to complain about him, but his normal joy for the new experience was missing. His smile was forced when-ever he had to interact with anyone, and he found himself looking for Ozen any time he left Mr. Van Buren's office. Mrs. Sable said he wouldn't be there, but Avery kept hoping anyway.

He was helping Mr. Van Buren by pouring through legal texts in search of something he needed when his phone rang. Mr. Van Buren answered it with a gruff, "Van Buren." Avery wasn't close enough to hear who was speaking on the other end, and he didn't much care until Mr. Van Buren said Ozen's name.

"Ozen... You know how I feel about you visiting that place."

Avery stopped breathing, trying not to let it show that he was listening in. He turned the pages of the book every once in a while and kept his eyes down, but he wasn't taking any of it in. He was desperate for any scraps of information on Ozen.

Mr. Van Buren grunted in response to whatever Ozen said. Avery felt the shifter's eyes on him and forced his face to remain neutral, flipping the page again and running his finger down the text like he was looking for what Mr. Van Buren wanted. He kept up the charade until Mr. Van Buren turned his chair fully around, his voice low.

"If you feel that's necessary, then I can't object. Yes, I'll watch over him. How long will you be gone?"

Avery's spine stiffened. If he was gone for a while, Ozen would need to feed eventually. And it was Avery's stupid idea to open up the contract so that Ozen could feed from anyone if Avery wasn't around. Avery didn't think it through at the time. If Ozen was avoiding him, then technically Avery wasn't around and Ozen wouldn't be breaking the contract if he fed from someone else.

"Yes. Do not fret, my friend. All will be handled here. I'll see you when you get back."

He hung up but didn't offer an explanation. Not that Avery expected him to. Mr. Van Buren was still as intimidating as ever. He didn't seem to do it consciously, and he was polite since Avery gave him no reason to get angry. But he heard the way Mr. Van Buren spoke to people on the phone, and twice that morning smoke filled the office when he got upset. Avery found it hard to imagine that the dragon shifter would give him the time of day if he asked for any information about Ozen.

The next few days were a blur. He found the information Mr. Van Buren needed, brought him coffee, spent some time organizing files for a case he was working on, but other than when Mr. Van Buren was explaining what he needed, they were both silent. Avery left the office each evening feeling worse and worse. The knowledge that Ozen would most likely be feeding from someone else was beyond depressing, and each day he didn't hear from him only solidified the idea that he was likely getting his feedings from someone else. Avery's crush had gotten out of control, but no matter how many times he said it was a good thing to have some time apart, it didn't make Avery feel any better.

"Mr. Whitman?"

Spinning around, Avery searched for the voice speaking to him. A chimera in a fancy suit stood not far behind him, all three heads focused intently on him. Avery swallowed hard. There weren't many supernaturals that he was afraid of, but chimeras used to hunt humans, and the few interactions he'd had with them weren't great. They were known to be ruthless and looked down on humans. Luckily, he was still outside the Spellbound building and in plain sight. Hopefully, that would keep him safe.

"Y-Yes?"

"My name is Walter Quinn. You're Ozen Hawksley's feeder, are you not?"

Avery stiffened. He didn't realize that was common knowledge. He wasn't sure who Walter Quinn was, but his instincts told him it wasn't a good thing that he was on his radar.

"I, uh–"

"Mr. Whitman, you don't need to lie to me. I'm not here to cause trouble for you. I'm here to discuss the lawsuit Mr. Hawksley's previous feeder filed against him. I'm a lawyer, you see. I'm only here to help."

Avery didn't question the lawyer thing, but he did question who this guy was here to help. It wasn't Ozen. Mr. Van Buren was Ozen's lawyer, and if he had questions he needed answered for the case, he would've asked Avery directly. Avery wanted to say as much, but that feeling like he was someone's prey skittered up his spine when the chimera came closer. This didn't feel like a simple conversation. The chimera was intimidating him. Avery's heartbeat picked up, and he took a step back automatically, bumping into someone behind him. A heavy hand landed on his shoulder and a familiar smokey scent filled the air. Oh, thank the gods.

"What are you doing here, Quinn?" Mr. Van Buren growled.

The chimera looked irritated at being interrupted, and his slow stalking stalled out as he hissed at Mr. Van Buren.

"I'm here to talk to a witness. You can't keep him from me."

"You have a copy of his deposition. Any questions you have regarding it can be discussed in a courtroom. Leave, or I'll file a motion to have you dismissed from the case for intimidating a witness."

Mr. Van Buren's tone was steady and clear, but Avery could tell his temper was only hanging on by a thread. He seemed to exude heat in general, but the angrier he got, the more heat he gave off. The office got stifling whenever he was angry. Avery could feel it now, despite the cool outdoor temperature. It was like a heater was pointed directly at his back.

Two of Walter's three faces morphed in fury, teeth bared, and low growls filling the air. Only the middle one remained calm. He blinked slowly before turning his attention back to Avery.

"It's for the best that we get this lawsuit dealt with quickly. I would hate for it to drag out." He pulled a card from his inside pocket, offering it to Avery. "I'm sure we can clear up this misunderstanding. Let's talk later."

He looked at Avery expectantly, but Avery refused to take the card, shaking his head and taking another step back until he was out of range and partially behind Mr. Van Buren. There was nothing the chimera could say that would make Avery change what he said. Ozen was the victim. Calvin shouldn't get away with hurting people like that.

Avery's response only angered Walter more, the hissing sound growing louder. That prey feeling got worse, and Avery felt the hairs on the back of his neck stand on end. Mr. Van Buren wasn't being dramatic. Walter wasn't here to talk. He was here to intimidate Avery. And with Ozen gone, Avery wasn't sure if he'd be protected outside of the office.

Mr. Van Buren growled out a warning, and the air shook with the vibrations of it. It was intense enough to make Walter back off. He shot them both one last scathing look before spinning on his heel and stalking off. Avery didn't let out a breath until he got in the back of a taxi and it sped away.

When Mr. Van Buren turned to face him, Avery worried he'd be blamed for the confrontation. He seemed to get blamed for a lot of things here when he wasn't around Ozen. He braced himself for it, but Mr. Van Buren's tone was gentle when he spoke.

"Are you alright?"

"Y-Yes... I– I didn't know who he was when he approached me."

"I'm aware. I was just inside when he showed up. I heard what he said. You're a very loyal employee. Most would have taken the card just to appease him. Maybe even considered calling to see what he had to say."

Avery's brow pinched tightly. "It doesn't matter what he has to say. I'm not going to change my statement. Ozen was a victim and Calvin got what he deserved by being blacklisted. Honestly, he got a lot less than he deserved, in my opinion. I think he should be punished more severely for starving Ozen like that."

Mr. Van Buren's rumbling hum of approval relaxed Avery's shoulders a little. At least he wasn't in trouble for the confrontation. It did make him nervous that the chimera approached him on the street. He knew Avery's full name. What if he knew where Avery lived as well?

"I'll need you to come with me. I want you to write a witness statement for the confrontation."

Avery nodded quickly. Anything to drag out going home. He probably wouldn't sleep well tonight. He'd never felt unsafe in his apartment before, but there was a first time for everything.

CHAPTER THIRTY

Ozen dreaded the choice he made the minute he stepped into his family home. If he wasn't so desperate for answers, he wouldn't be here. But his obsession with Avery was getting worse, and he needed to know if he had to break the contract early. The thought was abhorrent, but if there was some kind of magic involved that he was unfamiliar with pushing this kind of reaction, then he needed to know about it and end it before it affected Avery negatively. He couldn't keep pretending everything was fine. Not after the other night.

He had never planned on returning here after he left the first time. Ozen and his family... didn't see eye to eye. They were very traditional in that they didn't believe in hiding their true forms. They believed glamouring them was an affront to the creators. While at home, that never bothered him, but they refused to mask it even out in public, and the way people would actually stop what they were doing to follow around his father, especially, always made Ozen's hackles go up. Those people didn't consent to feeling that way.

Finding his father was always easy. He just had to follow the sounds of sex throughout the house. It led him to the den, where bodies writhed on the floor together while his father watched on with a smirk. He had a pretty male in his lap being tended to by a female with curly red hair on her knees in front of them both. The entire room reeked of sex, and yet Ozen's magic didn't even twitch. He had no urge to siphon any of the desire in the room, despite having gone a few days without feeding. He only wanted Avery.

When his father noticed him standing in the open doorway, he straightened and an enormous smile spread across his face. "Ozen, my son! This is a surprise!"

Ozen fought back a scowl. He was here for answers. Once he had those, he would leave. He purposely bit his tongue to avoid asking his father how many of the people in the room followed him home without giving their express consent first. It only ever led to an argument.

"Korath," Ozen replied blandly.

Korath patted the hip of the male in his lap, moving him out of the way so he could stand. Ozen rolled his eyes and looked away, waiting for his father to cover up. He'd lost count of the number of times he'd seen his father naked, incubi weren't shy about nudity, but it wasn't something he looked forward to. Korath knew this and was polite enough to pull on a robe before joining him.

"To what do I owe the pleasure?"

At the word pleasure, several of the bodies moaned, and Korath shivered with a grin. "Are you hungry? This is a good batch."

Ozen shot him a dry look. Even if he didn't face his current problem, he wouldn't share with his father. His cousins always called him a stick in the mud for preferring his privacy with his feeders.

"Is there somewhere we can talk?"

Korath's eyebrows drew together tightly, and his smile faded into a more serious expression. It was rare for him, Korath wasn't known to be serious, but he must've heard the severity of the situation in Ozen's tone because he didn't argue.

"Let's go to my office." He glanced over his shoulder and a surge of magic washed over the room. The moans dialed up a few levels as Korath shut the door behind them. "That should keep them busy for a while. Come, come. Do you want a drink? Your cousin Sandy brought me that good liquor from the kraken city beneath the ocean. I still don't know how they do it."

Ozen accepted a glass, mostly to be polite. When he tipped it back and swallowed it in one gulp, Korath looked surprised.

"It must be serious if you're indulging like this. So tell me. What draws my wayward son home?"

He ignored the barb, sitting in the chair in front of his father's desk. When Korath took his seat across from him, Ozen could almost pretend the man had pants on.

"I am having an unusual reaction to my newest feeder. I thought at first it was because of his inexperience, he was a virgin before meeting me, but—"

"That doesn't have any effect, magic wise," Korath interrupted. "It is great fun to introduce newbies to pleasure and watch their reactions, but it wouldn't cause any unusual reactions."

"I figured as much," Ozen replied with a nod. "I can't remember every feeder I've ever been with, but I doubted Avery was my first experience with a virgin."

That made Korath chuckle. "Can you imagine remembering every single one of them? That would be exhausting." He shook his head. "So it's nothing to do with that. What is the unusual reaction you're having, then?"

Ozen hesitated to continue. Korath was one of the oldest incubi that he knew. If anyone had any knowledge about this, it would be him. But not only was he uncomfortable talking to his father about any part of his private life, he was also incredibly reluctant to share information about Avery with anyone.

Korath leaned forward with a frown. "Son, whatever it is, you can tell me. I'll do what I can to help you. You know this."

Ozen sighed. He did know that. He didn't see eye to eye with his family and preferred to avoid them, but Korath was always a family man first and foremost. He doted on his children, all twelve of them, and was the first to offer help when someone needed it. He offered to back Ozen's company before it got off the ground, but Ozen had refused him, citing a need to do it on his own. Korath knew Ozen's feelings on their lifestyle and, unlike his siblings, kept his comments on the way Ozen lived to himself. He didn't do anything to change his ways, but neither did Ozen. They kept their distance to avoid arguments, but Korath wasn't being facetious when he said he'd do anything to help.

"My newest feeder is an... anomaly. I've never reacted this way with anyone else. He's potent, and I feel stronger after I've fed from him than I ever had in the past. I also don't need to do as much to feed. He's been my feeder for almost a month now, and we still haven't explored full penetration. But I also can't go very long without feeding again. Not only because of genuine hunger, but also because I crave being close to him. I saw a physician, thinking maybe it was linked to my two weeks' starvation, but—"

The lights in the room flickered and Korath looked furious when he demanded, "Say that again."

He sighed heavily. "It's hardly relevant. The only part of it that's relevant is that Avery saved me when I was close to feral. I've been feeding from him since. The physician says there are no physical explanations for my reactions to my feeder, and that it's most likely a mental block, but it's gotten to where I can't go a day without needing to feed again."

There was more, but he wasn't sure he wanted to mention what happened the other night with Avery. He was still reeling from it. And he wasn't sure it was pertinent, since he didn't actually feed that night.

"So let me get this straight. You were starved, which we will be discussing in a moment, then you met this new feeder, who feels more potent than usual. There's no magic involved?"

"None. I checked, and the physician agreed he saw no evidence of magic use."

Korath nodded. "Alright. What is his species? This feeder."

"He's human. No magic that I've noticed, and none in his family line, according to Dorian's research."

Yes, Dorian had looked up Avery's family line just to be certain, but there was nothing to indicate any dormant powers in Avery's past. Dorian told him about this information when Ozen called in a panic after the incident the other night. It was Dorian who told him to come see Korath. They needed the insight of an incubus.

Korath hummed, his expression thoughtful and a little clouded as he processed the information. "Well... a few things come to mind, but before I make any guesses, I want to know what drove you to come to me."

Ozen's head jerked back in surprise, and he frowned. "What do you mean?"

"I mean, you avoid coming home like the plague. Having a potent feeder sounds like a gift, and aside from being a curiosity, it wouldn't have chased you here seeking more information. Something happened to push you this far. I need to know what it was that did it."

Ozen ground his teeth together, his lip twitching against a scowl. "I hardly think that's necessary. You said you had ideas. You could just share those."

"I could," Korath agreed. "But until I know the full picture, I won't be able to tell you for sure. You didn't come all the way here for a guess." He gestured with his hand in an urge to continue. "Tell me what happened."

With a growl, Ozen shoved out of his seat and stormed for the door, only to spin around and pace back. His mind was at war between admitting his shame in front of his father and leaving without the information he needed. He'd avoided Avery for days already. Any longer and his hunger would drive him insane.

"I engaged in intimacy without feeding. I didn't even think of it. And I have no desire to feed from anyone but him," he finally admitted as he sat back down.

Shock made Korath's jaw drop, and his eyebrows disappeared into his hairline. "No one? Not even that delicious orgy in the other room? I mean, I figured you wouldn't indulge, since you prefer your privacy, but you weren't even slightly tempted?"

"No. And it's not a contract that's holding me back. Avery made sure to put fail safes in before signing, so I could feed if we were apart. It turned out to be irrelevant because the only one I want to feed from is him."

Korath huffed his surprise, his palms resting on his desk as his eyes darted back and forth. "I just... I've never heard of such a thing. I didn't even think it was possible for us to engage in sex acts without feeding. It happens naturally. You're sure you just didn't notice? Sometimes, if things are really intense—"

"I'm sure. I didn't feed that night. It's been days, and I'm hungry, but I don't have any urge to go to anyone else."

"Huh." Korath sat back in his chair, his expression matching the confusion in Ozen's gut. It made no sense to him either. Ozen had been banking on his father having the answers he needed, but he was just as stumped. Ozen's hope vanished, and he slumped a little in his chair. He wasn't sure what his next steps were, or if he could even break the hold

Avery had on him. There was a literal orgy down the hall, and he felt absolutely nothing.

"I don't have any answers for you, son. None of my first assumptions fit after that revelation. But if you're willing to wait a few days, I know someone who might. In the meantime, you can use this as an opportunity to test your control. Maybe your mind is unwilling, but your body should be able to tolerate feeding from someone else, even just temporarily. Perhaps some time apart from your feeder will help."

"Perhaps." But he doubted it. Still, it was better than nothing. He would wait and see who his father was so sure would have some answers and make an attempt to feed from somewhere else. It was better than blindly continuing whatever was happening between him and Avery. He didn't want things to get worse.

CHAPTER THIRTY-ONE

Rule Number 3 - If a feeder ever feels unsafe or unheard with their client, a report should be made to the local feeder protection agency immediately. A feeder's safety is paramount.

Mr. Van Buren drove Avery home after he wrote out his statement. It made Avery feel a little better not to be wandering around outside where the chimera could show up at any time, but he struggled to settle in his apartment. He left a message for his food to be delivered outside his door and waited until they walked away before fetching it. Then he spent the rest of the night jumping at every noise until finally falling into a fitful sleep.

He woke up with a start in the middle of the night when someone knocked on his door. There was no bleary period between waking and sleep after that. Avery was fully awake and terrified. He grabbed his phone, typing out the number for the police, but paused before pressing call. Tip toeing to the door, he peeked through the peephole and sucked in a sharp breath when he realized who was on the other side.

"Ozen?"

Hurrying to unlock the door, he barely had it open before Ozen stormed inside. He looked angry, and he barely looked behind him to lock the door before stalking forward. Avery took a few steps back on instinct, and Ozen paused for a moment before prowling forward again. For every step forward Ozen took, Avery took one backward until he tripped and nearly fell. Ozen lunged, catching Avery against his chest, startling a squeak from him as they both fell onto the mattress.

"O-Ozen, what—"

Ozen cut him off by crashing his mouth onto Avery's. Avery floundered, confused, but when Ozen's tongue shoved past his lips and tangled with his, Avery melted. The incubus could kiss. That shouldn't have surprised him, but with his rules against kissing, he hadn't been sure Ozen had ever done it before. But of course Ozen knew what he was doing. There was the perfect amount of lips, tongue, and teeth to drive Avery wild. It was against the rules in the contract to kiss, but since Ozen started it, Avery didn't think it'd be held against him. And it felt too good to stop and ask.

This time, he felt when Ozen's magic latched onto him. Every time it happened, it was like the pleasure dialed up a few degrees and Avery could feel Ozen's hunger tugging at his core. Between that and Ozen's lips, Avery was lost in what was happening. He barely felt Ozen pulling his pajamas off until they were skin on skin. The shock of it made Avery groan and his kisses turned desperate. His hands skimmed along Ozen's skin, only to be caught and pinned above his head by one of Ozen's hands. His other hand held Avery's jaw, moving him however he wanted while he continued to plunder Avery's mouth. Avery couldn't move without Ozen's permission, and he was completely fine with that.

He wasn't sure how long they spent kissing like that. Long enough for Avery to grow needy and start tugging helplessly at Ozen's hold on his wrists. Ozen was straddling him, but he hovered just out of range to give Avery any sort of friction. It was maddening, and Avery could do nothing about it with his hands pinned.

When he whimpered, Ozen finally broke away, trailing hot kisses along Avery's jaw. He had so many questions, but he was so delirious with lust that he couldn't ask any of them at that exact moment. He could only watch as Ozen straddled his waist, positioned Avery's cock at his entrance, and sank down onto it.

Every nerve in his body lit up like a fireworks display, and he threw his head back on a shout.

"Ozen!"

They hadn't discussed penetration of any kind. Ozen was determined to take it slow, so this came out of nowhere, and Avery wasn't prepared for the onslaught of pleasure that slammed into his system. Ozen didn't give him a chance to catch his breath before he was riding Avery's cock like he was just as desperate as Avery felt. The slick heat of Ozen's body wrapped around his cock made his eyes roll into his head, his body going taut from the pleasure.

He wasn't going to last long. It was too good, and he'd had no time to mentally prepare for it. His balls drew up tight and his head lashed side to side as he fought back his release, but it was no use. It slammed into him so hard, it felt like his soul left his body and he went blind from the pleasure. It dragged on and on with each grind of Ozen's hips, and when he whimpered from the overwhelming sensitivity, Ozen's magic flooded him, bringing him back to full hardness in seconds.

"O-Ozen, please!" Avery sobbed.

It felt so good. Too good. And he could do nothing but feel with the way he was pinned beneath Ozen's body. He considered for a moment asking Ozen to stop, but when he opened his eyes to do so, he saw Ozen's expression. He had never seen such ferocious bliss before. It felt good for Ozen, too. That knowledge sent Avery's desire skyrocketing and Ozen groaned heavily, his hips stuttering for a moment before he picked up speed again.

Time was a difficult concept while Ozen was riding him like this. It felt like it lasted hours and only minutes at the same time. He felt another release barreling down on him, and his toes curled in anticipation. He wanted to come with Ozen, wanted to hold out long enough, but he wasn't sure he could. He tugged at his wrists again, but Ozen wouldn't budge. He dipped and crushed their mouths together, and when Ozen's tongue stroked along his, it was all over. Ozen's body tightened around him, ripping his orgasm from him without warning. Ozen was quick to follow, his release splashing over Avery's belly and chest.

Avery was panting and felt fatigue drag at his senses. He fought it, desperately wanting to ask Ozen what all this was about, but blackness swirled on the edges of his vision and he passed out before he had a chance.

————

He was alone when he woke up the following morning to the sound of his alarm. He almost wondered if the night prior had been a dream, but he recognized the exhausted feeling tugging at him. A restless night's sleep wasn't enough to combat a quick feed. It answered his question on whether last night lasted minutes or hours, though.

Forcing his tired body to sit up took work. It felt like a dozen sandbags were dumped into his eyes and his limbs were heavy. He stumbled to the bathroom, hoping a shower would get him moving. He had to get to work. Hopefully Mr. Van Buren would be more understanding than the research floor had been with Avery's sluggishness.

Lifting his arms to wash his hair was surprisingly difficult. His muscles were sore from trying to tug free of Ozen's grasp. His whole body felt out of sorts, and he wished Ozen were still there to comfort him. Last night was entirely consensual and Avery had no issues with that part, but waking up alone after something so intense was hard on him, and he felt a little like he needed a cuddle to set him to rights. Not to mention the weepy feeling he always got from over exhaustion after a quick feed. It wasn't pleasant, and he wasn't looking forward to working today in the slightest.

A familiar town car was waiting out front when he stepped out of his apartment building. His chest tightened momentarily, foolishly hoping it was Ozen there to pick him up, but the back seat was empty when the driver ushered him inside with a smile.

"Where's Mr. Hawksley?"

The driver frowned at him through the rearview mirror. "Away on personal business."

His frown said Avery was supposed to know that, but Ozen was at his apartment last night, so he wasn't sure what to believe. He was confused and exhausted and contemplating calling in sick when they pulled up in front of Spellbound. When a few of the golems from security met him at the car, Avery's confusion compounded.

He forced a polite smile for the driver when he opened the door for him, hugging his messenger bag to his chest. "Uh... Thank you. For the ride. And my door..."

"You're welcome, Mr. Whitman. I'll see you this evening."

"You will?" Avery questioned, turning to track the driver, but he was back in the car and driving away before Avery could blink. That left him alone with the golems, who looked down at him curiously. Avery had to crane his neck to look them in the eyes.

"Good morning," he said uncertainly.

"G'mornin'," one of them drawled. Learning new languages wasn't easy for golems, and Avery wasn't familiar enough with their language to attempt to reproduce it, so after a few more seconds of staring, he headed awkwardly inside with the golems following behind him. They left him alone after he reached the front desk, leaving him even more confused than before.

"Good morning, Avery," Clarita greeted. Well, one of her heads did. Another was busy answering the phone, and a few more were on the computer. It always fascinated Avery that they could all think independently. He wished he could split his attention that efficiently.

"Good morning, Clarita. How are you?"

She tipped her head back and forth, and if she had shoulders, Avery would probably have seen her shrugging them in reply.

"Mr. Cunningham requested you meet him in his office. Do you know where it is?"

"Uh... Yes. One floor below Mr. Hawksley's office. Did he say why?"

She snorted, and several of her heads rolled their eyes. "He never does. He barely stands still long enough to give me a message before he's off again. If he wasn't such an amazing ideas man, I'd be questioning his position in this company. If you don't mind, this package came for him this morning. It'd save the mail pixies the effort if you brought it up with you." She pointed to a box with the tip of her tail.

"No problem," Avery assured her, taking the box. He felt like he just needed to accept that he was going to be confused today. He was too tired to sort out why he wasn't going to Mr. Van Buren's office like before. He gave Clarita a wave and scanned his ID to get past the turnstiles.

While waiting for the elevator, he heard the familiar voice of those jerks from research. Today was just getting worse and worse. He debated turning tail and using the elevator to Ozen's office and taking the stairs down one floor, but they spotted him before he could decide.

"Ugh. Let's take the next one. I wouldn't want to catch anything."

Avery's shoulders went up, and he stared intently at the label on the box. He was not going to embarrass himself by crying, no matter how tired and out of sorts he was.

"Did you hear he ditched out last Friday? Just completely abandoned his job and got away with it too. Must be nice to bend over for special treatment."

"Mr. Varzin. Who, exactly, are you speaking to?"

Avery hadn't noticed Mr. Martell standing next to him. The goblin was glaring at the men behind them, practically seething. The one who seemed to hate Avery the most, Varzin, was quick to feign innocence and he and his friends hurried into the elevator to avoid answering. Avery chose to wait for the next one, and Mr. Martell joined him, glaring at the group as the door slid closed.

"Does that happen often?"

"It's fine," Avery mumbled.

"That's not what I asked."

The goblin was at least a foot shorter than him, but he didn't lack any backbone because of it. He had a stern look on his face, and he wouldn't let Avery squirm out of the conversation until he admitted the truth.

"Sometimes. Not all species like humans. I'm fine, though."

"Have you told Hawksley?"

"Yes," Avery said with a quick jerk of his head. It technically wasn't a lie, because Avery had told Ozen people were harassing him. He just didn't mention who. Or what was being said. Or any real details. Ozen had enough to deal with, and Avery wasn't looking to cause trouble. He didn't want to lose his job. If he had a job for much longer. With the way Ozen was avoiding him, he wasn't sure what was going to happen. Especially after the confusing feeding last night.

CHAPTER THIRTY-TWO

Rule Number 59- In general, it is considered good practice to take a day to recover after a difficult feed. Accommodations should be made for feeders in these instances.

Taron's assistant was a friendly-looking woman with dark brown skin and a shaved head. She smiled brightly when Avery came in, and it almost felt like she gave off calming energy. It settled him a little, and he offered her a weak smile in return.

"Hello. I'm Avery Whitman. I was told Mr. Cunningham asked to see me?"

"You were told correctly. He's in his office, so you can go right in. Can I get you something to drink?"

It felt weird for him to be on the receiving end of that kind of care and attention. It was always him in the support role. He wasn't entirely sure he liked it. He didn't want to appear rude, though, so he gave her a polite smile as he shook his head.

"No thank you, I'm fine. I, uh... I can just go in?"

"Yep. He's been waiting for you."

Waiting for him? Why?

As he headed for the door, he remembered the package in his hands and did an about face, offering it to her with a grimace. "I forgot. Clarita asked me to deliver this. Can I leave it with you, or should I give it to Mr. Cunningham?"

She put out her hands, taking the box with a frown. "Oh gods, what did he order now? Thank you, I'll take care of this. If you see him ordering something online, please tell him to stop. The man can't seem to help himself."

Avery was still befuddled, but he forced himself to get a move on and knocked before entering Taron's office. It was a lot more chaotic than Ozen's office. Just as large, with floor to ceiling windows and lots of natural light. But the furniture was all random and his desk was messy, and the room smelled surprisingly like incense.

A man was on the phone when he came in, but he waved Avery over and pointed at the couch near the windows before putting up a finger to ask him to wait. It took Avery a second to recognize him. Only his eyes gave him away. Since Avery had last seen him, Taron had gone through some major changes. He was shorter, with wide shoulders and more muscle. He reminded Avery of a gymnast. His facial features were different, too. His skin was lighter, more caramel colored, and his hair was short and wavy. Avery was surprised by the change, but it wasn't a bad one. He was still quite handsome.

Avery perched awkwardly on the edge of one cushion, fiddling with the zipper of his messenger bag until Taron dropped onto the couch beside him.

"Sorry about that. Maverick was none too pleased about me stealing you this morning, but I'm on strict orders. And technically, I outrank him."

"Strict orders about what?" He couldn't help but ask. He was still confused about what was happening.

"I got a call this morning. Apparently, our fearless leader can't seem to follow his own rules when it comes to you. He said he visited you last night?"

It sounded like a question, but Taron already knew the answer. Avery felt his cheeks flush anyway. Being friends with Ozen, Taron knew plenty about feeders and he didn't seem as judgmental as the people from the research team, but Avery still didn't want to discuss it.

Avery's refusal to answer didn't bother Taron in the slightest. He waited just long enough to make Avery blush before continuing.

"Ozen is under the impression that if you're left unattended, you won't actually rest. I didn't believe him until you showed up to work this morning. Did he not discuss the effects of quick feeds with you after last time? You're supposed to take a day off if he needs something like that."

He lifted a shoulder helplessly. He thought about taking a day off, but then the sneering comments of the research team filtered through his mind, and he couldn't make himself do it. People already had low opinions of humans. He didn't want to make things worse simply because he wasn't feeling one hundred percent.

"Hmm... I can see now why he called me. You've got a few choices. You can either lay down on this very comfy couch, or I can bring you to Ozen's office to use the bedroom. Ozen wasn't happy with either option, he would prefer you go home, but I get the feeling if I suggest that, you won't take it. Am I right?"

Avery grimaced. "I don't need a day off. I'm fine. I'm expected downstairs to help Mr. Van Buren, and—"

"Not anymore, you're not," Taron interjected. "I told you, I stole you for the day." He grinned, completely unrepentant. "You're important to Ozen. He needs you healthy to stay alive. So you're important to me too. Now you can either get some rest, or I'll make you."

Avery didn't see that as possible, and he was just tired enough that his patience ran thin. He huffed out a breath, pushing to his feet. "I'm going back downstairs. I appreciate your concern, but—"

"Avanna, my beautiful assistant. Can you come in here for a second?"

The woman from before came in, raising an eyebrow at Taron. "What now?"

Taron gestured at Avery with a smile. "I could use a hand. Avery here needs a nap."

Avery protested, his face bright red, but Taron caught him by the arms before he could storm out. Then Avanna started to sing, and it was like he couldn't keep his eyes open any longer. He went limp in Taron's arms, and after a few seconds of struggling, he was out like a light.

———

"I can't believe you used a siren song on him."

"What? Would you have preferred I sit on him until he went to sleep? It would've been funny, but I'm pretty sure Ozen would kill me if he found out," Taron replied, his smirk clear in his voice without Avery even opening his eyes.

"So instead, you used magic to get your way. You realize he could sue you for that, right? Non consensual magic use is illegal," Mr. Van Buren growled.

"He won't sue," another voice chimed in. It sounded like Mr. Martell, but it was hard for Avery to be sure. He wanted to open his eyes and look, but it felt like his eyes were weighed down by sandbags.

"What makes you so certain?" Mr. Van Buren demanded.

"He doesn't overreact. I saw him when he was being harassed this morning. He ignored comments that I would have lost my temper over. He's incredibly patient."

"Of course he is. He's Ozen's feeder. Not just anyone can pull off that job. The only one who was even a little successful was Tristan, and he only lasted the year," Taron commented.

Avery didn't know who that was, but an uncomfortable feeling twisted in his gut. It felt a little like jealousy, but he stuffed it down before he could take a good look at it. He wasn't allowed to be jealous or possessive over Ozen. They weren't in a relationship.

"Did he say when he'd come back?" Mr. Van Buren asked.

"No," Taron scoffed. "His old man is being vague as hell. You know how he is. The asshole tried to convince Ozen to feed outside his contract as a 'test'. I'm glad Ozen turned him down."

Avery tried to keep his breathing even so no one would notice he was awake and he could hear everything they were saying. It was rude to eavesdrop, but Avery was desperate for any scraps of information about Ozen. He was still confused about what was happening with him.

"He'll be gone as long as he needs to be," Mr. Martell's craggy voice snapped. "Don't rush him. He gave you a week to handle your issues. You should give him the same courtesy."

"It's not the same and you know it. I needed a boost to handle the transition. He's being stubborn. I don't understand what the big deal is. So he's got feelings for his feeder. So what?"

Avery's heart stuttered in his chest, and he froze, listening intently.

"He didn't say that," Mr. Van Buren argued. Avery's heart sank. "He said he's attached."

"Same difference," Taron complained. "He's got feelings that don't fit into his little contract and he's doing whatever he can to turn back time. It's stupid. There's nothing wrong with dating."

Mr. Martell scoffed. "You can say that. You aren't reliant on your romantic partner to feed you. If Ozen gives in to his attachment and things go wrong, he'll lose the most dedicated feeder he's ever had. It's smart to leave feelings out of it."

"How long does he have to be alone before he—"

"Enough," Mr. Van Buren growled. "He's listening."

Crap.

There was no point in pretending if Mr. Van Buren had already noticed he was awake, so Avery slowly opened his eyes and looked up at the supernaturals surrounding him. He was on Taron's couch, tucked tightly in the fluffy blanket from Ozen's office bedroom. Mr. Van Buren stood behind the couch, and Taron and Mr. Martell sat on the coffee table in front of him. It was a little weird, them hanging around him like this, and Avery considered hiding under the covers to escape their staring.

"Feeling any better?" Taron asked, his smile coming back.

Although, yes, he was a lot more alert than before, Avery didn't answer, instead glaring at the shapeshifter who magically forced him to sleep.

Mr. Martell chuckled and shot a pointed look at Taron. "You deserve his wrath. There were other ways to get him to listen. Now that I know he's alive and I won't need to be writing up a new contract, I'm going back to work. No using your assistant to manhandle the feeder. And call me when you hear from Ozen. I want an update."

Taron still looked unrepentant, and he grinned with all his teeth when Mr. Van Buren gave him a dirty look.

"I'm not going anywhere. I don't trust you. He can rest just fine in my office."

"And die from smoke inhalation. There's a reason Ozen asked me to watch him."

Smoke billowed from Mr. Van Buren's nostrils as he glared at Taron. "I can control myself. You're the troublemaker here."

Taron raised his eyebrows, giving a significant look to the smoke filling the room. "You're only proving my point right now. Don't you have a lawsuit to work on?"

Avery sat up, wriggling free of the blankets, desperate to escape this weird situation. "I don't need a babysitter. If no one needs me today, I think I'll go home."

It was better than sitting around here being treated like a toddler who needed supervision.

"Great," Taron said as he bounced to his feet. "I'll go with you."

Mr. Van Buren made a face. "You have a company to run in Ozen's absence. Or did you forget that?"

Taron rolled his eyes. "Unlike my dear friend, I know how to delegate. I've got it covered. Come on, Avery. Let's book it."

For some reason, Avery felt like this might be the worst possible outcome, and it didn't take a psychic to know that no amount of arguing was going to change Taron's mind. If he wasn't so uncertain about his place with Ozen, he'd be calling him for backup. Instead, he silently prayed for patience.

CHAPTER THIRTY-THREE

Ozen sat in his father's office, his face buried in his hands. His attempt at feeding from another source backfired so spectacularly, he basically attacked Avery in the middle of the night. Trying to feed from one of Korath's guests, who assured Ozen several times he was there of his own volition, ended up making Ozen physically ill. He couldn't touch the man, and his magic stubbornly refused to latch on. Not only that, but that feeling like he was going feral hit him so hard, he panicked and went straight to Avery's apartment to combat it. In his rush, he bypassed every rule he had set in place to protect himself and Avery from getting attached.

The feel of Avery's lips, though...

Ozen used to kiss when he was with his first feeders. He was young and foolish, and didn't worry about feeders getting attached. He didn't have the same issues he had now, since no feeder wanted to stick around a young incubus with nothing more to offer than a good time. These days, with the amount of money they were given and the cushy lifestyle, feeders wanted to nail down a relationship to keep what they earned ongoing, even if they had to fake feelings to do it.

Avery didn't fake his reactions to Ozen. His kisses were eager and needy, like he was with every session. Ozen could taste his confusion in the air, he knew Avery had questions, but his desperation made him reckless and he didn't give Avery a chance to talk before riding him ruthlessly. Ozen nearly came when Avery did the first time, his pleasure and desire so thick that Ozen felt like he was drowning in it. It was physically painful to hold back. The feeding was rushed as it was. If it was too rushed, he risked actually hurting Avery. So he dragged it out a few more minutes to protect Avery, and he called his friends to ensure Avery was taken care of once Ozen was finally clear headed enough to realize what he'd done.

He hadn't called since. He itched to check in and see how Avery was doing, but he couldn't risk it. He didn't want to give himself another reason to go after Avery again. The feeding had been so intense, Avery passed out afterward. Ozen didn't trust himself near Avery right now.

"Where is he?"

Ozen lifted his head and straightened his back. It took a while for him to get his father to admit who he was inviting to talk to him. In all honesty, Ozen hadn't realized his grandfather was still alive. He disappeared when Ozen was just barely of age, and Ozen had heard no one talk about him since. Korath said it was hard to track him down since he was always on the move, which meant Ozen was stuck here for days, waiting for him to show up.

The office doors opened and Korath strode in, actually dressed this time. Apparently there were limits, even for him. He wouldn't greet his father in nothing but a robe. Ozen just wished he'd afford the same courtesy to his son.

Ozen's grandfather followed behind him. His hair was fully white now, and he had wrinkles around his eyes, but that was the extent of his aging. Incubi aged incredibly slowly. In human standards, his grandfather looked barely sixty, even though he'd been alive for nearly six thousand years.

"Ozen, my child."

"Grandfather," Ozen replied, pushing to his feet. He clasped hands with his grandfather, bowing to rest his forehead against their hands, which was customary when greeting elders. Korath didn't bother with those traditions, but Grandfather Sylix was a formal man when Ozen last knew him, and the proud smile on Sylix's face when Ozen straightened again told him he'd gotten this tradition right.

"At least someone knows how to greet their elders. How are you, my boy? You look tired."

Ozen hummed, joining his grandfather on the couch. "I've been better. I'm assuming Korath didn't tell you why you were asked to come?"

"Not much. Only that something was wrong with you and you needed an expert. Have you taken ill? Do you need a transfusion?"

Blood from the ancients, like Sylix, could cure all sorts of illnesses, but it wasn't a pleasant process for either party. Ozen hoped it wouldn't come to that.

"I'm not sure. I've asked around, but no one can tell me what's happening."

Sylix gripped Ozen's shoulder a little roughly, but his smile was reassuring. "Tell me. We'll figure it out together."

With a sigh, he started from the beginning. It was a slow process. He didn't want to leave anything out. He even included his reaction to the feeders from Korath's little party, just to be safe. When he finished, he felt defeated. Nothing about this looked like it had a good outcome. Being dependent on a feeder was difficult enough. Only being able to use one feeder for the foreseeable future was daunting. It removed Avery's ability to break the contract or move on when the contract was done. Ozen knew he'd never do it if he knew the consequences. Ozen didn't want him to feel obligated to stay if he was unhappy. And with the way he'd been treated lately, Ozen was sure that was the case.

"Well, that's easy enough," Sylix commented after a moment.

Ozen whipped his head up, searching his grandfather's face. There wasn't a hint of teasing. He was completely serious.

"So you know what's wrong with him, then?" Korath demanded. He was sitting on the armchair beside Ozen, trying to be supportive. It might've helped if he wasn't making comments the whole way through until Sylix glared at him to make him stop.

"There's nothing wrong with him," Sylix answered. "He's found his mate."

Ozen and Korath both gaped at the older man. Korath found his voice first, stammering as he tried to get the words out.

"His– But– Incubi don't have mates!"

Sylix gave his son a bland look. "No. *You* don't have one. Yet. That isn't to say that you won't find one or more than one in the future. You're still young, after all. But all supernaturals have a mate or mates. It's the way of our world. And it's not a bad thing." He gave his attention fully to Ozen. "You are describing what's happening with an air of defeat. You're failing to see the positives. When you feed from your mate, he strengthens you. He reminded you of the pleasure of the action, and your feedings are more potent when you share pleasure together. These are good things."

"But... What about the fact that I can't go a day without? It's difficult for him when I'm busy and in a hurry."

Sylix rolled his eyes, which looked odd on such a formal man. "For one thing, if you bit your mate like you should have, you wouldn't need daily feedings. Blood sharing will take away that demanding urge to feed. It won't take away the need to be near him. That will actually grow with time. But that's normal for mates. And if you were living together like you should be, you wouldn't need to resort to quick feeds. You'd be able to go home together and take your time after the work day was over. I've watched your company grow, and I know you must be busy, but you'll need to make time for your mate. It will help, I promise."

Ozen sat with that for a moment. Avery was... his mate? He'd never even considered it. He valued Avery, both as his feeder and his assistant, and he wanted to make him happy, but he thought that was just to keep Avery in his position longer. He didn't think he was destined for a mate. He'd been alive for thousands of years. A mate was a nice idea when he was young, but he'd long since given up the fanciful idea.

"You're not serious. So you're saying he'll never be able to feed from anyone else again? I saw his attempt the other night. It made him ill!" Korath screeched.

"Why in the world would he try to do that?" Sylix demanded.

"I thought it'd help! You didn't see him! He looked gaunt and pale!"

"Much like he does right now?" Sylix asked blandly. "No. He won't be able to feed from anyone else. He won't want to, either. A mate is a great blessing. His mate will give him everything he needs. Feeding from someone else won't even cross his mind."

Based on Korath's expression, the idea of feeding from only one person for the rest of his life sounded like the worst thing that could happen. To Ozen, it sounded like heaven. He'd never have to search for a feeder again, or wonder if he'd be starved by a petulant feeder's tantrums. Avery was dedicated and cared about his well being. He wouldn't let Ozen suffer.

His grandfather's explanation cleared up a lot of Ozen's confusion. It all made sense. His increasing need to be close to Avery. The itch under his skin when he hadn't seen him in a while. The struggles he had finding Avery a new place to live. Nothing was ever good enough. Probably because he never considered asking Avery to move in with him.

But... Avery never agreed to that. He was professional, and he enjoyed their sessions, but he'd given no indication that he'd be interested in something more. It was one of Ozen's favorite things about him. He didn't cross that boundary. Instead, it was Ozen who continued to cross it time and time again. There was no telling if Avery would be interested in mating with him. To his knowledge, humans didn't have mates. And even if he had been interested, after the way Ozen had acted recently, he'd probably scared Avery away from the idea entirely.

Ozen's hopes rose and sank in quick succession. His emotions felt turbulent because of it. Sylix picked up on it and put his hand on Ozen's forearm, drawing his attention.

"What's wrong?"

Ozen shook his head slowly. "I know Avery. He'll agree to a mating just to make sure I'm taken care of. But he never signed on to be my mate. I don't want him to feel obligated to be with me. And with the way I've treated him as of late..."

Sylix smiled indulgently. "Let me guess. You panicked and pushed him away, only to need to feed so badly you basically mauled him."

Ozen's eyes widened. "How did you—" He studied his grandfather carefully. "You too?"

Sylix dipped his chin once. "Yes. My mating was... chaotic, for lack of a better word. They are both so very young compared to me. It felt wrong. But they are both adults, and once they had a grip on me, they refused to let go. I needed that. My mates needed a strong will to keep me in line." He chuckled to himself. "They still do from time to time. I'll introduce you to them one day. *After* you fix things with your own mate."

Korath made a spluttering noise. "You're mated?" he asked incredulously.

Sylix made a face at Ozen, rolling his eyes at his son's dramatics before answering. "Yes. You'd know that if you contacted your father every once in a while. Don't pretend you don't know how. I gave you the tools to do it the day I left. Now, perhaps we should discuss my other grandchildren. I've been informed by your brother that one of them is in jail."

Ozen snorted. That wouldn't surprise him in the slightest. He left his father to explain his messy family life to Sylix. Ozen had better things to do. Namely, apologizing to his mate.

CHAPTER THIRTY-FOUR

Rule Number 80- Feeders are allowed to cancel contracts at any given time, though it is customary to give two weeks notice.

Avery was going insane. He didn't believe Taron anymore when he said Ozen asked Taron to watch over him. Avery knew without a doubt that Ozen wouldn't ask Taron to sleep on his couch every night. And he only slept there because Avery refused to go home with him. Taron never tried anything untoward, but it was getting rather frustrating trying to balance entertaining the shapeshifter while trying to figure out everything else.

Ozen had been gone for nearly a week now, minus the night he showed up and fucked Avery into unconsciousness. No text, no calls, nothing that wasn't a message passed through one of his friends. And gods, they'd gotten annoying. They wouldn't leave him alone. He was almost certain that they were making up tasks to keep him occupied. Mr. Martell had Avery reorganizing his entire office. Which would be a fun challenge if the goblin didn't complain every time Avery moved something. Avery almost missed suffocating on smoke working with Mr. Van Buren. At least with the dragon shifter, he didn't feel like he was going around in circles.

Their antics led to a rather frustrating few days. He'd hoped by the week's end, they'd back off and give him some space, but Taron refused to leave. He was camped out on Avery's couch, poking through his miniscule book collection and complaining that he was bored. Avery couldn't even work on his book because he knew Taron would read over his shoulder if given half the chance.

"You live in a shoe box. Can't you afford something nicer?"

"Not really," Avery replied offhandedly. He was trying to read one of his favorite books in an effort to distract himself, but Taron was hellbent on keeping all of his attention.

"Why not? You can't be paying a lot to live here. What do you spend your money on?"

"I've spent most of my adult life paying off my mother's hospital bills. I couldn't afford to save until I became Ozen's feeder. And there's nothing wrong with my apartment. I live alone. I don't need a lot of space."

Taron went uncharacteristically quiet when he asked, "Is she okay?"

Avery looked up. Taron actually looked concerned, and he felt a little bad for bringing it up. It'd been almost ten years now, so it didn't hurt to talk about anymore, but it still took people off guard when he brought it up.

"She died. Breast cancer. She and my dad tried for years to find a cure, racking up hundreds of thousands of dollars in medical debt. Medical care for humans is really expensive without insurance, and most human companies won't offer insurance outright. They basically demand a third of your paycheck to cover it and it doesn't cover everything. Experimental treatments, hospice care, those kinds of things aren't covered. She died despite their best efforts to save her, and my dad followed soon after from a broken heart. All their debt passed to me. They didn't have anything to sell, so I got the first job I could find as a temp and moved in here. It's not the greatest apartment in the world, but it's better than living on the streets, and the rent is cheap. I don't hate it."

Taron listened intently and looked close to tears when Avery finished. He cleared his throat, looking away with a frown.

"Your story is a little cruel. You make me want to call my mother."

A smile tugged at Avery's lips. "Would that be such a bad thing?"

Taron scoffed. "Yes. She's a tyrant. She's been trying to manipulate me into moving home for years. And not because she misses me, either. She has her own business, and she was pissed when I left to partner up with Ozen. She won't even acknowledge the fact that my company is doing way better than hers. I'm a failure for ignoring my duties to my family."

Avery tipped his head from side to side. "Okay, that does sound annoying. But if you found out she was going to die, would you still want to avoid her?"

Taron made a face. "Low blow. I thought you were my friend."

That made him snicker. "We're not friends. You're friends with Ozen. I'm basically your captive. I don't need a babysitter, you know. The effects of the quick feed wore off days ago. I'm fine."

"Yeah, yeah. You said that already. Maybe I could send her some chocolate or something. If I go visit, she'll hog tie me into staying or something. Long distance is the only way I can deal with her." He hoisted himself off the couch, going straight for Avery's computer. It proved how distracted Avery was with what was going on with Ozen that he forgot entirely why he didn't want Taron near his computer until Taron made a curious sound. "What's this?"

Horror dumped into his gut, and he launched off the bed, scrambling to shut the computer off. "Nothing! That's nothing! Don't–"

Taron's arms lengthened enough to keep Avery at a distance so he could read the page that was still pulled up on Avery's screen. No amount of fighting was helping and Avery eventually gave up, flopping face first onto his bed and burying his head under the pillows with a groan.

"Hey, this is hot. What is it? A diary?"

"No!" Avery shouted, though the sound was muffled from the pillows. "It's nothing! Just a hobby! Can you stop now?"

"No can do, buckeroo. This is interesting. And damn, it's long. This is a novel, isn't it? You write romance novels?"

Avery didn't reply, but his face was burning so hot he was worried his pillows would burst into flames.

"I'm emailing this to myself."

"What? No!"

That got Avery moving, and he launched off the bed again, yanking the chair away from the desk. Taron saw it coming and stood before he could be yanked away as well, cackling to himself as he attached Avery's novel to an email to himself. Avery let out a frustrated growl and tried to tackle

Taron away from his desk, but all he really managed to do was give the shapeshifter a hug.

"Aw, you do love me," Taron cooed. "I should send this to Ozen, too. He'll want to know what you're into."

"I hate you! Seriously! Don't you dare send that to him! I know where your office is! I'll mess up all your files! I—"

A knock on the door cut off his rant and the sound of the email being sent followed right after it. Taron smiled brightly down at him, tipping his head with an innocent look.

"Should I get that?"

Avery shoved away from him, his shoulders slumped in defeat. He'd never be able to face Taron again if he read that. And Taron probably wasn't lying when he said he'd send it to Ozen, too. Avery would be too embarrassed to face him, which meant Ozen would starve and Avery would never forgive himself. He whimpered, contemplating fleeing the country when he opened the door. He lifted his gaze for a second, doing a double take when he realized who stood there.

"Ozen..."

"Ozen's back?" Taron asked, poking his head out of the main room. He beamed at his friend, jerking his thumb over his shoulder. "Glad you're here. You should see what I found—"

"What are you doing here?" Ozen demanded. His voice was rough, like a growl, and he was shooting daggers at Taron. Avery wasn't sure what to make of his mood. Especially when Ozen reached for him and yanked him against his side. Avery gasped at the position. Being plastered against Ozen didn't do great things for keeping his libido or his crush at bay. But aside from the confusion and the butterflies that always showed up whenever he was around Ozen, Avery was also pissed. He shouldn't have been, the feeling wasn't professional in the slightest, but it didn't change how Avery felt.

"I asked you a question," Ozen demanded.

Taron, at least, didn't look bothered by Ozen's growls. If anything, he looked overjoyed with the development, and his grin grew impossibly wider.

"Woah. Someone's possessive. Finally going to admit you've got a thing for him? I mean, my back suffered a lot, but it was worth the effort if—"

Ozen's snarl wasn't human, and his glamor fell away in his fury. That made Taron shut up and his smile fell a little.

"Relax. I was just doing what you asked."

"Get out."

Taron raised his hands in surrender and didn't argue, edging past a seething Ozen without a fuss. It was only when he made it into the hall that he spoke again.

"He writes sexy books in his spare time. That's how he relaxes. You should read it. It's—"

Ozen slammed the door before Taron could finish, and Avery could hear him cackle in the hallway as he left. The shock finally wore off, the noise of the door slamming startling Avery back to reality. He shoved away from Ozen with a glower, giving them enough space to breathe without starting up the chasing thing that happened the last time he backed up too far. As much as his body wanted a repeat, Avery's mind was buzzing like a hive of angry hornets.

"What was that?"

Ozen's face turned slowly to Avery, and he growled low. "I could ask the same thing. Why was Taron here so late?"

Avery rolled his eyes hard. "Because he wouldn't leave me alone. None of your friends would. You disappeared, and they decided I couldn't be trusted by myself. Even though I'm not the problem here. You're the one who disappears without a word except to show up to maul me before leaving again."

To his credit, Ozen looked ashamed when Avery reminded him of that. His anger faded and regret took its place, his frown so deep it looked like it was carved into his face.

"I understand that you're busy and things come up, but I would've thought I would be afforded the courtesy of an explanation. You're the one who invited me to your home. I don't understand why you're treating me like I'm the one who did something wrong."

A lump formed in Avery's throat that no amount of swallowing would remove. Tears burned his eyes, and he jerked away to face the wall so Ozen wouldn't see them fall. He didn't actually care about courtesy. He was hurt that Ozen left without a word and wouldn't speak to him for a week. He was sure the entire week that they were making sure he stuck around long enough for Ozen to come back and fire him. And because of the stupid crush that wouldn't go away, Avery missed him terribly.

When Ozen's arms came around him, Avery wanted to push him away. He told himself to do it. But he melted into it, choking back sobs as he leaned against Ozen's chest.

"You have every right to be angry with me, firefly. The way I acted was childish and cruel. I'm not going to ask you to forgive me yet. That will take time. I would, however, like a chance to explain. I've come to realize a few things, and it's important we discuss them."

Dread filled Avery's stomach. Ozen must've figured out about Avery's crush. He was going to break the contract and send him on his way. He squeezed his eyes shut, trying to brace himself for the worst. Tears spilled down his cheeks onto Ozen's arms, and there was nothing Avery could do to stop it. He broke the contract first and fell for his boss. He deserved whatever Ozen had coming for him. Maybe he'd be blacklisted like Calvin. Maybe he'd even be dismissed from his temp job because of his unprofessionalism. The possibilities were endless, but the most gut wrenching one was the thought of losing Ozen.

CHAPTER THIRTY-FIVE

Ozen hated that he caused Avery so much distress. He wanted to explain, but he couldn't do that with Avery shaking and sobbing in his arms. He wouldn't hear him properly. Instead, Ozen scooped him off his feet and brought him to bed. Ozen laid down beside him, much like that night so long ago when he accidentally slept over for the first time. Except this time, Avery was awake and upset, and Ozen needed to reassure him before he selfishly threw out words like mate.

"Avery... I'm so sorry. I never meant to ignore you. You're right, you deserved to be treated better than the way I've been treating you. I can't guarantee I'll be perfect going forward, but I'll spend the rest of my life trying to be better."

Avery's tears subsided a little, and he looked up at Ozen with a frown. "Your... life?"

Ozen hummed, carding his fingers through Avery's messy curls. He must've been running his fingers through them, because they were more wild than normal. Ozen smoothed them out, trying to settle his unhappy mate.

"It's a long story, and I fully intend to share it with you, but I need you to know first and foremost that you aren't obligated to agree to any of this.

It's complicated and messy, but you still get a choice in the matter. It's not permanent." Yet. Once Ozen bit him and tasted his blood, there would be no going back. Not for him, anyway. And when they shared blood, Avery would change as well. His lifespan would match Ozen's, and he'd gain a little more insight into Ozen's emotions. Ozen did some research on the trip home. There weren't only benefits for the incubus during mating; their mates gained things as well.

"What... What are you talking about?"

Ozen studied the beautiful man beside him. Avery gave no indication that he understood or fully agreed with Ozen's comment about him not being obligated. He wouldn't, either. Not until he knew the whole story. Even Ozen knew that. So, despite not knowing how he'd react or what the outcome would be, Ozen told him the truth.

"You're my mate, firefly. It's why I've been so addicted to you. You're my perfect match."

Avery looked dumbfounded, staring up at him like he'd said something truly unbelievable. It was a little disheartening. Ozen had hoped Avery felt the same way that he did, that his feelings weren't one-sided, but that was a little too much to ask. Especially after the last two weeks.

"I understand if this comes as a shock. It was a shock to me as well. Again, you're in no way obligated to agree to this. If you'd rather cancel the contract and move on, I..." He trailed off with a frown. "I can't say I'd be happy to do it, but I would understand. To my knowledge, humans don't have mates. This won't affect you."

"W-Wait... I'm your– You're my– How–"

He looked confused, his wide eyes searching Ozen's face for answers to questions he couldn't quite get out. Ozen offered him a small smile.

"I know. It's a lot to process. You're in no rush to make any decisions. But I've been unfair to you these past few weeks, and you deserve to be treated better than you have been. It had nothing to do with anything you did. It was entirely on me, and I want to make amends for that."

He had to fight the urge to kiss away the confusion on Avery's face. He refused to push his agenda in any way. He was hungry, but just being in Avery's presence helped with that. He'd survive at least a little while before bringing up a feeding.

"H-How do you know?" Avery finally asked, his voice trembling ever so slightly.

"There were things happening whenever I was with you that confused me. I went home to confer with my family on the matter. It was my grandfather who told me what those things meant."

"What things?" Avery asked.

Ozen knew he'd need to explain this carefully. He took a deep breath, locking eyes with Avery so he could see the sincerity in Ozen's expression.

"From day one, feeding from you made me feel stronger. None of my other feeders ever satisfied me like you can. I've actually made plans with the research team to help with some of their development because I seem to be overflowing with magic since I've started feeding from you regularly. I'm also drawn to you in ways I couldn't explain. Not once since its creation have I ever felt the urge to deviate from the terms of the contract. Not until I met you."

"Not even with Tristan?"

There was a hint of jealousy in Avery's tone that thrilled Ozen to no end. He wasn't sure how Avery found out about Tristan, but if Avery did agree to become Ozen's mate, there would be no secrets between them. He had no wish to lie to his mate.

"Not even with Tristan. What do you know about him?"

Avery shrugged, looking a little embarrassed when he admitted, "Not a lot. I overheard your friends talking about him. He sounded important."

Ozen hummed thoughtfully. "He was, in a way. He was the only other feeder I've had in my lifetime who respected the contract. He maintained professionalism and always showed up when I needed him. He set the standard for what I wanted in a feeder."

"What happened to him?"

"He left," Ozen replied easily. "He found someone who made him happy and wanted to be in a relationship with them. He was polite enough to wait until the end of his contract term, but I wasn't going to stop him from finding his happiness to keep him as my feeder. Our contract ended, and he got married a few months later. Last I heard, they've adopted a set of twins and moved to the suburbs."

"Do you miss him?" Avery whispered.

Ozen was quick to reassure him with a shake of his head. "No. Before you came along, I missed the ease of our working relationship, but I had no feelings for the man himself. I'm happy for him. He was a kind and thoughtful man, and he deserved to find someone who could provide him with what he needed. That never would have been me. There were no feelings involved with either of us. Nothing like the way I feel about you."

Avery sucked in a sharp breath, but Ozen couldn't tell yet if the barely banked hope in Avery's eyes was wishful thinking or not. He could be imagining it because of his own wants.

"I do have a confession to make," Ozen continued. "Up until your weekend at my home, I'd been curious but not overly concerned about what was happening between us. I still would have put in the effort to figure it out, but the mistake that I made sent me into a panic and I went home looking for answers. I wanted to protect you, to prevent it from happening again, but I didn't know how."

Avery frowned. "What mistake?"

Ozen dreaded admitting it. While technically what they did together was consensual, Avery only agreed to those acts as a way to feed him. He never agreed to do anything like that for fun. It still felt wrong.

"I..." He grimaced and forced himself to tell the truth. "You weren't wrong when you mentioned not feeling my magic that night. I never used it."

"You didn't feed?"

Ozen shook his head, shamefaced. "No. I lost myself in the pleasure of the act and completely forgot. I'm sorry. I know you never agreed to that outside of feeding. I wasn't even aware of it until you mentioned it. I promise, I never would have—"

Avery put his fingers over Ozen's lips, silencing him. His face was pensive, and Ozen held his breath, worried this would be the final straw to push Avery away. His stomach clenched and fear filled his veins with ice. He didn't want to lose Avery. He'd do anything to take it back.

"I'm not angry with you about that."

Shock hit Ozen hard, and he wanted to ask questions, but Avery's hand was still over his mouth.

"I mean, it's a little hot that you were so into it that you forgot to feed. If you would've told me, I might've suggested trying again so you ate, though. Was that why you were so wild when you showed up in the middle of the week? You were starving again?"

Ozen nodded once. He still felt ashamed about that as well. It was a rough feeding and Ozen was so worried about the effects of it, he sent his friends to watch over Avery because Ozen himself was too ashamed to face him.

"Well, you couldn't really help that. You said you didn't even realize until afterward. I'm more angry about what happened after your so-called mistake." Avery's frown deepened and hurt filled his voice. "You were really dismissive, and then you disappeared without a word. I thought I'd done something wrong, or maybe I overstayed my welcome. And when you didn't come back, I was sure you wanted nothing more to do with me."

It pained him to hear Avery's side of it. He hated himself for making such a sweet man feel that way. But he stayed silent, letting Avery speak his peace.

"When you showed up in the middle of the week, I was really confused. You didn't offer me any explanation and—"

"I couldn't," Ozen interrupted, gently pulling Avery's fingers away. "I wasn't... all there that night. I made the mistake of taking my father's advice and trying to feed from someone else. It backfired quite severely. It wasn't until after we were finished that I was clear enough to realize what I'd done."

"You tried to feed from someone else?" Avery murmured, pain etched across his face. Ozen cupped his cheek, desperately wishing he could take back the last week entirely.

"I never meant to hurt you. I was in a panic. I thought I'd become addicted to your energy and that I wouldn't be able to let you walk away when your contract was up. I never wanted to force you to be with me. I thought if I made myself feed from someone else, I'd break the cycle and keep you safe from me."

"I don't want to be kept safe from you," Avery argued. "You should've talked to me about it. I—" He swallowed and Ozen was surprised to see the shame on Avery's face that matched his own. "You weren't the only one who broke the contract. I have the biggest stupid crush on you, and I was trying to hide it from you for weeks. I didn't want you to fire me for being unprofessional and be left without a feeder again, so I pushed the feelings away. Every jealous, hopeful, needy feeling got shoved down. But when you disappeared, it wasn't courtesy that upset me. I missed you and it hurt my feelings when you didn't even call to explain things to me."

Hope swelled in Ozen'schest, and his heart hammered uncontrollably. "You... You have feelings for me?"

Avery flushed bright red and deflected, glaring at the wall. "Well, you have feelings for me, so it's only fair."

CHAPTER THIRTY-SIX

Rule Number 43 - In the event of a change in dynamic, i.e. a relationship is established between feeder and client, the contract is considered void.

Avery seriously needed to look into why he had no filter around Ozen. He regretted his stupid comment the minute it came out of his mouth, but he was embarrassed and confused. And stupidly hopeful that what Ozen was saying was true. He was Ozen's mate? It didn't feel possible. Avery didn't deserve someone so perfect, not after lying to him for weeks about what he was feeling.

"No, firefly. The way I feel about you is so much more than a crush," Ozen assured him. Then he followed it up with a kiss so full of passion that Avery moaned in response.

Ozen ripped his mouth away suddenly, his breathing harsh and a pained look crossing over his face. It took Avery a second to remember that Ozen hadn't fed since that night in the middle of the week when he showed up and rode him. He had to be hungry. Avery cupped his cheek, soothing him with a chaste kiss.

"You should feed. It's been a while. We can keep talking afterward."

Ozen looked torn, and it soothed a little of Avery's hurt feelings to see how much Ozen cared about making things right with him. But Avery wouldn't be able to focus, knowing that Ozen was starving the whole time.

Since Ozen didn't seem willing to make the first move, Avery decided to take the lead for once. He nudged Ozen's shoulder, forcing him onto his back. He straddled Ozen's waist, leaning to give him a slow and passionate kiss. Now that Ozen had broken the seal on that particular act, Avery never wanted to stop. He loved kissing Ozen, loved the way their tongues tangled, and the way his belly clenched with need whenever Ozen sucked on his tongue. He nipped teasingly at Ozen's bottom lip, drawing a groan from the incubus. It seemed to be the tipping point, and Ozen finally relaxed, his hands coming into play, sliding up Avery's legs to grip the cheeks of his behind.

Avery groaned when Ozen's magic latched onto him. His kisses grew more needy, and when Ozen tugged at the hem of his shirt, he lifted his arms eagerly. Ozen was in a suit, sans a tie, and it took a few minutes of hasty movements to get all the buttons undone without ripping the shirt open like he wanted to. Ozen wasn't helping, breaking the kiss to trail more down Avery's neck and shoulder. Ozen knew all the right places to make Avery moan, and it was really hard to concentrate when Ozen was licking his neck.

He finally got Ozen's shirt and jacket off, and this time, when he ran his hands over Ozen's skin, the incubus didn't stop him. He smiled indulgently, letting Avery explore, and he didn't rush him to hurry things along. Avery took advantage of his charitable mood, kissing and touching every inch of him until Ozen's slacks got in his way. Frustrated with the interruption, Avery wrestled with the button and zipper, his face flushing when it took a little too long.

Ozen's hands came up to stop him, and he cupped Avery's cheek with a look of adoration on his face that made Avery's heart skip a beat.

"We've got all the time in the world, firefly. I'm not going anywhere."

Avery hadn't realized he needed to hear that until Ozen said it. He melted, leaning into Ozen's hand and moving willingly when Ozen pulled him back down for another kiss. With Ozen's help this time, Avery managed to strip them both, groaning at the delightful feeling of skin on skin. Their cocks brushed together, making Avery moan and Ozen shiver.

His grip on Avery's ass tightened encouragingly, and Avery slowly rolled his hips, gasping at the sensation.

They stayed that way for a while, mouths fused and hips grinding, until Avery was breathless and desperate for release. When Ozen's fingers teased over his hole, Avery shuddered and pulled away with a whimper.

"I want you..."

"You have me, firefly."

He shook his head. That wasn't what he meant, but it was hard to get the words right when his mind was all lust fogged and horny. He came willingly for another kiss, but pulled away again when Ozen teased over his hole again.

"Ozen..." Avery whined.

"Tell me what you want. I'll give you anything."

"I want you inside me," Avery begged. Fingers weren't enough this time. Avery hadn't stopped thinking about what it'd be like since Ozen rode him the other night. He wanted to feel Ozen inside him, to know what that ribbed skin felt like against his hole. He felt almost desperate for it. He reached between them, trying to mimic what Ozen had done the other night, but Ozen stopped him before he could sink down.

"Incubi don't need prep, firefly, but humans do. Lie on your back. Let me get you ready for me."

Avery didn't have a chance to feel embarrassed before he was flipped onto his back and distracted with Ozen's mouth on his. His mouth nipped and teased, keeping Avery distracted while Ozen's fingers played with his ass. Avery loved Ozen's fingers. The incubus knew just how to play him to get him the most amount of pleasure. But Avery wanted more than just fingers, and it didn't take long for Ozen to get him close. He tried to push Ozen's fingers away with a whine.

"I don't want to come yet. I want you inside me first."

Ozen's chuckle sent shivers up his spine. "Even if you came now, I wouldn't deny you what you want. I would keep going until you were delirious with pleasure."

"Getting there," Avery admitted, moaning when Ozen teased his prostate. "Still want you inside me first."

"As you wish," Ozen purred. Literally purred. It was the sexiest thing Avery had ever heard, but he didn't have time to enjoy it. Ozen's fingers slipped free and Avery tensed when the head of his cock brushed against him instead. It was entirely instinctual, Avery knew Ozen wouldn't actually hurt him, but his body still tensed automatically.

"Relax, firefly. I won't hurt you. I would never hurt you."

Avery let himself be distracted by Ozen's mouth, wrapping his arms around Ozen's shoulders to keep him close. Ozen waited until he was relaxed, making needy noises against his lips, before sinking slowly inside of him.

Ozen didn't lie when he said he wouldn't hurt him, but he failed to mention just how much Avery would enjoy it. His back arched and his mouth fell open in surprise, his fingers scrambling for purchase on Ozen's shoulders as the incubus sank in to the hilt.

"O-Ozen!"

He thought their last encounter had been good, but it was nothing compared to this. Avery's hole throbbed with the ridges of Ozen's cock. It was so intense, he nearly came instantly. It was Ozen's hand around the base of his cock that kept him from exploding.

"Oh gods, oh gods, oh gods!"

Ozen's chuckle was deep and throaty, his voice gone all husky as he murmured against Avery's ear. "You like my cock in your ass?"

"Yes! Yes! Ohhhh..."

Desperation filled Avery's veins with every thrust of Ozen's hips. It took no time at all before he couldn't take any more. He pleaded for Ozen to let him come, wailing so loud the windows rattled when Ozen finally released Avery's cock. It only took one stroke of Ozen's hand for Avery to come, his eyes going blind from the pleasure.

Instead of feeling relief, though, the continued thrust of Ozen's hips only dragged things out. Avery didn't have a chance to soften, his dick staying rock hard despite his explosive finish. He whimpered, clinging to Ozen's back when Ozen slowed and grimaced.

"What's... wrong...?" he panted.

"Nothing," Ozen gritted out, but his face said otherwise. His fangs were back, his eyes looked wild, and his glamor kept flickering on and off. Something was definitely wrong.

Avery cupped his cheek, drawing Ozen's attention. The kiss he gave him was soft, more reassuring, and Ozen melted into it with a sigh.

"Tell me what's wrong."

"I... I want to bite you. It's something only mates do, and I've felt the urge since we met, but–"

"Do it," Avery urged.

Ozen looked stunned, his whole body tense. "Avery, you don't understand–"

"Yes, I do," Avery protested. "We still have a lot to talk about, because I'm sure there's more, but it won't change anything. I want you. I have since the day I met you. I'd be happy to be your mate."

———

Ozen had never heard more perfect words. He stared at Avery, looking for any signs of apprehension or dishonesty, but there were none. His smile was soft and reassuring, and he stroked a thumb over Ozen's cheek, soothing his anxiety. When Ozen crashed his lips against Avery's, his mate met him just as enthusiastically, moaning in delight as Ozen's hips began moving again. He couldn't help himself. There was nothing more perfect than being inside his mate.

Like every time he was with Avery, the urge to sink his teeth into Avery's creamy skin was overwhelming. It was even worse now that he had Avery's permission. He could only hold out for a few moments before the need was too great to ignore. He dragged his mouth from the sinful delight of Avery's lips, kissing his way down the column of Avery's neck. His heart thundered in his ears at the implication of biting Avery, and he questioned himself on whether it was truly the right thing to do to accept Avery's encouragement while he was in the throes of passion. But then Avery tipped his head to the side to give Ozen more room and instinct took over.

Avery flinched for only a moment before his body stiffened and his nails dug into Ozen's shoulders. Ozen felt it, too. Each pull of suction, each swallow of Avery's blood, sent waves of pleasure crashing against them both. Avery was silent at first, the shock of it catching him off guard, but when Ozen's hips started moving again, his pleasured cries filled the room. It was too intense for either of them to bear for long, and they came together, Ozen's cum filling Avery's channel as Avery's covered his chest and stomach. It dragged on and on until Ozen finally released Avery's neck. Avery melted into the mattress, but before he fell into a sex coma, Ozen needed to finish what they'd started.

He quickly pierced his tongue with his fang, kissing Avery hard to share his blood. He didn't need much, just enough to start the bonding process. Avery was too tired to question him, his kisses lazy and his body pliant and sated.

Ozen would have been content to stay like that all night, trading languid kisses and just being close with him, but a pounding at the door made them both tense.

"Police! Open up!"

A snarl ripped through him, fury filling his veins at being interrupted. Avery went rigid beneath him, fear and worry erasing all his relaxed energy. That only pissed him off more, and he pulled away from Avery, storming to answer the door without pausing to get dressed. The officers, a griffin and a wolf shifter, both jumped back in surprise at Ozen's growl.

"What?"

Both men zeroed in on Ozen's mouth, no doubt still covered in blood. The wolf shifter reached for his weapon, but before he could touch it and piss Ozen off any further, the griffin stopped him with a hand raised.

"Hold on. You wouldn't be in the middle of a mating, would you?"

"That's correct," Ozen snapped. He had no patience right now and wanted nothing more than to climb back into bed with his Avery. The lights flickered with his annoyance. He'd been starving before they started, but truly being with his mate for the first time left him full of energy and magic and beyond satisfied. It also made him dangerous, and the griffin recognized that.

He cleared his throat, wincing when Ozen snarled when his gaze shifted in Avery's direction. They wouldn't be able to see Avery from here, but mated pairs were notoriously possessive, and he didn't want either man looking at his mate.

"Are they awake?" the griffin asked carefully.

Ozen dipped his chin once, still glaring at the pair.

The griffin raised his voice, his eyes locked on Ozen even as he called out into the apartment. "Uh, sorry to interrupt. We got a few phone calls. Your neighbors were worried you were being hurt. If I could just get you to confirm that you are in fact mating and not in any danger, we can be out of your hair."

A shuffling sound alerted Ozen that Avery was moving, though he didn't look away from the two at the door, not while his instincts were telling him they were a threat to his mate. He waited for Avery to approach, wrapped in a sheet and blushing dark red, his own mouth smeared with blood.

"Uh, yes. We were, um... mating. Sorry. I didn't realize—"

The griffin shook his head, cutting him off. "No need to apologize. Extenuating circumstances and all that. You two have a pleasant night."

Ozen didn't wait for them to leave before he slammed the door. He turned, pulling Avery into his arms, and listened to the officers bickering as they walked away.

"What the hell? We're just going to leave? You're not even going to cite them for noise violations?"

"You're young, kid. A good rule of thumb I've learned over the years is that you never ever interrupt a mating unless you want to die. Let's go. The neighbors will understand once we explain it to 'em."

Ozen didn't really care what the neighbors said or thought. And it didn't really matter. After tonight, Avery would come home with him. His wards also included sound proofing. Avery could be as loud as he wanted once they were home. Then it would be Ozen's goal to make his mate scream in pleasure every night.

CHAPTER THIRTY-SEVEN

Rule Number 14- A feeder should smartly separate what must be done well now and what can be improved later.

Avery was torn between embarrassment and amusement. He completely forgot about things like neighbors once he and Ozen started, and he would probably never stop blushing whenever he bumped into them in the hall. It was a little funny to see the stunned faces of the police staring at his very naked mate blocking the doorway, though. The griffin seemed like he understood, but the other officer's eyes were as wide as dinner plates, and he seemed incredulous when his partner made him walk away.

Ozen's growls faded the longer Avery was cuddled against him. There were still dozens of things to discuss, and Avery wasn't overly familiar with mates in general, much less about mates of incubi. But luckily, they had the rest of the weekend to figure it out before they had to go back to work. For now, Avery was too tired to grill Ozen anymore. Leaning against him, Avery sighed and closed his eyes. He needed a nap.

When Ozen scooped him off his feet, Avery didn't protest, throwing his arms around Ozen's neck as he made his way back to the bed. They got comfortable, returning to the position they'd been in when their conversation started, but Avery didn't have to keep his distance anymore and pretend to be professional. He rolled into Ozen's chest, snuggling close.

Ozen chuckled, running his fingers through Avery's hair. "Tired, firefly?"

Avery hummed, melting against Ozen's warmth. "Haven't slept well this week. Too worried about you."

Ozen sighed, and Avery could hear the regret in his voice. "I'm sorry about that. I'll make it up to you. Get some sleep."

Avery wanted to, but something made him pause, and he reached up to grab Ozen's hand. "You won't... You won't leave, right? I... I really want you to stay."

Ozen's fingers laced with his and he kissed the back of Avery's hand, waiting until Avery looked up at him to answer.

"I won't go anywhere without you. I promise."

Relief flooded through him, and exhaustion quickly followed. He cuddled close, sighing happily when Ozen wrapped his arms tightly around him, and he was out like a light a minute later.

Ozen was still there when he woke up, lying on his back with Avery's head pillowed on his chest. His arms were still around Avery's shoulders, keeping him close. Avery never wanted to leave that spot. Unfortunately, his bladder had other ideas, and he eventually had to wriggle free to use the restroom. He took a second to brush his teeth and wash the blood off his face. He hadn't realized that would be part of the mating, but he didn't hate it. It wasn't like licking a paper cut; there was no copper taste to it. Avery made a note to ask Ozen why once he was awake.

His phone rang before he could climb back into bed, and he rolled his eyes when he saw Taron's name on the caller ID. He considered ignoring it, but knowing Taron, he'd keep calling until someone picked up. Sneaking into the kitchen, Avery kept his voice at a whisper when he answered.

"Hello?"

"Good morning, sunshine! How'd it go last night?"

Avery summoned every ounce of patience he possessed to deal with Taron's lack of boundaries. He was Ozen's friend and business partner. As Ozen's mate, Avery had to get along with the shapeshifter, even if he was slightly obnoxious and nosy.

"We're fine. Is there a reason you're calling so early?"

Taron snorted. "Early? It's almost lunch time. Don't tell me you're just waking up now. How late were you two going at it?"

Frowning, he pulled the phone away from his ear to look at the clock. Sure enough, it was after eleven. He didn't remember the last time he'd slept that late. Even on weekends, he got up early so he could have as much time to work on his book as he could muster.

"Hello? Avery? You didn't fall asleep, did you?"

Putting the phone back to his ear, he replied, "No. Just checking the time. I didn't realize it was this late. Is there a reason that you're calling other than to bug me?"

Taron chuckled, but his tone turned serious as he explained, "I know I can be a bit much, but Ozen has been my friend for eons. I care about him, and I was worried when he disappeared the way he did. He's okay, right?"

The sincerity in Taron's voice made Avery smile. "Yeah. He's okay. He's still asleep."

"Seriously? Damn, you wore him out. And... he fed? You don't need to tell me details. I just want to make sure he's not punishing himself."

"He fed," Avery assured him. "I'll have him call you once he gets up. Will that help?"

"Nah, he doesn't have to do that. I trust you. Thank you, Avery, for taking care of him. I was truly worried before he found you."

Warm arms wrapped around Avery's waist and he leaned into Ozen's embrace. "I'm glad I found him, too. Enjoy the rest of your weekend."

Ozen nuzzled his neck, pressing a gentle kiss on the bite mark from last night. It made Avery shiver, and he felt torn between going back to bed and ordering food. Ozen's friends forced him to eat while Ozen was gone, but after last night, he felt starved. His stomach rumbling decided for him. Ozen straightened, turning Avery to face him.

"Would you prefer breakfast here, or would you like to go out?"

"It's almost noon," Avery pointed out with a smirk.

"Brunch, then," Ozen amended with a smile. He looked better than he had the day before. He didn't look pale and exhausted anymore, and his expression was relaxed. He was also not shy about walking around naked. Avery had at least pulled on some briefs. Feeling every inch of Ozen's flawless skin pressed against him sealed the deal for him.

"Let's order in. That way, when we're done eating brunch, you can eat me."

Ozen's grin turned wicked, and he yanked Avery off his feet, palming his ass as Avery wrapped his legs around Ozen's hips.

"I can agree to that."

———

Avery was drifting in and out when Ozen got out of bed. They'd had an amazing brunch, followed by a delicious frot in the shower and cuddles in bed afterward. Avery was feeling lazy and planned on taking a short nap when Ozen pulled away. Fear seized in his chest and he sat up in a rush, looking around wildly. Ozen froze by the foot of the bed, surprise and confusion written on his face.

"Avery? What's wrong?"

It was hard to hear him over the sound of his heartbeat pounding in his ears. Ozen sat on the edge of the bed, running soothing fingers through Avery's hair until he settled enough to speak.

"I... I thought..." Avery grimaced. Now that he wasn't in the middle of panic, he realized how ridiculous he sounded when he admitted, "I thought last night was a dream and you would leave again."

Ozen didn't seem to judge him or get annoyed with his clinginess. He pulled Avery into his lap and surrounded him with his warmth, whispering reassurances in his ear.

"I know it's hard to trust me after everything that happened, but I promise I'm not going anywhere. I was just going to get a glass of water."

"Oh." Now he felt a little stupid. There was no reason to panic, and he didn't want to be the kind of guy who wouldn't let his boyfriend go anywhere without knowing where he was going first. That was creepy.

Ozen pressed a kiss to his forehead, and he didn't seem to be in any rush to leave. He made sure Avery was calm and comforted before getting up to get them both a drink. When he sat back down, Avery cuddled close, frowning at the glass in his hand.

"Will it always be this way? The idea of you leaving scares me."

Ozen hummed, tipping his head thoughtfully. "If my grandfather is correct, the desperation will fade, but the urge to be around each other will only get worse. Since he was the one who told me what you were to me, I'm inclined to believe him."

Avery's mouth fell open. "Worse? I– Wha– How will we function?"

Ozen chuckled, lifting a shoulder with way too much nonchalance. "Together, I suppose." He must've noticed the worry on Avery's face, because he set their drinks down on the floor and took Avery's hands, kissing the backs of them. "I'm not one hundred percent certain what will happen because I've never had a mate before. Neither has my father. My grandfather has two, but he travels a lot, and I hadn't heard from him in a long while, so I've never met them before. He promised we could meet them and that he'd be there to answer any questions we had. I'm sure we'll figure it out. We're in no rush, firefly. After last night, your life span now matches mine. And by incubi's standards, I'm still quite young."

Avery pursed his lips, wondering if it was considered rude to ask how old he was. Again, Ozen seemed to pick up on that and answered without him asking.

"I've lost track of the exact years, but I'm well over two thousand now. My father, Korath, will enter his fourth millenia soon, and my grandfather is well into his sixth. We've got plenty of time to figure everything out."

Avery could only gape at him. He knew supernaturals lived longer lives than humans. You had to be incredibly healthy to even make it to one hundred as a human. But living over six thousand years? The concept was dizzying.

Still... It made him feel better to know he had so much time with Ozen. If he was going to spend thousands of years on this earth, he'd rather do it with the man beside him. Ozen was right. They'd figure it out. Together.

CHAPTER THIRTY-EIGHT

Convincing Avery to move in with him was a lot less harrowing than Ozen expected. Avery didn't have a strong attachment to his apartment, and with the anxiety he was having at the thought of being away from Ozen, he didn't argue about the idea of living together. Ozen had a sneaking suspicion the library had a small part to do with Avery's easy acceptance. Avery looked giddy when Ozen said there were open shelves for him to add his own books to the collection.

He thought moving in together would be the hard part. As it turned out, work was the more troublesome matter. Ozen could tell it made Avery just as uncomfortable as Ozen to be apart from one another, but Avery refused to give up his job as a temp. His working contract as Ozen's feeder was void now that they were mated, and Avery wasn't the type to be a kept man. He wanted to work. So despite it still being early in their mating, he accepted when Brennus told him IT needed an assistant to keep track of things while they updated the company systems. It meant he was all the way down on the third floor, and Ozen wasn't pleased about that. His foul mood was felt throughout the entire office, and Collette was careful to keep his meetings to a minimum to spare people from his wrath.

Ozen was distracted for most of the morning, his eyes constantly flicking to the clock on his computer screen. Avery told him he'd come upstairs to eat lunch with him, but time moved too damn slowly. No matter how much effort Ozen put in trying to distract himself with work, he'd end up looking at the clock again and only minutes would have passed.

His desk phone rang, and his voice was too terse when he answered. "Hawksley."

"So the rumors are true, then."

Taron's voice made Ozen roll his eyes. "What rumors?"

"The rumors that the CEO is seething, and that people needed to avoid him. What's going on? I thought you'd be in a better mood now that you're mated."

Ozen made an irritated sound and tossed his pen onto his desk, giving up the false pretense of getting any work done. "I'd be in a better mood if he wasn't so far away from me."

"What do you mean? Where is he?"

"He's helping IT with their systems upgrade. He doesn't want to be a kept man, so he insists that he keep working, despite the fact that I can tell it's bothering him just as much as it bothers me to be separated."

Taron sighed. "He is a stubborn one. I spent half the week with him. Getting him to relax was a colossal pain in the ass, I hope you know."

"Yes, I've been meaning to ask about that. What were you doing at Avery's apartment the other night?"

Taron snickered, obviously amused at Ozen's jealousy. Ozen trusted his friends implicitly, but when it came to Avery, he was turning out to be a possessive asshole. One of the movers smiled at Avery when packing up his things, and Ozen very nearly lost his temper.

"You told me he wouldn't relax on his own. I was making sure he did. I didn't want you worrying about him while you pulled your head out of your ass."

Ozen's face flattened. If Taron were around, he'd consider hurting him. Which was probably why Taron was smart enough to call this time instead of visiting Ozen's office like he normally did.

"Considering what Avery believes is relaxing, it's a good thing I hung around."

"What do you mean?" Ozen demanded.

"You probably don't remember because you were too busy glaring at me, but I told you about Avery's writing, right? He's really good. The book isn't finished yet, but I read the whole thing in one sitting. It was that good, and you know how hard it is to get me to focus and sit still. He's basically working three jobs—temp, feeder, and writer. You should ask him about it. And don't leave him alone to relax, because he's just going to work on his book if he's not being watched. It's no wonder you're mated to him. You're both workaholics."

Ozen vaguely remembered Taron mentioning Avery's writing, but he had been a little distracted at the time. If he was as good as Taron suggested, then it might be worth talking to Avery about. As a writer, he could work anywhere. Namely, as close to Ozen as possible. He just had to convince Avery to make his hobby his full-time job.

———

The day moved at a crawl, but lunch finally came around, and Avery showed up right when he said he would. He looked... strained, and his smile was forced. He didn't relax until he was cuddled in Ozen's arms. Ozen felt the tension of being separated from his mate slowly fade the longer he held Avery close.

"Missed you," Avery murmured.

Ozen wanted to point out that he didn't have to miss him if Avery would just come upstairs, but that wouldn't help matters. He and Taron had made a plan to get Avery to switch careers, and if Ozen wanted him to be open to the idea, he had to be patient.

"I missed you too, firefly. Are you hungry?"

Avery hummed, burying his face against Ozen's chest. Now that he was no longer hindered by the contract, Avery was incredibly cuddly. Ozen loved the easy affection, and he would never complain about having his mate close to him. Lifting Avery's face, Ozen pressed a soft kiss to his lips. He'd denied himself the pleasure of kissing for years, and he couldn't resist kissing his mate any chance he got.

Avery had a dreamy smile when Ozen pulled away, and his tension was gone. Ozen almost considered dragging him into the bedroom, but his need to feed him overrode the desire to fuck him. He'd indulge in that in their bed tonight.

"What are you hungry for?"

Avery thought about it, his head tipped slightly. "Something light, I think. You kept me up late last night, and I don't want to eat something heavy and need a nap to get through the day."

Ozen couldn't help the smug smile on his face. He didn't feel an ounce of guilt about that. He couldn't resist when Avery was next to him all night. The first time it was because he was hungry. The other three times were just because he enjoyed making Avery scream in pleasure. Ozen couldn't get enough.

Avery rolled his eyes when he noticed the look on his face. "Don't look so smug. You came just as many times as I did."

Ozen chuckled, stealing a quick kiss before making a few suggestions. They decided on a restaurant close by that had amazing wraps, light but still filling and very healthy. They sat close, enjoying each other's company as they ate, and Ozen wondered for the hundredth time how he got so lucky.

He was paying for their meal when his phone rang. He handed the waiter his card as he put his phone to his ear, lacing his fingers with Avery's as they waited for the receipt.

"Hawksley."

"I'm sorry to interrupt your lunch, Mr. Hawksley," Collette ground out. "I can't get them to leave."

He sat up straighter, listening intently to the other end of the line. "Who?"

"Calvin and his lawyer are here to see you. They're insisting you meet with them."

"Tell them I'll be right there. Are you in any danger?"

Collette scoffed at his concern. "I'm fine, sir. I'll let them know you're on your way."

When he hung up, Avery shot him a worried look, tipping his head. "What's wrong?"

"Apparently, instead of waiting for court, Calvin and his lawyer have decided to confront me directly. Do me a favor and tell the waiter we're in a hurry. I need to call Maverick and tell him to meet us upstairs."

Avery was quick to action, popping out of his seat and scurrying away to find the waiter. Ozen appreciated the fact that he never had to ask

Avery twice to assist him. He set aside his adoration for his mate for now, dialing Maverick as he tossed his napkin onto the table and stood.

"Van Buren."

"Maverick. There's a little weasel in my office, causing trouble. Do me a favor and make sure he doesn't leave."

A low growl filled the line, and Ozen could almost hear the dragon itching to play. Legally speaking, if they irritated a dragon, it wasn't held against him if he killed them, as long as they got a fair shot at running away first. Dragons were temperamental and the government was firmly in the belief that if you were stupid enough to pull their tails, you deserved to face the consequences.

"I'm on my way up now. How far out are you?"

"Maybe ten minutes. We walked here."

"Good."

Ozen fought back a grin. He got the feeling that Maverick was hoping they poked the dragon. He was tired of dealing with them.

Avery appeared at his side again, card in hand, and he took Ozen's hand when he offered it.

"We're on our way."

Ozen hung up, and they made a beeline for the door. A part of him wanted to leave them to face the dragon alone, but he also wanted to confront the little shit himself. Calvin had avoided being face to face with Ozen since his attempt to kill him. He wanted to see what kind of idiocy would make him brave enough to come to Ozen's office directly.

"Do we need to call the police?" Avery asked, hustling to keep up with Ozen's long strides. He never complained, but Ozen slowed just a little so Avery could more easily keep up.

"Not yet. It wouldn't hurt for you to record the interaction, though."

"On it," Avery said with a sharp nod. He had his phone out, and the camera pulled up before they even entered the building. They got a few curious looks as he stormed past the turnstiles. One of the security guys opened the gate at the end for him and Avery, so they skipped the lines in front of the turnstiles entirely. Perks of owning the company.

The wait for the elevator to his floor was short, and Avery bounced on his toes the entire way up, watching the numbers rise on the screen above them. It was only when they stepped into the office that Avery hesitated.

His grip on Ozen's hand tightened and fear tinged the air. The reaction set Ozen off and he glowered at the chimera, who was glaring at his mate.

"Finally," Calvin snapped. "What? Did you crawl here?"

"Watch it," Maverick warned him with a growl.

"Or what? You can't do anything to me! I've got proof that he fired me to hide the fact that he broke the contract first!"

Ozen resisted the urge to snort. This ought to be good.

He wanted to hear what the idiot had to say, but first, he had to settle Avery. He strode around the group, keeping Avery against his side and as far from the chimera as possible. Once they were on the other side of his desk, Avery relaxed a little. Ozen didn't release his hold on him, but he gave his attention to the men across from him, gesturing for them to go ahead and prove it.

"My client brought to my attention that you fed from another before the contract was formally terminated." He shot a pointed look at Avery. "And you're still using that feeder now. We have reason to believe you set my client up so that you could tarnish his reputation and choose a new feeder."

Ozen sighed heavily. "There are two flaws with your accusation. The first being the idea that I would need an out to find a new feeder. It's written in the contract that if we lacked compatibility, we'd go our separate ways. Considering the tantrum your client threw merely because I wouldn't make my assistant cater to him, our compatibility was immediately called into question. I was patient and gave Calvin a chance to cool off before participating in a feeding, but his refusal to show up when called voided the contract automatically. Which negates your second point, I believe. Once he voided the contract, I was free to feed from whoever I liked."

The chimera frowned, ripping open the file in his hand to check the contract. While it would have been difficult for Ozen to break the contract without paying through the nose, he wasn't completely locked into it. There were some outs, including incompatibility. Ozen usually only used that when he and a feeder couldn't get comfortable enough with one another, but it still fit here. Maverick pointed that out to him during their first meeting after Calvin's lawsuit was brought to their attention.

"That clause is too vague. It's open to interpretation," the chimera complained.

"Feel free to put it in front of a judge and ask for their interpretation of the matter, then," Ozen offered. He knew they wouldn't. They wouldn't be here if they thought they actually had a decent case. They were here to try and force a settlement. They were targeting the wrong incubus for that.

CHAPTER THIRTY-NINE

Rule Number 10 - A client/feeder relationship should be fair on both sides. If you feel you are being taken advantage of, legal action should be taken.

"What about emotional damage?" Calvin shot out. "You refused to touch me for days, and barely even looked at me. It was an attack on my self esteem!"

That made Avery snort, and he rolled his lips between his teeth to hide his smile. He noticed Ozen fighting back a smile as well, but he was looking at Avery, so that might've been a response to Avery's reaction as opposed to the stupidity coming out of Calvin's mouth.

"Your emotional state was not part of the contract," Mr. Van Buren interjected. "It's not my client's job to cater to your whims. He feeds when he needs it, you offer yourself to provide for him, and you go about your day. It's not a relationship where he was to ensure your self esteem is intact."

From the look on Walter's face, he'd already covered that with his client, and he didn't appreciate him bringing it up in front of the group. Still, Calvin wouldn't let it go, pointing an accusing finger at Avery.

"He caters to *him*! Why would I be treated any differently?"

"He's my mate," Ozen answered evenly. It still thrilled Avery every time he said it, and he had to fight to keep his face neutral and not grin like an idiot. Avery got the feeling it wouldn't help the situation.

Calvin's mouth fell open, and Walter made a choking sound. Avery didn't understand their reaction, but Maverick didn't look bothered that Ozen had brought it up. If anything, he looked smug.

"W-Well, then there is definitely motive for Mr. Hawksley to treat my client unfairly to get him to leave so that Mr. Hawksley could be with his mate," Walter said in an attempt to get the situation back under his control. "It brings forward the question of when Mr. Hawksley knew that information and if he signed the contract with malicious intent while knowing his mate was available."

Avery couldn't help making a face. "You really think Ozen knew I was his mate and chose to sign a contract with someone else anyway? Do you know anything about mates?"

"He has a point," Taron commented. He breezed into the room and joined the group, dropping onto the sofa with his feet on the coffee table. Completely relaxed despite the situation. "No one would see their mate and choose another. That's not physically possible."

"But he fed from his assistant before signing with me!" Calvin demanded.

That made Avery pause. That was true. Ozen did feed from Avery first, but neither one of them was aware of the connection for at least a month. It started off so slowly that they didn't notice until they were both so obsessed with each other that they couldn't ignore it anymore.

"That's not relevant," Mr. Van Buren argued. "Had my client known he'd met his mate, he wouldn't have signed the contract. We all know mating isn't instantaneous. And there would have been a payout if my client realized and needed to break the contract early. Your client was the one who voided the entire thing by choosing to not show up in an attempt to starve my client." Before either man could open their mouth to argue, Mr. Van Buren put up his hand to stop them. "I'm not interested in hearing more of this without a judge present. I'll be presenting a counterclaim to the judge for attempted murder. We'll see you in court."

Calvin visibly paled and Walter looked like he swallowed a lemon. "Now wait just a minute. You can't just–"

"Taron, please contact security and have these two removed for trespassing," Ozen demanded. The threat got Walter moving, and he grabbed Calvin by the arm to drag him along.

"We'll see you in court!" Calvin screamed on his way out. "I didn't do anything! You were the one who wouldn't touch me! I would've been the best you ever had! You'll rue the day—"

His voice cut off as the door to the office closed behind him. Avery ended the recording, sending it immediately to Ozen and Mr. Van Buren so he wouldn't forget.

"Well, that was fun. Did he seriously think he could come in here and intimidate you into giving in?" Taron asked, raising an eyebrow.

"Apparently," Ozen replied dryly. "You just had to come enjoy the show, didn't you?"

Taron scoffed, waving a hand dismissively. "You assume I came here to see you." He turned to face Avery with a scowl. "I've got a bone to pick with you."

Avery felt his spine stiffen. He wasn't sure what he could've done to upset the shapeshifter, but it made him nervous all the same. He didn't want Ozen's best friend to dislike him.

"W-What did I do?"

"You haven't finished that book! I'm going to die if I don't find out what happens. Seriously. Just keel over. The scene you stopped in was just cruel. He was about to fu—"

Avery squeaked, waving his hands wildly. "O-Okay! I know what you're referring to! I'm working on it! I just don't have a lot of free time!"

"Working on what?" Mr. Van Buren asked with a deep frown.

"His novel," Taron replied, still scowling at Avery. "It's amazing, but he hasn't finished it yet. I can't believe you sent that to me when it wasn't done."

Avery's jaw dropped. "I didn't! You stole it!"

"What kind of novel?"

Mr. Van Buren actually looked interested, and Avery felt his face flush dark red. It was bad enough that Taron read it. He didn't want to share it with Mr. Van Buren, too. It was too humiliating to consider.

"I didn't realize you were writing a novel. Can I read it?" Ozen asked curiously.

Avery took back his previous statement. This was worse. Having others read it wasn't nearly as bad as having Ozen do it. Avery may have used him as a reference when rewriting all the spicy scenes. It wouldn't take him long to figure it out. He covered his face with his hands, at a loss for what to say. He couldn't just tell him no. That would be mean. But he was too embarrassed to show him.

"Seriously, you need to read the sex scenes. They're so hot, even I was blushing," Taron commented.

When Avery whimpered, Ozen decided to spare him from further humiliation, tucking Avery against his side.

"Alright, enough teasing. Leave my mate alone. Maverick, do you need us to write a statement on what just occurred?"

"No. I got the video from Avery. It's plenty. I'll let you know when I have a court date."

"Good. Take Taron with you. He's caused enough trouble for one day."

"Hey, I resent that!" Taron complained, his voice fading as he was no doubt dragged away by Mr. Van Buren. Once the door shut behind them, the room went quiet again and Ozen turned Avery so he could hide his face against Ozen's chest.

"Do you not want me to read your novel?"

"No! Yes... No. I don't know!"

He chuckled, and Avery soaked in the noise. He was a lot more open and playful now that they were mated. Getting rid of the contract gave them both the freedom to be themselves around each other. Ozen didn't seem to mind Avery's constant need for physical touch, and Avery loved Ozen's teasing, even if it drove him nuts.

"After everything we've done together, I'm surprised you have anything to be embarrassed about."

"Not helping," Avery whined, gently thumping Ozen's chest. It only made him laugh again.

"How did you intend to publish it if you were this embarrassed?"

"I was going to use a pen name," Avery admitted. "It's easier to hide the fact that I'm human if I do."

Avery heard the frown in Ozen's voice when he asked, "Why would you need to hide that?"

Avery sighed, shifting back so he could look up at Ozen. "The amount of books written by humans published every year is less than one percent of the overall total. I figured if I didn't do things like book signings and published under a pen name, I'd have more of a shot to actually get my book out there. It doesn't matter, really. It's more of a hobby."

Ozen's fingers combing through his hair made him melt, and he rested his cheek against Ozen's chest again. He was quick to claim this as his spot, and Ozen never seemed to mind having him there.

"Do you enjoy writing?"

"Yes. I like creating new worlds and writing things I think people would enjoy. But it's mostly just for me. I never had high hopes it'd get me anywhere. I would probably never have the courage to send it out anyway. It's taken me years to get the book as far as I have."

It was a dream. Probably unattainable, but nice to think about. Avery wanted to try, but he put very little stock into the idea.

Ozen seemed to disagree with his approach, though. "If you enjoy it and you're as good as Taron says, then you should focus on that. You never know. You might just be one of those one percent who make it."

"Taron is being dramatic," Avery argued. "I'm not that good."

"Let me read it then. I'll give you my honest opinion. I won't sugar coat it for you. And if it's as good as he says, I want you to at least consider making it your main focus. The odds were against me and Taron when we started this business. We didn't let distractions get in our way, and look where we ended up. You can't say it will fail if you've never given it an honest try."

Avery wrapped his arms around Ozen's middle, hugging him tightly. It'd been a long time since he had support like that. He wasn't sure what to do with it. As embarrassing as it was to share it, Avery believed that Ozen would give his honest opinion. Maybe if he hated it, Avery could move on from the idea. No point wasting more time if it was an impossible dream.

"Fine. You can read it. But not while I'm in the same room."

"We live together, firefly," Ozen chuckled. "Are you suggesting I ignore my work to read yours?"

Avery's shoulders slumped. He'd forgotten about that. In his defense, he only moved in yesterday. It was still new.

"Fine... just don't tell me you're reading it."

"I'll save all comments for the end," Ozen assured him.

Great. That meant Avery would be on edge until Ozen finished.

"How fast do you read?"

CHAPTER FORTY

Avery was pacing. He'd been pacing for the past two days. He started when they got home and Ozen went to his office to read his book. Ozen had suggested he go to the library as a distraction, but it hadn't lasted very long. When Ozen took a break for dinner each night, Avery kept eyeing him for any clue on Ozen's opinion of the novel, but he had promised he wouldn't say anything until he was finished. Now, as it got closer to bedtime, Ozen wasn't sure Avery could take the suspense much longer.

It was distracting, but not distracting enough to pull Ozen out of the story. Avery was a talented writer, and he knew exactly when the story needed comedic relief and when it wasn't appropriate. Taron wasn't lying about the sex scenes either. Ozen spent thousands of years partaking in all kinds of sex, and still Avery's scenes left him hot under the collar. Masking his reaction to not give away his opinions on the novel was difficult, especially when sharing a bed with his mate. Sylix was right that Ozen no longer needed to feed daily now that they were fully mated, but he had to keep lying to Avery and saying he was hungry to have an excuse to maul him after reading a few of those scenes.

He finished what was available of the story and faced a heavy amount of disappointment that he didn't get to know the story's conclusion yet. He understood better why Taron was getting so demanding about it. Ozen was curious, too.

When he closed his laptop, Avery's pacing stalled, and he stared uneasily at him through the open door.

"Come here, firefly."

The combination of eagerness and anxiety made Avery's footsteps hurried. He didn't hesitate to round the desk, crawling into Ozen's lap when he opened his arms for him.

"You hate it, right? That's why you're cuddling me. To soften the blow. I knew it. Taron was just being nice. I—"

Ozen silenced him with a fierce kiss, pouring every ounce of sexual frustration into it until Avery was dazed enough to stall his panic. Only once he was certain Avery would listen did Ozen pull away.

"I loved it, firefly. You have true talent."

Avery sucked in a sharp breath, the dazed look vanishing in an instant as his gaze snapped to Ozen's. "Wait. Really?"

Ozen dipped his chin. "Really. It was intriguing. I found I didn't want to put it down. Taron didn't lie to you. You could make this your career."

Avery might not have fully trusted Taron not to lie to him, but he knew Ozen would tell him the truth. He would never lie to his mate, especially not with something as important as this. Ozen liked the idea of keeping Avery close by and having him work on his book instead of leaving for a temp job, but he wouldn't give Avery false hope if he thought his writing wasn't ready.

Avery still looked uncertain, but Ozen figured it'd take more than a single conversation to convince him. In the meantime, he had something more pressing to discuss. He ran his hand along Avery's thigh before gripping his ass.

"I've been lying to you."

Avery's smile fell, and he looked worried. "You didn't like it?"

"Not about that. I've been making excuses about needing to feed to get you into bed. Those scenes you wrote were... tantalizing."

A slow grin spread across Avery's face, making Ozen's cock swell. He did enjoy his mate's enthusiasm in the bedroom.

"Really? I tempted the great Ozen Hawksley? Did you recognize any of it?"

Ozen hummed, readjusting Avery in his lap until they were chest to chest with Avery straddling him. It brought their cocks together, teasing the both of them with seductive friction.

"A few scenes seemed familiar. You realize if you do make this your career, I can help you research those scenes beforehand."

Avery nibbled on his bottom lip, drawing Ozen's focus to his mouth. Those scenes explained the day in the office when Ozen had come back to Avery's desire soaking the air. He'd been working on his novel during his break. Ozen was beyond curious about which scene he'd been working on at the time.

"I didn't think of that," Avery murmured.

"Perhaps you need a demonstration, then. Should we recreate one of your scenes?"

Ozen felt Avery's cock twitch and desire filled the air. It made Ozen shudder, but he felt no need to feed from it. He wanted to enjoy the moment with his mate without distraction.

"Which one?"

"Well... we do have a desk right here..." Ozen suggested with a purr. Avery's grin was gone now, replaced with heated lust, his eyes locked on Ozen's mouth. The scene didn't start with kissing, but Ozen wasn't going to deny himself the pleasure of Avery's mouth.

Cupping the side of his neck, he drew Avery closer, nipping at his lip to demand entrance. Avery gave it with a gasp, moaning as he sank into the kiss. They started slow, savoring each other, but when Avery started to fidget and whine, Ozen decided to get on with his plan. He helped Avery stand, spinning him around to face the desk.

"Pants off and bend over."

When he'd first started reading that scene, he was surprised how similar it was to their own encounter, but it thrilled him to no end that Avery liked it enough to include it in his novel. He would recreate it over and over again if Avery asked him to. Avery trembled as he bent over the desk, spreading his legs a little to give Ozen room.

"The lead character doesn't finish until his lover is buried inside him. Do you think you can hold out?"

"No," Avery answered honestly. "But I'll do my best."

And Ozen would do his best to make him come before he lost the race with his desire to sink into his mate. They would see who could hold out the longest.

———

One of Avery's favorite things about living with Ozen was that he could be as loud as he wanted. Ozen explained the wards on the building, including the one that prevented people from eavesdropping. Avery didn't think it was possible to stay quiet while Ozen was torturing him like this.

That wicked tongue was twisting inside him, paying special attention to his prostate. Avery was holding on to his release by a thread, babbling nonsense as he clutched the edge of the desk. He wanted so badly to hold out until Ozen was inside him, but it was almost impossible to stop the orgasm that was barreling down on him like a freight train.

"Please! Please! Ozen!"

Ozen ripped himself away without warning, leaving Avery trembling against the desk. He choked on a sob, his cock throbbing and dripping precum all over the floor. He heard Ozen moving, and he took a few precious seconds of reprieve to draw in a deep breath. He was considering rewriting this scene in his book. There was no way his character could hold out that long without losing his mind. Avery felt close to losing his, especially when Ozen's fingers dipped inside him, making sure he was stretched and ready.

"Are you ready for me, firefly?"

"Yes. Please," Avery begged. He needed relief.

Ozen didn't make him wait, and the familiar stretch made Avery's toes curl. He moaned, rocking his hips when Ozen wouldn't move fast enough. It made Ozen growl, and he punished Avery with a rougher thrust that had stars bursting behind his eyes.

"A-Again! Please!"

Ozen didn't reply, aside from giving Avery what he asked for. He drove into Avery's ass, burying his length entirely, barely pausing to allow him to adjust before pulling out to the tip and slamming back in. Avery cried out, staring blindly ahead as bolts of pleasure slammed into him with every thrust.

"You're perfect. My firefly. My mate. There's nothing better than being inside you. I– Ah!"

Avery clenched in response to Ozen's words, clamping down on Ozen's cock. It made his hips stutter and Ozen's fingers dug into the skin of his ass, his growl of pleasure making the hair stand up on the back of Avery's neck. Avery wasn't sure how long he would last, but the rougher Ozen got, the louder he got, and Ozen seemed determined to get him to shatter the windows.

"Ozen!"

Ozen's voice came out in a husky growl, and goosebumps spread along Avery's neck. "That's it, firefly. Come for me. Let me hear how much you like it."

"I love it. I love you! I–" Avery sucked in a sharp breath when Ozen's fangs sank into his neck, time freezing for a moment as a massive tidal wave of pleasure tore through Avery's system. He wailed, his back arching from the force of his release, and he took Ozen right along with him. The incubus released his neck to roar his pleasure, thrusting twice more before he dropped back into his chair, dragging Avery with him.

They were covered in sweat, both fighting for breath, with Ozen's cock still inside him. Avery was always reluctant to end the contact, and Ozen never rushed. They savored the closeness. Sometimes it led to another round, but this time Avery was too wiped out.

"That was... amazing."

"Good enough for your book?" Ozen queried with a smirk.

Avery dropped his head back against Ozen's shoulder and shook it once, his breathing still heavy like he'd run a marathon. "I'm going to have to rewrite it. It's so much better than I described."

Ozen chuckled, wrapping his arms tighter around Avery's body. Avery craved this whenever they were intimate. He needed Ozen to keep him together when it felt like he came so hard that he exploded into a million tiny pieces. He told Ozen how out of sorts he felt when he'd left right after that intense middle of the night visit. Ozen apologized profusely and since then refused to let Avery go until he was sure Avery felt okay again.

"I know you don't have much faith in the idea, but I think you should give your writing a real chance," Ozen murmured. "You can always go back to temping if it doesn't work out, but unless you give it your all, you'll never truly know if it could be a success."

"Do you really think I could do it?" Avery asked, his voice trembling with barely contained hope. He'd wanted to publish his book for so long, but he dragged his feet on it. He knew how the book would end, but he avoided actually writing the ending because then he'd have no more excuses for not trying to publish it. If he took extra jobs and worked until he was too tired to function, then he could pretend he didn't have the time to finish it and keep lying to himself that he'd do it one day.

"I do, firefly. You have a way with words. I want you to achieve your dreams."

"How much of you is saying that so I'll be with you throughout the day?" It was as much a deflection as it was a tease, but Ozen didn't let him get away with changing the subject.

"I do want you close. It's difficult for me when you aren't by my side. But if your dream was to continue temping, I wouldn't stand in your way. I want you to do what makes you happy, and I think writing truly makes you happy."

It did. It was Avery's favorite time of day when he was working on his writing. At least... It was before he met Ozen. And being apart for work wasn't easy on him, either. He felt anxious when they were apart for too long.

"I'm scared..." Avery admitted.

"You have nothing to be afraid of. I'll be with you every step of the way. Always."

Trusting Ozen had been the smartest decision Avery had ever made. He wouldn't start doubting him now.

EPILOGUE

"I think I'm going to throw up."

Taron snorted, pointing in the opposite direction. "Do me a favor and face that way when you do. I just got this suit dry cleaned."

Dorian smacked him upside the head while offering Avery a small trash can. "Ignore him. You'll be alright. Just breathe."

Once Avery dedicated his full attention to his book, it only took a week to finally finish it. It might've been sooner if Taron wasn't harassing him every day to get it done. He was trying to help, but in the most distracting way possible. Ozen's friend Dorian introduced him to a publisher once he finished, and things took off like a rocket. Avery hadn't actually thought he'd ever publish, but not only did he sign a deal with the phoenix publisher, he was scheduled for an entire series. Apparently, supernaturals liked smutty office romance.

Which was how he ended up here—backstage at a writer's conference, where he was going to do an interview in front of a huge audience in less than half an hour. His stomach tightened uncomfortably, and saliva filled his mouth. He really was going to throw up.

"W-Where's Ozen?"

"He'll be here soon. Court took longer than expected. He said he left twenty minutes ago," Dorian reassured him.

Calvin went ahead with his baseless lawsuit and it was thrown out almost immediately. It was the attempted murder charge that was taking so long to process. Apparently, this wasn't the first time Calvin tried something like this. Usually, it ended with an incubus feeding from someone else to survive and Calvin suing them for breach of contract. Maverick mentioned something about laws changing because of this kind of precedent. Ozen and several of Calvin's other victims wanted to be there during his sentencing, which meant Ozen was busy when Avery needed him most. Avery couldn't be mad about it, he wanted Ozen to get justice, but doing this without his person was unfathomable.

"Mr. Whitman? Five minutes," his agent's assistant informed him. Because he had an agent now. Ozen was also trying to talk him into an assistant of his own to keep him on track with his writing schedule and marketing and everything else an author needed to do. Apparently, it wasn't as simple as writing the book and giving it to someone else to sell.

Avery shot a panicked look at Dorian. He couldn't do this without Ozen.

"Deep breaths. You can do this."

"Want me to go out there with you?" Taron offered. "I am your biggest fan, after all. I feel like that should be acknowledged."

Avery's laugh was strangled and his hands shook as Dorian handed him a bottle of water. If Ozen was here, he could use his magic to settle him. Stupid Calvin ruining lives and making him late.

When his chin trembled, Taron finally got serious. He rolled off the couch and stood, putting his hands on Avery's shoulders and leveling him with a look. "You can do this. Ozen says you're the greatest assistant he's ever had. Just imagine you're doing this for someone else. Ozen asked you to do this because he's too busy, or something like that. It's just another work task. Got it?"

Avery nodded, latching onto the idea. If it was for Ozen, he could do it. He made Ozen promise that if Collette was ever out sick or had to go away for her vacation, he'd only let Avery step in to help him. If Avery focused, he could pretend she was out of the office and Ozen asked him to do this interview because he was busy. It would definitely work. Maybe.

"Alright, Avery. Let's get this thing started," Winnie, Avery's agent, flut-

tered into the room. Avery almost never saw her feet on the ground. She
was always flitting around, talking a mile a minute.

Avery looked around helplessly, but Ozen didn't appear out of thin air.
Dorian and Taron both gripped his shoulders supportively, walking him
towards the side of the stage. Avery could hear the murmur of the crowd.
He suddenly felt dizzy, and sweat gathered at his temples.

"You can do this. We'll be right in front. If you feel panicked, just look
at us," Dorian encouraged.

They couldn't stay and were quickly ushered to their seats when the
introductions started. Avery swallowed heavily, staring at the place he'd be
sitting in a few moments, talking in front of a crowd. His vision swam, and
he took a step back. He couldn't do this. It was too much.

Right as he was about to back out, heat filled his chest, warming him
from the inside out. Avery sucked in a sharp breath, blinking rapidly as his
gaze darted around. He knew that feeling. Only Ozen could do that. It was
one of the things his grandfather taught them over their many lunch dates.
They got to meet his mates, and all three of them taught Ozen and Avery
the tricks they'd learned over the years to better support each other. Ozen
was sending him comfort and love through their bond, soothing Avery's
frayed nerves.

"... And now, we'll introduce you to our best-selling romance author,
whose debut novel sold over a million copies in the first week. Please
welcome the author of 'The Incubus's Assistant,' Avery Whitman!"

Another pulse of support got his feet moving, and he stepped out
onto the stage, forcing a smile as he shook the host's hand. He wanted
to grimace, he knew his palms were sweaty, but the host didn't say a
word, smiling brightly as they sat in the cushioned chair across
from him.

Avery's eyes darted around the room for a brief second, and when they
caught on the most important person in his life, he let out a shaky breath.
Ozen stood in the middle of the aisle, smiling supportively, his hand on his
chest over his heart, sending waves of support and love Avery's way. Just
seeing him helped, and Avery's smile lost some of its tension. He gave his
attention back to the host and felt himself relax.

Ozen was here. He believed in Avery, and his support was unwavering.
Avery thought once that them getting together was impossible. Then he

thought finding a publisher would never happen. It all came true. With his mate by his side, Avery could accomplish anything.

————

"So, Avery. Where do you get your inspiration for your writing?"

There he goes. Ozen watched Avery's shoulders come down. His spine straightened and his smile was more genuine. Ozen knew he was scared; he felt it the entire way over here. It killed him that he couldn't be here sooner, but Avery was stronger than he believed himself to be. Ozen knew he could do it. He just needed a little support.

Taron waved him over and Ozen took his seat in the front row where Avery could see him easily. Pride filled his chest as he watched his mate answer questions and banter with the host. The crowd unnerved him, but Ozen coached him before they left that morning. He only had to focus on the host and the front row where Ozen sat. No one else existed. Avery begged him to come on stage with him, but this was Avery's accomplishment, not Ozen's. He needed to do this on his own.

As Avery regaled the host and the crowd about his work as a temp and the many office romance stories he'd heard over the years, Ozen thought back to the first time Avery showed up in his office. Stubborn pride warred with nerves, but he pushed through and forced Ozen to give him a chance. He hadn't expected that chance to end up with him laying across Ozen's desk, but he met even that challenge with avid enthusiasm. He'd stunned Ozen, even then, with how brilliantly determined he was to do his job well. That reflected in his writing as well. He refused to send it to a publisher until he was certain it was done to the best of his ability. He met all life's challenges with the same determination.

"And what about those intimate scenes? I'll admit some of those scenes made me blush. Was there someone who inspired those?"

Avery's gaze flicked to him for half a second, not long enough for anyone to catch on, but long enough for Ozen to notice. He fought off a grin and Avery's face flushed dark red as he replied, "I, uh... may have someone who fits the bill."

The host wheedled him for more, but Avery gave nothing away. He preferred to keep their private life private, for which Ozen was very appreciative. He didn't hide his relationship, and most people knew who they were to each other, but Avery didn't want to share any details. People could come to their own conclusions on Ozen's participation in Avery's intimate writing.

The host moved on eventually, asking about the next books in the series and the struggles Avery had as a human author. Avery was very honest about how privileged he was to have connections to his publisher, and he knew it wouldn't have been that easy if he hadn't had help. Avery never pretended to be anyone but himself, and a lot of his fans appreciated that. They liked his honesty, and when the host allowed questions from the crowd, he got a lot of praise for being so approachable compared to some authors.

The interview finally ended with a roaring round of applause. The host mentioned a book signing table that was being set up down the hall, and people were already headed that way to get in line. Avery's day wasn't quite done, but the hard part was over. Ozen had no intention of sitting on the sidelines while Avery signed books. He'd be right next to him to make sure he felt safe and loved.

The host led Avery off stage, and Ozen followed Taron's directions to meet him backstage. His mate was sipping water, listening to the host praise him for his bravery, when Ozen approached.

"Ozen!"

Avery nearly dropped his water in his haste to get to him, and Ozen wrapped himself around Avery's smaller frame the second he was close enough.

"I'm so proud of you, firefly."

Avery hugged him tightly for a second before thumping him on the chest. "You're late!"

He barked out a laugh, gripping Avery's wrist to protect himself from any further abuse. He knew Avery wasn't truly angry with him. He would be able to feel that through their bond. Avery was just teasing.

"I'm sorry, love. I got caught in traffic. I got here in time, though."

"In time for the interview, maybe. You missed his freak out before-hand," Taron drawled as he sidled up to them. He shot a wink to the host, who flushed in response, and narrowly avoided a swat from Maverick.

"Ignore him. You did great. When is the next book coming out?"

Maverick was one of Avery's more surprising fans. No one, not even Ozen, thought the gruff dragon shifter would be into smutty office romance. He probably wouldn't have admitted he enjoyed it if he hadn't been caught by Avery when he was delivering a file for Ozen. Avery had been delighted, and Maverick begrudgingly admitted he found the story addictive. Since Avery was willing to share little details about the characters with him, he stopped pretending he wasn't interested and they'd become fast friends.

Avery laughed, shaking his head. "I already told you. Next year."

"Okay, but when do we get to read it?" Taron wheedled.

Apparently, Taron was still listening. He said since he was Avery's first fan, he deserved special privileges, like being the first to read the next installment.

Ozen rolled his eyes. "Leave him be. Let him enjoy his success."

Avery cuddled closer, and with a final glare from Ozen, the group dispersed, finally giving them a minute alone.

"Did I mention how proud I am of you?"

"You might've," Avery said with a chuckle. "Did you read the dedication?"

Ozen's brows drew together. "No. I read the version you emailed me. Why? What does it say?"

Avery waved a hand dismissively. "You can read it later. Come on. We need to get to the table to start signing books, or my agent will have a hairy fit."

Curiosity drove Ozen forward, but Avery wouldn't let him check his phone, and when people brought their books up for him to sign, none of them opened them to the dedication page. He'd have to figure it out later.

That was the way things worked with them, though. His mate was full of surprises. From showing up when Ozen needed him most to catching on to Ozen's reactions to being called sir and running with it, he was constantly stunning Ozen speechless. Ozen knew without a shadow of a doubt, it would always be that way with Avery. And he looked forward to every surprise headed his way.

DEDICATION

Rule # 1: Never fall in love with your incubus.
   (Unless he's really, really perfect for you)

The End

COMING SOON

The Dragon's Aide

"Isaac! Your phone is ringing!"

Isaac jumped, jerking the eyeliner brush in his surprise. It left a line on his cheek, which was more than a little frustrating. He didn't overindulge in makeup, but what he did wear, he wore perfectly, if he did say so himself. And it bothered him to no end that it was messed up. He sighed, wetting a tissue in the sink to wipe it off. Whoever was calling could wait. If he left it to sit, the liquid eyeliner would dry, and he'd have more difficulty getting it off later. He was just fixing his foundation when his roommate popped her head into the bathroom.

"Hey! Did you hear me?"

"Who is it?"

She shrugged unhelpfully. "I didn't look. Do you have work today?"

Pursing his lips, he thought about his schedule. "No. They didn't need me this week. Can you answer that? It could be my boss."

Maeve disappeared from sight to answer Isaac's phone without complaint. He heard her murmuring from the other room, but as a mage, he didn't have heightened senses like shifters did and couldn't hear her without a spell. He quickly finished up his makeup, rinsing his hands before he scurried to meet her. They nearly collided in the hallway, and she thrust his phone out with a laugh when they both jumped.

"It's your boss."

"Oh, thanks." He quickly put the phone to his ear, keeping his voice upbeat. "Good morning, Morana."

"Hello, Isaac. Is this a bad time?"

"Of course not," he reassured her. "I was just getting ready for the day. How can I help?"

Her sigh was long suffering, and it was more than obvious that this wasn't the first phone call she'd made that day. There were a few people at the temp company he'd worked at the past few months that were unreliable, and Morana was constantly dealing with their screw ups.

"I have a job for you, if you're interested. It's a legal assistant position, so you'll get some hands-on experience for your degree."

A bright smile lit up Isaac's face. "Absolutely. I'll take it."

"I was hoping you'd say that. I asked Charlotte to go since she has more experience, but she is taking another leave of absence for her mental health." There was a level of irritation in her tone. Not that Morana didn't care about her workers' mental health, but Charlotte was flaky at the best of times and it was inconvenient just how often she turned down jobs. She only showed up often enough to have money for rent before she started calling out again. Isaac didn't know why Morana put up with her, but he'd only been working there for a few months, hired as part of a large influx of newbies that summer. The more experienced personnel were obviously important for big jobs, but only if they deigned to show up.

"Happy to help. When do I start?"

"Monday," Morana replied. He heard paper shuffling in the background, probably Morana looking over the information of the job before relaying it to him. "You'll have to come in this week to fill out the paperwork. You won't have time on Monday. The man you're going to assist is fastidious about not wasting time, and he won't take kindly to you being late." She paused and when she spoke again, Isaac could hear the apprehension in her voice. "I should warn you, the man you're going to be working for has been known to have a bit of a temper. I won't ask you to stay if he's being unprofessional, but…"

But sometimes when people work with temps, they know exactly how to straddle the line between being unprofessional and over the line. Isaac was familiar. It didn't happen with him often, he put one hundred percent into his work and very rarely had complaints, but he appreciated the warning.

"I'm sure I can handle it."

"I'm sure you can," she said with a sigh. "You've been a great asset since you started. But if you're ever uncomfortable or feel like you've been mistreated, I want you to promise you'll call me. I don't want my employees being harassed, no matter how big the contract is."

Curiosity swelled, and Isaac bounced on his toes a little. "What contract?"

"Spellbound Corps. You'll be working with their top lawyer, a Mr. Van Buren."

Isaac's heartbeat kicked up, and he had to bite back a squeal of excitement. Spellbound Corps was one of the biggest supernatural companies in the world. Their products helped make the world more accessible to all supernaturals, sorcerers included. Some sorcerers whose powers were more difficult to manage used products made by Spellbound to focus their powers so they could function normally. It wasn't something Isaac had any trouble with, but his cousin Parker was dangerous to everyone around him before those products were made. Now, he had his own apartment in the city and a job in government helping other supernaturals who committed crimes accidentally as a result of untamed magic. All thanks to Spellbound.

Putting on his most professional tone, Isaac said, "That sounds good to me. I'll come in this afternoon to do the paperwork."

"No rush. You've got a few days to prepare. But I appreciate your promptness. I'll have the paperwork ready for you at reception. Thank you, Isaac."

When she hung up, Isaac's ability to hold back his excitement finally broke and he let out a squeal, dashing toward the living room where Maeve was sitting watching TV. Her eyebrows flew up in surprise, and she smiled curiously at him when he plopped himself onto the cushion beside her.

"What is it? A job?"

Isaac nodded exuberantly, bouncing in his seat. "At Spellbound! As a legal assistant!"

Her eyes widened in surprise and her joy rose to match his own, a bright smile on her face. "Really? That's like the dream! That's so exciting!"

Isaac couldn't sit still, he was so excited. Since he was only a little over half way into his law degree, he thought they'd assign him regular temp jobs like secretary or office manager until he graduated. He never thought he'd actually get to spend time in a legal office so soon. Especially at a company like Spellbound. He launched himself off the couch, snagging his laptop before he sat back down next to Maeve.

"What are you doing?"

"Looking up who I'll be working for," he answered, his eyes glued to the screen. "Morana said I'd be assistant a Mr. Van Buren. I've never heard of him before."

Maeve made an incredulous sound, catching Isaac's attention. He looked up, frowning at her stunned expression.

"You haven't heard of Maverick Van Buren? He's like the top corporate lawyer in the country! He cuts through any red tape to make sure the products made at Spellbound can be brought to fruition. That company wouldn't have gotten nearly as far without him."

Impressed, Isaac turned back to his laptop, pulling up a search engine. Maverick Van Buren was the top hit, and when Isaac saw his picture, he sucked in a sharp breath.

"Goddess..."

Maeve scooted closer to look. "Oh, my..."

Isaac could only nod in agreement. Not only was Mr. Van Buren a top class lawyer, he was also gorgeous. The company photo alone was something to swoon over. Silky looking jet black hair, sharp dark eyes, thick eyebrows, a square jaw that looked like it was chiseled from marble, clean shaven because it would be a crime to cover up a face like that. The company photo was only from the chest up, so Isaac couldn't get any details on the man's body, but his shoulders looked broad and the suit he wore was well tailored to his muscles. Isaac lifted a hand absentmindedly to check for drool. The man was certainly drool worthy.

"How are you going to get any work done?" Maeve breathed, her gaze locked on the screen, much like Isaac's was.

"Sheer force of will," Isaac replied. Though he questioned that. He'd need to use every ounce of self control he had to not stare at that man day in and day out. It was hard to imagine someone that gorgeous having a temper, but maybe his personality would be enough of a turn off that Isaac could get his work done. One could hope, anyway. He didn't want to embarrass himself at a company he one day hoped to work for.

He and Maeve spent some time looking up more information about the man Isaac would be working for come Monday. She knew about him from her law classes.

Maeve was a year ahead of him in her classes, she'd be graduating in spring, but they both worked so they could afford the basics. Neither of them came from family money, and Isaac would never ask his parents to pay for his law degree. They couldn't afford it. Instead, he worked during the day and took classes at night. It was exhausting, but completely worth it once he got his degree. One and a half more years to go.

After lunch, Isaac headed into the temp agency to fill out the paperwork for his new assignment. The temp agency paid better than working at a cafe or in fast food, but going a week without work made him nervous and he was eager to claim the job offered to him so he could make his wages this month.

Since he was hired along with a dozen other newbies, the office was pretty busy. People didn't spend much time in the office itself, given that they were hired out to other jobs, but they always came and went to fill out paperwork or sign off on jobs. Isaac grabbed the paperwork from reception, smiling politely at the receptionist before finding an empty desk to work at. He plopped himself down, skimming through the contract, and bounced in his seat a little from excitement.

"Got a good one?" a quiet and somewhat gruff voice asked him.

Isaac looked up, searching for the speaker. He didn't know everyone who worked in the office, too many people came and went, but he recognized the man across from him because they were hired at the same time and trained together. Tony was a kind of intimidating looking human at first glance, especially with the scarring across one cheek and down his neck, but he was actually a huge cinnamon roll.

"Hey, Tony. How's it going?"

Tony lifted one shoulder. "I'm working, so I'm good. You?"

Isaac glanced down at the contract again and beamed. "I'm perfect."

"What've you got?" It was surprising sometimes to hear such shyness out of such a big dude. But humans weren't exactly powerful. Even humans as big as Tony.

"Legal aid at Spellbound. You?"

Tony frowned down at his own paperwork. "Supposed to be maintenance, but I'm not sure it'll stick. Can't do any heavy lifting."

Yeah, Isaac would have guessed that. Tony favored his scarred side and Isaac got the feeling the damage went a lot farther than just the scars on his face. Still, Morana wouldn't assign him something he couldn't handle. At least, that was the impression he got off of her the last few months.

"If you're worried about it, then you can talk to Morana. She probably didn't even think about it much."

Tony nodded slowly. "Yeah. Maybe."

Isaac got the feeling that Tony wasn't the type to stand up for himself. Since he had to meet with Morana while handing in the paperwork, he made a mental note to mention Tony's apprehension. Someone needed to stand up for the poor guy. He was only human. They had it rough as it was. He didn't need to suffer doing a job he couldn't handle.

Isaac thought about the job offered to him while he filled out the paperwork. It wasn't a difficult job, legal aid was basically a secretary with more legal background than the average assistant. But Morana's warnings flashed through his head. The job might be doable, but working with Mr. Van Buren would put his patience to the test. It was a good thing Isaac knew how to handle difficult people. Mr. Van Buren wouldn't know what hit him.

Check it out now!

DID YOU FIND A TYPO?

This book has been edited and reviewed to find any typos and mistakes, but alas, we are only human. If you spot an error, please let me know! I want to hear from you so I can fix it!

Send me an email at authoramypadilla@gmail.com or send me a message on my Facebook group page.

ALSO BY AMY PADILLA

DALLYING WITH DEMONS

Dating a Demon

Taming a Demon

Claiming a Demon

Loving a Demon

Saving a Demon

———

CHARMED AWAY TEMP AGENCY

The Incubus's Assistant

The Dragon's Aide

The Shapeshifter's Secretary

The Vampire's Receptionist

The Telepath's Associate

———

NOT-SO-SAVAGE BARBARIANS

The Barbarian's Tribute

Saved by a Barbarian

Seducing a Barbarian

The Barbarian's Claim

The Physician's Barbarian

Prince of the Barbarians

ABOUT THE AUTHOR

Amy is an introverted squish who loves Happily Ever Afters, Magic, and True Love. While she doesn't stick with one specific subgenre, her favorite tends to be fluffy paranormal romance. In between writing books (like several. At one time. Because squirrel.) Amy likes to read and play relaxing video games. Her kindle is stuffed with romance and she hoards trophy books on her shelves. You can find her most nights pretending to be fancy with a glass of sparkling cider and a good book.

Send her a message. She might be an introvert, but she won't resist being adopted by an extrovert.

Don't forget to join her Facebook group for the latest updates and more!

Sign up for her newsletter on her website to get more news, access to WIPs, and occasional shorts.

www.ingramcontent.com/pod-product-compliance
Lightning Source LLC
Chambersburg PA
CBHW030039020825
30520CB00009B/125